turning of the TIDES

DAUGHTERS OF THE HIGH SEAS
BOOK 2

turning of the TIDES

RACHEL CHERIE

This novel is a work of fiction. Names, descriptions, entities, and incidents included in the story are products of the author's imagination. Any resemblance to actual persons, events, and entities is entirely coincidental.

Book design copyright © 2014
Cover design by Gian Philipp Rufin
Interior design by Jomar Ouano

Published in the United States of America

ISBN: 978-0-99988-181-1
1. Fiction / Action & Adventure
2. Fiction / Historical
14.10.13

Dedicated to all my family and friends who encouraged me to write this sequel. You all have a special place in my heart—CLP, CJM, TKW, KDP, & ELP.

Chapter 1

"She went this way!" a deep voice called out into the rosy colored sky.

Clutching the collar of her shirt closed as she sat precariously between the roots of an old tree, a young woman, streaked with dirt, took in gasps of air. A short distance away, a twig snapped. Her ragged, hurried breathing all but stopped, making her body involuntarily shudder. Every noise in the dense forest seemed to fade and listen for her to gasp again.

Wincing at the pain in her lungs, the young woman slowly leaned back further into the little cove created by the aboveground roots. Pushing back a lock of her honey colored hair, she smeared more dirt onto her forehead. "What could I have possibly done to deserve this?" she whispered to herself, closing her eyes for a moment.

Snap! sounded another twig, closer than the one before.

"Edgar! Ya lug! She ain't deaf!" a voice growled, sounding as though it was being discharged from behind the very tree she was trying to bury herself within.

"Then what ya yellin' at me fer, John?" Edgar yelled in return.

Snap!

"Edgar!"

"John!"

Pulling her legs as close to herself as possible, the filth-covered girl, concentrating on keeping her breathing steady, peered over the tops of the roots. The burly silhouette of a man stood stark against the illuminated foliage of the morning forest canopy. Ducking back behind the gnarled tree, she glanced about herself, her hazel eyes taking in the fact that she had no conceivable way of escape. Her breathing having almost regulated, she forced herself to creep forward. *Why am I always running short on time?* she asked inwardly in agitation.

"Oi! John! I found a footprint!" Edgar called out.

Rolling her eyes irritably, the girl took one last glance about and, seeing a gap between them, bounded away from her cubby, wildly scrambling to get deeper into the forest.

"*Teishi!* Avast! Not so fast, *shōjo!*" a different voice yelled.

Her heart stopping, she skidded to a stop in front of a man no taller than she, clad in completely unsoiled white clothes beneath a purple knee length cape and a white hat flaunting a large violet feather that trailed out the back. His dark hair, impeccably straight and long, shimmered about his angular face while his tiny mustache twitched as he stared down at the young woman. His eyes, like slanted onyxes set flawlessly in his well-tanned, high-cheekboned face, ripped coldly through her face and bore straight into her soul. "Hello, Jacq," his accented voice mocked.

Her eyes darkened immediately. *Blackguard...* she sneered fearlessly in her mind. Feeling her lip curl instinctively at his presence, Jacq straightened slowly, her nostrils flaring slightly in disgust, and flagrantly took a deep breath only to expectorate

forcefully on the man's shoe.

His mouth forming a thin line of anger, he raised his left hand mercilessly over his right shoulder, letting it fall soundly and squarely against the side of Jacq's head. He smiled devilishly as he watched her fall to the ground at the force of his blow, hitting it with a dull thud. For a few seconds he watched her still figure lie on the forest floor, observing her dirt-smeared blouse and pants. His keen eye, however, also noticed a shiny golden locket lying above her shoulder, connected to her by a thin gold chain that went around her neck. Not altering his gawk, the man ordered in a voice much bigger than he looked capable of, "John! Edgar!"

"Aye, Captain?" the two men, both almost a foot taller than the Easterner, asked breathlessly as they ran up beside him.

"Bring her," he commanded shortly, gesturing towards her motionless body.

"Have ya killed her?" questioned Edgar, hesitantly reaching for her.

"Nay, *baka!* That was what ye thought last time!" spat the Captain, sending the man a condescending glare. "Bring her promptly, now. We do not have time to be late. And," he motioned to the pristinely lustrous locket, "make sure that gets put in my cabin." With that, he spun around, tossing his cape gallantly aside, and marched off in the direction the group had come.

Exchanging glances, the two men then looked down again at the mud-caked, unconscious figure that was lying shallowly breathing at their feet. "Well, ya heard the Cap'n!" John said awkwardly. "Pick up the lass and off with us!"

Rolling his cold blue eyes, Edgar leaned down, grabbing Jacq's wrist and hauling her to his shoulders. "What do we

want with her anyway?" he asked under his breath as he trudged off after his cohort.

Glumly opening her listless eyes, Jacq watched the forest trees pass her by as she was lugged off towards Captain Ming's boat. *Run, Alex,* she thought, tears of frustration welling up in her eyes. *Run as you never knew you could...* Then her vision blurred to blackness.

On the other side of the forest, a nearly identical girl dressed in equally battered clothes flopped wheezing to the ground. Forcing her weak limbs to pull her body out of the open meadow and amidst the nearby tall grasses, she laid still, trying to catch her breath. Glancing down at her tattered and torn dress, the girl grimaced. "Heartless blackguards," she said in a bitter mutter. "This was brand new." Then, glancing at the sky, she sighed heavily. "Why am I always running short on time?" She coughed, struggling to stand up, and hobbled sorely forward. As she moved ahead with her uneven gait, she felt a steady *thump thump* against her heaving chest. Pausing, she put her thin hand to the top of her dress, feeling a unique semi-oval shaped object between the fabric and her body. Hooking her finger in the chain around her neck, she produced a locket almost identical to the one dangling around Jacq's throat. Holding it in the palm of her hand, she ran her thumb over its flawless surface. "Oh, Jacq...How did this happen?"

Gulping sullenly, she dropped it back beneath her dress and gazed warily at her surroundings. Off to her left, the ocean shimmered in the early day's light. Heaving a laden sigh, she shuffled in the direction of the gigantic body of water, her uneasy breathing reflecting the pain in her chest. Happy scents of spring goodness reached up her nostrils and into her brain, summoning a weak smile and attempting to provide her with a strange sense that everything would be all right. Her practical logic, however, denied her such fantasies. *I must hurry*, she thought, *before all is lost and we are stranded apart for the rest of our lives. Heartless pirates…*

After what seemed like half an eternity, she came to the edge of what was actually a flat shelf of dirt. Walking painfully to the edge of the terrain, she smiled halfheartedly at the downward slope to the small village of Port Gilgallad. From here, she and Jacq were to meet up with their sister and friends so as to begin their journey home. So much for that. Sighing dolefully, she stood watching the quiet town a moment when suddenly the ground beneath her feet shifted slightly. Inhaling sharply, she froze, holding her breath.

Picking up her foot up with the utmost caution, she moved to step back from the edge. However, despite her efforts, the ledge gave way, abruptly dropping Alex down the slope as she squealed, throwing her plummeting down the hill. End over end she tumbled down the hillside's face as it watched the ocean to the east of it. When she rolled to a stop, still a fair distance from the village, Alex whimpered, touching her tousled hair as she wincingly dragged herself to a sitting position. Her brow furrowing, she stared down at her dress… stained, torn, and everything except entirely and unbearably ruined. "I look awful," she said miserably.

"I have seen much worse," a well-spoken voice commented from behind her.

Whirling about, Alex gasped at the blue eyes that stared warmly into her soul. "Hello," she said, punctuated with an awkward laugh as she touched her ratted hair in self-conscious mortification.

Kneeling in front of her and holding out his hand, the

young man smiled gently and said in a low inflection, "Are you quite all right?"

"Well," she started, glancing up at the hill she'd just tumbled down, "no…We are on our way to Swansea – at least we were…But, now we are separated and everything is going terribly wrong and the ground gave way and dropped me down this dreadful hill and my sister…" She stopped herself, breathing deeply as she tried to regain her composure.

"Just take it easy, Miss. I know just the place for you to obtain soap and water." He held his hand out further to try and convince her. "Come with me."

Blushing uncontrollably, Alex took his hand and laughed nervously. "Thank you, sir. Pray tell me, would you happen to know if a ship by name of the *Queen's Pride* has docked in the ports here?" She smiled, pushing the pain to the back of her mind as she rose in unison with him.

Releasing her hand, he shook his head. "No, m'lady, but I know where to inquire so that I might be able to tell you."

Her face unveiled a beautiful smile that she usually kept hidden from strangers. "That would be quite splendid if you could," she returned. Moving to take a step forward, she was unpleasantly surprised by a shooting pain in her ankle when she put her full weight on her foot, causing her to nearly collapse.

Catching her, the man smiled. "Allow me to help you to the inn."

He has the most gentlemanly voice I have ever heard, Alex thought to herself. Giggling again, she shrugged. "Very well, but I do not even know your name in order that I might thank you once we get there."

What are you doing? Do you not remember Jim? Hello! part

of Alex ranted inside.

Oh poppycock! He is just being a gentleman. Nothing more, she countered herself dreamily. Smiling politely, her glittery eyes completely hid the turmoil within her mind as she waited for him to answer.

Grinning with such glorious brilliance as Alex had never before seen, the man answered courteously, "My name is Nicholas Dunne, m'lady, and may I ask yours?"

Finding herself blushing at the impeccable manner in which he asked, she inwardly chided herself. Of all the times to fawn over a man, now was certainly not one of them! Taking a deep breath as they began to slowly move forward to the village she replied, "Of course, sir. Alexandria Thorpe Luray, but you may call me Alex, if you wish. Most of my friends know me as such."

"Very well," he agreed, chuckling at her demure behavior. "And please don't call me sir. It is a title I do not deserve in the presence of one such as yourself." He watched, pleased, as her cheeks became nearly scarlet. "And pray, Miss Luray, tell me what a lady was doing fallen and tattered at the bottom of a hill?"

"Well, Mr. Dunne," Alex complied, "my twin sister and I were coming to this village to meet up with the rest of our company. However, we had slight complications along the way and became…" She abruptly stopped, choking on the words sticking in her throat. Reality was suddenly threatening to overwhelm her. *No,* she resolved. *I will be stronger than this.* Halting a moment, she took a deep breath before continuing. "We became separated." Her eyes glazing over, she smiled again, trying to hide her quickening intense desire to burst into a blubbering little girl in need of a handkerchief the size of a topsail.

"I see," he returned, patting her hand gently and pausing a moment to look at her sorrowful eyes. "May I inquire as to how?"

"It is," she paused, unwilling to entirely trust this stranger under the circumstances, "complicated."

Perceiving she did not want to discuss it further, he acquiesced to her silent request. "I am sure you two will find each other, but in the mean time, being able to wash will make you feel much better. And, please, call me Nicholas."

Smiling, Alex nodded in thanks and they continued towards the inn at the edge of the village. "Thank you for your kindness."

He nodded her direction. "Of course. Think nothing of it." Then he added another reassuring smile.

Blinking her eyes open, Jacq found herself flat on her back, staring at a wall. There was a pounding pain on the right side of her head in synchronized rhythm with the sting of her left cheek. Opening her jaw and moving it back and forth, she was relieved to find that it was still mobile. *Blackguard...* she thought, annoyed. Reaching up to the pounding pain of her skull, she frowned at the discovery of a scabbed over gash at the very edge of her eye socket. It felt like an extension of her eyebrow. Pushing slowly up until she was propped up on her elbows, she squinted in the tar-smell filled air. Instinctively, her fingers wandered to her throat, where the necklace should have been. When she found it missing, her eyes narrowed and she snorted in disgust. "What does this Captain Ming want with us anyway?" she muttered, wanting to cough, but forcing herself to resist in order to avoid the pain that would come of it. Then, she stopped. *What is that? No!* She glanced around. Crawling to the bars of the cell, she pulled herself up and peered around for any sort of portal. Though she couldn't visually verify, there was one thing her nose was never wrong about–the salty mistiness of the ocean air. Her heart skipped a beat and her soul shivered.

"My, my..." a deep voice said in a husky breath near her cell.

At the sound of his voice, she drew back to the middle of her cell, watching for the man to show his face.

"What the devil did the bloody captain drag aboard this time?" With a swagger of confidence, the owner of the voice stepped from the shadows, and Jacq found herself staring at the face of an ebony-haired, green-eyed man dressed entirely in black, from the cravat around his neck to the knee-high boots that covered the lower half of his trousers. He was smiling what would have been a very attractive smile, had he not obviously been a member of Ming's miscreant crew.

"Does it matter?" she asked, the sharpness of her comment diminished by the hoarseness of her voice. Folding her arms over her chest, she stuck her chin out in defiance and ire. *Just go away you black-hearted, troublesome, piratical scalawag.*

"I heard you were quite difficult for ol' Ming to actually catch," he continued quietly.

But he did catch me. Jacq sighed and averted her gaze to the floor.

"And I just wanted to congratulate you on that," the darkly dressed pirate concluded, giving the bars a strong shake before turning to walk away.

What? What kind of deception is this? Jacq couldn't help but turn and look at him again.

Catching her glance, he smiled a wickedly handsome smile.

Throwing a scowling glare to the floor, she considered his comment. *Fine! I shall play this game...* Clearing her throat awkwardly, Jacq replied, "Thank you."

Sauntering comfortably back towards her cage, he inquired in a very low voice, "Would you fancy a drink?"

Lifting her eyes to meet his, she said nothing, but stood as straight as she could and slowly walked up to him, not saying a word.

His mouth tilting in a rather amused smile, he handed her a flask through the bars, not breaking eye contact with her. *The captain has no idea what he's picked up.* The pirate laughed inwardly.

Not backing down from his incessant stare, Jacq twisted open the cap and placed the container to her lips, drinking it as she continued to watch him wordlessly. *What do you want?* she found herself demanding. After letting the water quench her parched throat and tongue, Jacq pulled the flask from her mouth and, recapping it, held it back to him through the bars.

"Where are you from?" he asked easily, taking the water container from her hand.

"Of my original home I am yet to know," she returned in a riddle. "However, I've spent half my life aboard a ship and the other half in *Port de Couler de Bateaux*. Yourself?"

His smirk tugging a little wider, he nodded. "I was born in France, spent most of my life growing up in London," the pirate explained simply and casually.

"And you decided life as a pirate was better than life in London?" she asked, incredulous.

"Well, it's never so simple, is it, lass?" He grinned at her. "Nay, my father died of a prolonged illness and my mother was left to try and tend me by herself."

"So you left your mother and became a pirate?" Jacq interpreted, raising an eyebrow at the outrageous idea of such a thing. *To have a family and throw it away for this?! What a positively unimaginable, thoroughly maniac thing to do!*

"Aye. She was having difficulty supporting my brother and me, and her parents would not give her aid enough for the both of us because they had not approved of the union of my mother to my father," he continued shamelessly. "I wanted to repay her for all the hardship she went through for me."

"I see," Jacq replied uneasily, backing nonchalantly away from the bars and sitting herself down against the back wall of her cell. *And becoming a pirate was the best possible way to repay her for her hardship?* she questioned sarcastically.

"And what of you? There must be something special about you for the bloody captain to go through all the trouble to capture you more than once *and* keep you alive," he prodded curiously.

"Surely your captain has gone out of his way to find others to ransom off or some such thing afore," Jacq retorted, shrugging off this seemingly honorary notion.

"Nay," the man said, leaning fully on the cell bars. "If they run as you, he either lets them go or eliminates them."

"And you're not going to use me as a strumpet?" she queried, wincing at the possibility.

"Haha! Nay, lass! 'Tis against the code." He laughed again, smiling at her between the bars.

A rather bemused smile twisted Jacq's mouth as she rose and sauntered towards him. "I have heard stories of this

Captain Ming, but he does not frighten me. He is the same height as I am!"

Chuckling at her naive audacity, the man shook his head and returned, "You are a bold lass for certain, but ol' Ming is the bloody devil himself." His voice dropped to a very low, dangerously appealing tone. "He has no remorse for the blood he's shed in all the years of his life, and it is rumored that he was born without the ability to have righteous emotions…and possibly without even a soul…"

Jacq's heart beat more slowly as she listened to the miscreant unwind tales of the malicious pirate captain who had become notorious in Africa and India for his reprehensible iniquities. Her face paled as the Frenchman continued plunging into the seemingly endless recesses of the deep reservoir of evil that this captain had so proudly dammed up for himself.

"How old are you?" the man abruptly questioned, breaking the smooth flow of his voice and causing Jacq to start a little.

"I recently celebrated my nineteenth birthday," she admitted quietly.

"And do you really go by Jacq?" he asked, sounding skeptical.

"Aye," she acknowledged dully.

Nodding, he smiled softly and turned to walk away.

What?! Walk off and not tell me your name?! How uncouth! Jacq rolled her eyes and inquired with a tone of indifference, "And yours?"

"Jean-Pierre Legard is my Christian name, but everybody aboard knows me as Pike," he answered, readily turning back and smiling because she had asked.

She eyed him a moment, retaining an aloof air that would have made Alex proud. "Am I to be kept locked up for the entire voyage?" she questioned, looking down and then back up at him with big hazel eyes that pleaded for him to just unlock her right now. *What is the real reason you are a pirate? Is it for the doxies?* Jacq's forehead contorting slightly; she glanced at the floor. *Why do I care?*

Feeling his hand touch her shoulder through the bars, she shrunk away from the weight of it and stared up at him. *Why do you seem so nice?*

"I think the captain will release you onto the ship, but I believe you will be put under the charge of one of the crew members," he said, letting his hand drop back to his side. "He seems determined to bring you into our company."

She scoffed, rolling her eyes. "That's preposterous."

Jean-Pierre smiled. "Well, I wouldn't argue that." He chuckled, eyeing the lock on the cell door before turning nonchalantly on his heel, striding down the corridor, and then clunking up the stairs.

Returning to the back of the cell, she sank to the ground once again, letting her head fall back and land soundly against the wall. Wincing she sighed. "Fraternizing with a pirate? Alex would want to kill me," she muttered, a devilish smile stretching her mouth. Taking a deep breath, she bent her knees, pulling them to her chin, and rested her forehead on them, only to pass out of consciousness again.

Staring trancelike out the window of the room the town innkeeper had graciously given her for the afternoon at the behest of Mr. Dunne, Alex hypnotically brushed her long, clean hair. "I just don't understand," she said in a low voice, her brow furrowing while trying to figure out why the previous events had taken place as they had. Tearing her gaze away from the hill she had tumbled down, Alex fixed it on where a new violet dress Mr. Dunne had so graciously gone to the market to get for her lay on the bed, and she stopped brushing her hair. Glancing down at her undergarments, she straightened her petticoat then returned to brushing her luxurious strawberry blond hair. Then, forcing herself to stop, she put it up in a fashionable bun, leaving a few wavy tresses down to frame her face. As she finished, her eye caught the locket from her neck resting beside her brush.

Picking up the golden piece of jewelry between her thumb and index finger, she held it up to look it over. How it shone so unabashedly in the sunlight! Its luster was at the very heart of greed…so welcoming and calling to the soul of anyone minutely interested in wealth and beauty. *It is strange*, she thought as she clutched the helpless gold piece, *how soothing it is to hold this.* Somehow, it made her feel like Jacq was still with her, which gave her a sense of strength and sanity. As she stared at it, running her thumb over its textured surface in a trancelike state, there was a harsh rap on the door of her room.

"Yes?" she called out, not breaking her blank gaze.

"Are you clothed?" Nicholas Dunne's voice questioned politely.

His voice snapping her back to reality, Alex vaulted to a standing position, hurriedly grabbing up the dress. "Just one moment and I shall be decent enough for you to enter!" Nearly jumping into the dress, she expertly shoved her arms into the sleeves and pulled the dress up over her corset. Then she suddenly stopped, staring down at her brush. "I cannot fasten my own dress!" She paused, gawking at the brush as if she expected a solution. "Jacq usually does this for me. In fact,

I believe it to be the only part of putting on a dress she knows!" Why didn't she think of a solution to this before she agreed to take her old dress off? A sense of panic began taking hold of her mind as she glanced about the room wildly for a solution.

"Miss Luray?" Mr. Dunne's voiced inquired, sounding slightly concerned.

His voice startled her, a small gasp escaping her lungs as she reached her nimble fingers to try and tie herself. Whirling about to face the door, she gulped. "I…uh…cannot…fasten…" she paced back and forth around the bed as she explained, searching for words that would allude to the problem without making her actually say it, "uh…my…my dress." She stopped, utterly embarrassed. Biting her lower lip, she stared, mortified, at the door.

"I can do that for you," he offered casually in a quiet voice through the door. "Or I could go down and ask the innkeeper if his wife is around, but I think she stepped out to go to the market." He smiled softly, pushing his ear to the door to listen for her footsteps, knowing her type would never agree to his offer out loud. Ever so quietly, the rustle of her dress and the subtle sound of her footfall approached the door. Backing up, he folded his hands behind his back and waited.

Shyly, she pulled the door just wide enough to peer out. "You must never speak of this," she said in a cool, commanding tone.

He nodded, doing his best to maintain a respectfully straight face.

Taking a deep breath, she opened the door barely wide enough for him to walk through. Poking her head out first to make sure nobody else was around, she moved away so he could enter as she said to herself, "Jacq would be laughing at

me if she were here right now. Of course, if she were here, I would not be in this predicament."

Despite his efforts to be a polite and proper gentleman, he could not help but stare at her a moment as he entered. The sunlight streaming in the window was hitting her from behind, illuminating her golden hair like an illusion from a dream. Shaking his head, he stepped inside and waited for her to turn her back to him. "You, m'lady, are a vision of beauty," he said in an almost breathless whisper. "The dress fits you perfectly."

"Thank you," she returned sheepishly, pivoting so her back was to him just in time so he didn't see her face turn scarlet.

As she did, he smiled and acknowledged, "I was coming to tell you that the ship of your inquiry is just a few moments from docking. Your timing was almost perfect."

Breathing a sigh of relief, Alex shook her head. "No. It was perfect." She thought again of Jacq. *It is always perfect.*

"Yes, perhaps you're right. After all, a few moments difference and I may not have been there to witness you tumble down the hill." He chuckled, pulling the last of her dress together with an efficiency that suggested he had done it many times before. "There you are."

"Thank you, sir." She exhaled, smiling up at him.

My, but he is tall and handsome, is he not? Half of her sighed wistfully.

Alex! her other half retorted, appalled.

Stifling her internal squabbling and forcing even larger grin onto her face, she questioned further, "And where, exactly, is this dock? I have never afore been to Port Gilgallad."

"Then to be in this village is a new experience for the both of us," he said, his grin broadening. "I shall escort m'lady to the

harbor so that you will not have to perform the inquiry that I have already done." At this he bowed slightly and offered her his arm.

Still surprised by his unceasing thoughtfulness, Alex's mind did cartwheels. *How can I possibly say no?* She stared at this storybook gentleman, absolutely flattered by his guarded attention. "Of course!" she said, smiling as though she had just fallen in love for the first time. "That would be splendid!" Taking his arm, the two then left the quarters, thanking the innkeeper on the way out, and made quickly to the dock.

Upon arrival, Alex saw a rangy man with shaggy dark hair reclining on a barrel, eating an apple. Her eyes narrowing immediately, she marched up to him, leaving the benevolent Nicholas Dunne behind, and whispered into his ear, "You better have paid for that, Miata!"

Jumping so quickly off the barrel that he almost dropped the piece of fruit, Miata turned his bright blue eyes to stare defensively at the young woman. "Now, what be ye meanin' by that, Alex?" he retorted, deliberately taking a rather large bite of it only inches from her face. "It were from the ship we be sailin' on, thank ye very much." He chewed his bite a few seconds as they glared at each other. "Where be Jacq?"

Well, he has certainly gained a bit of confidence. Amy must be wearing off on him, Alex noted uncomfortably. "We must speak in private regarding my sister," she said in a low tone. "And, speaking of sisters…" Her voice jumped suddenly from private muttering to demanding mother as she shoved her fists onto her hips and asked, "Where is my younger sister?"

"Amy? She be 'round about somewhere," he returned, shrugging casually at the question. "What be the trouble with me mate, Jacq?" The small mustache he had decorating his upper lip twitched involuntarily as he waited patiently for

Alex to continue with the story.

"She is…missing," Alex admitted as Nicholas came up behind her.

Noticing Dunne approaching, Miata's eyes darkened. "Who be this, Alex?"

"What? Oh. This, Miata, is Mr. Nicholas Dunne," she introduced, gesturing between them.

"How do you do?" Nicholas greeted him cordially, offering his hand.

Alex sighed inwardly until she realized that Miata was being hesitant in shaking her rescuer's hand. Her eyes narrowed and she eyed him menacingly.

Noticing her glare, the young man smiled mildly and took Nicholas' hand, returning, "Oh no, Mr. Dunne. The pleasure be all mine." Then, releasing the grip and turning back to Alex, asked, "What be his purpose on our venture?"

"Mr. Dunne has been so kind as to assist me," Alex returned sharply.

Miata sent him another distrustful glance. "If ye be sayin' so. Now, be tellin' me about Jacq."

"Well," Alex began, holding herself tightly together, "we did not send you and Amy the message to get on the *Queen's Pride*."

Miata chuckled. "Actually, to be honest, I were thinkin' it a might odd that ye be sendin' me off with yer sister alone an' unattended."

"Yes, well, someone else sent that note, and then Jacq and I were trying to find out where you two were going when we got intercepted by pirates."

"Pirates? More o' them?" he asked, nearly dropping his apple again.

"Quit interrupting me and allow me to finish!" she demanded.

Rolling his eyes, Miata crossed his arms over his chest and turned his eyes unwaveringly at her.

"So," she continued, trying to ignore his exaggerated, incessant, wide-eyed stare, "after Jacq and I found out that the ship was making a stop at this port, we somehow managed to evade the miscreants and got out of town. However, when we were on the other side of the forest," she gestured back behind her at the forest in which Jacq had been captured, "the pirates arrived for us again. They chased us deep into the forest, but Jacq kept making loud noises and then disappearing so as to keep them occupied and not looking so much for a girl in a skirt. As near as I can tell they caught her. I am quite certain of it. The last I saw of her, they were chasing her back the direction we had come; but I am here, and we must find her!" Alex concluded breathlessly, all but caving into an emotional wreck right at Miata's feet.

The young man blinked several times. "Aye. We will get our Jacq back, but Amy should not come with," he stated calmly.

Alex started at this, surprised at his calm and intelligent suggestion. "Yes. I agree. She shall return home to our father while we turn around and find Jacq."

Just then, Amy came bounding up, her curly golden locks bobbing up and down with her chipper step, a blue parrot on her shoulder and a furry monkey clutching her waist. "Alex!" she called out cheerfully, rushing up and embracing her.

Squawking loudly, the bird flew to Miata and began flapping in irritation.

"Amy!" Alex greeted, reaching down to pet the creature around her sister's waist as she returned the hug. "How are

Frank and Bill?" she sighed, glancing first at the monkey, then at the parrot.

"They are splendid. Well, mostly splendid. Bill is most unhappy with Jacq sending him off without her," the younger girl said. Seeing Nicholas, her eyes lit up and, pointing at him, she asked, "Oh, Alex! Is this gentleman with you? I approve! He is more handsome than Jim!"

"Amy!" Alex laughed, teeth clenched as she slapped her hand over her sister's mouth. "We have had a change of plans. Miata and I have to return to pick up Jacq, but we believe it would be wise for you to continue onward and meet our father so that he knows his daughters are alive and on their way to see him." Glancing at the bird, who Miata had managed to calm down by giving him his apple, Alex then added as she let her hand drop, "And take Frank and Bill with you."

Nodding, Amy agreed, "Very well. If you think that is best, then I shall do so. The ship leaves soon, so I should get back on board." Backing away from Alex, the girl crossed over to Miata and, taking his hand in hers, stared up at him. "I shall miss you."

He smiled back at her, just as starry-eyed as she. "And I be missin' ye too," he admitted, touching her cheek softly with his fingertips.

A chill ran down Alex's spine as she watched the two stare lovingly at each other. "Ahem! Miata," she interrupted, snatching his arm, "we have no time to linger."

Chapter 2

Tracing the tar-coated grain of the wooden floor, Jacq hung her head glumly as she listened to the muted sound of ocean waves slapping at the exterior of the boat. Her mind kept oscillating between worrying about Alex and the awful things Pike had told her of her apparently ruthless captor. *How can one be so filled with hate?* Scowling down at the floor, she inclined her ear for the footsteps of the strange French pirate that had so easily talked with her earlier. Above her were the sounds of a normal crew mulling about as day turned to night, swabbing the decks, adjusting this rope and that…She sighed bitterly. *Out at sea…Kidnapped by pirates…And locked below deck where I can't even feel the sea breeze.*

As she listened, a rather difficult sounding footfall reached her ears. *Thump. Clunk. Thump. Clunk. Thump. Clunk.* Her brow furrowing, she turned and found herself staring at another pirate with naught but a peg leg! His baldric, strapped across his chest, held his cutlass at his side and a flintlock at the bottom of his sternum. A striped sock decorated the portion of leg left exposed between his leather buckle shoe and mid-calf length trousers. A jacket which looked as though it had once belonged to a naval officer of some kind fit perfectly on his broad shoulders over the top of a shabby shirt. Though he was rather unkempt with his long dreadlocked hair and beard, the style which he displayed was striking and flashy.

A sharp intake of breath that she could not keep quiet sounded in the silence that had otherwise hushed the air about them. Though she wished she wasn't, she was immediately intrigued and continued watching him wordlessly as he came to a stop in front of her cell.

Smiling heartily, the man shrugged and greeted, "Me brother said ye were a perty lass, but I had to come see fer meself."

My, but his diction sounds a lot like Miata's, she thought in amusement. Tilting her head and laughing softly, Jacq returned, "And who is this brother of yours?"

"Jean-Pierre," he returned. "Me name is Jean-Paul, but all aboard the *Wind Hawke* be knowin' me as Peg Leg Paul," he admitted just as freely as his brother. As he spoke, chuckling lightly about his statement, he gestured at the wooden extension of his leg.

How creative, she thought sardonically. "Do all pirates have such nicknames?" She laughed nervously, unsure of the joke he made about himself. Tilting her head the other direction, she crossed her legs and waited for a response.

"Nay. Not all be havin' the names o' nick that ye be speakin' o'...but even ye be havin' a second name aboard the *Wind Hawke*," he shared, smiling as though it was something to be proud of.

"Is this so?" Jacq asked, suddenly feeling quite interested even though she knew deep down that curiosity in any part of such debauchery was outrageously uncouth and wrong.

"Aye, it are!" He chuckled, glancing about the room. " It be..."

"Jean-Paul!" Jean-Pierre's voice yelled from the top of the stairs that led down to the corridor. "Are you down here?"

"I be!" he replied, turning his back to her.

Jacq's eyes widened. *What is my pirate name?* she mentally demanded to know.

"Come hither, brother!" Jean-Pierre called jovially.

Her heart leapt into her throat. *You're not leaving me, are you?*

Without comment or concern, Jean-Paul began his slow, awkward walk to the deck, not even bothering to look back at her.

Jacq's heart sank. *What is wrong with me?* Leaning against the wall, she stared fixedly at the cell across from her, which was as empty as the eyes of the buccaneer brothers she had just met. *Grow up, Jacq,* she chided herself. *This is serious. I should be worried about Alex and focus on getting off this vessel.* Her mind paused a moment, allowing her to concentrate...on absolutely nothing.

The scent of the tar covered boards beneath her suddenly filled her nostrils almost overwhelmingly. She allowed herself to be swept away by the rocking of the ship in the waters, and she found that she could not deny herself the pleasure of singing along with the choir above her that sang unabashedly, regardless of voice quality, into the air:

What shall we do with a drunken sailor?
What shall we do with a drunken sailor?
What shall we do with a drunken sailor Earl-eye in the mornin'?
Way hey and up she rises

Way hey and up she rises
Way hey and up she rises Earl-eye in the mornin'!

Put 'im in a longboat 'til he's sober!
Put 'im in a longboat 'til he's sober!
Put 'im in a longboat 'til he's sober Earl-eye in the mornin'!
Way hey and up she rises
Way hey and up she rises
Way hey and up she rises Earl-eye in the mornin'!

Put 'im in bed with the captain's daughter
Put 'im in bed with the captain's daughter
Put 'im in bed with the captain's daughter Earl-eye in the mornin'!
Way hey and up she rises
Way hey and up she rises
Way hey and up she rises Earl-eye in the mornin'!
That's what we do with a drunken sailor!
That's what we do with a drunken sailor!
That's what we do with a drunken sailor Earl-eye in the mornin'!

"Ya have a might pretty voice, lass," a voice interrupted her.

Jacq's eyes flew open and she bound to her feet, hovering by the wall as a caged cat. The icy eyes of Edgar Jones came into view, the miscreant who had lugged her aboard. Pressing herself further into the wall, she stared back at him with a coldness that would have sent chills down a normal man's spine. Edgar, however, simply ignored her snarling gaze. Apprehension built like a crescendo in her mind as he stood in front of her cage door, holding something that looked to be a pile of cloth in one hand and a bucket of water in the other. "What did you do with my locket?" she questioned, her eyes

growing with surprise as she never intended on asking the question aloud.

"The captain has that, lassy."

The snarl on her face deepened. *And why would he want that?* she asked herself, as much puzzled as she was on edge.

Edgar, however, seemingly unaffected by the sneering expression that had enveloped Jacq's pretty face, simply noted, "I did my best to find ya some clothes that should fit ya." Placing a key in the lock, the metallic sound of the key clicking open the lock echoed in the quiet. Dropping the clothes in his hand near the door and setting the bucket beside them, he smiled at her, three gold teeth sparkling in the dim light that pervaded the downstairs of the ship. "The captain wants to see ya, after ya change and wash up a might."

Swallowing an iron lump that had somehow accumulated in her throat without her knowing, Jacq came forward slowly as a stray dog approaches one who is trying to feed it chunks of bread. "What does he want with me? Why am I a captive aboard this ship?" she demanded once she had the new clothing in her clutches and was beginning to back away from the bars with the bucket.

"Of that I know not, lass," Edgar replied in a grumble, glaring at her as if annoyed for the inquisition. "That's why he be wantin' to talk to ya, says I," the pirate said as he turned his back to her. "Hurry up, now. I haven't all day for ya to change, lass. I snuck down here quiet afore without any o' the lads knowin'."

Narrowing her eyes, Jacq hurriedly discarded her shirt and plunged her face into the mildly warmed liquid. Finding a rag inside, she scrubbed her arms and upper body before putting the other shirt on and following suit with the rest of her.

Before too long, she was hurriedly put back together. "Have you a brush?" she inquired dryly after she was fully clothed once again and eyeing her matted braid.

"Nay, lass," he admitted, sounding almost disappointed.

Her eye caught the light glinting off of something near his belt and, looking up at him, she sighed deeply. "Might I borrow your knife to cut my hair, then?"

His eyes growing in size, he backed up slightly at such an inquiry. "What?"

Gesturing at the knife that hung at his side, she explained, "If there is no brush aboard this vessel, then I wish to have my hair easier to maintain."

The glaciers in his eyes melting slightly at this decision, he opened her cell door again. Walking slowly and solemnly to her back, he took her long, filthy braid and asked, "How long, lassy?"

She gulped. "Two palm widths should do it," she returned.

"Very well." He hesitated a moment, a small part of him deep down somehow feeling bad about it. But, pushing those aside, he began to saw through the braid with the sharp knife.

As she listened to the *shr shr shr* of the knife ridding her of inches of knots and dirt, she could not help but close her eyes in order to hold back the tears that wanted to spring forth from the very depths of her breaking heart. *What have you done?* she sobbed inwardly. *Do you think you're going to be here a long time?* Opening her eyes, glassy with tears that she had barely been able to stop from streaming down her face, she stared dejectedly at the wall that helped contain her in this cell.

"Cap'n!" she could hear someone bellowing above them. "The winds be changin' as I ne'er afore seen!"

Smiling a strange, sad smile, Jacq felt a combination of frustration and sorrow. *I wonder*, she thought, *what my odds of survival would be if a storm were to sink this wretched ship?*

"Finished," Edgar sighed gruffly, backing up and tilting his head to observe his work.

"Cap'n!" she heard the man yell again. "We ain't gonna be seein' nothin' in just a moment! The winds be blowin' in the thickest clouds I e'er seen afore!"

Sniffing calmly in order to continue to restrain the tears that were pushing themselves forcefully forward, Jacq reached back with tentative fingers to undo the tangled mess that remained, now reaching just to the bottom of her shoulder blades. It wasn't so bad, really. Turning to Edgar and swallowing an iron lump that had developed along with the tears, whispered in a voice he found to be barely audible, "Thank you, Edgar."

The ship began to rock as the waves below changed to match the winds above. Nodding, Edgar returned his knife to his belt and stumbled slightly on his way to the cell door.

Exhaling heavily and wiping her eyes with the sleeve of her clean shirt, she straightened and said, "Let me finish my hair, and then I will be ready to see your captain."

"Cap'n!" shouted a voice shaky with superstitious fears. "The winds and waves be calmin' again as if they were tol' to stop by Circe herself…I can't be explainin' it…"

"Strange," Edgar muttered under his breath as he waited in the corridor. "I've never heard of the weather changin' so much in such a short time afore. It were as if it be havin' a mind of its own…"

A smirk of devilish delight curled Jacq's lips up at the corner. "But I have…" she murmured, splashing water over her hair.

"Are you quite certain this shall not be troublesome for you?" Alex inquired meekly, her cheeks still burning with the rosy radiance that had caught them on fire when she had asked Nicholas to fasten her dress.

"Quite certain, m'lady," Nicholas said to her pleasantly, nodding in her direction. As he nodded, he bent slightly at the waist, smiling all the while with his hands clasped ever-so gentlemanly at the small of his back.

Chewing on a long piece of grass he'd plucked from the nearby field, Miata rolled his eyes at their flirtatious antics. "I be not likin' this idea so much," he retorted loudly, crossing his arms in annoyance at the fact that Alex would not listen to him.

"Look," Alex returned in a growl, "Amy is going home with Bill and Frank, and Mr. Dunne said that his friend, Captain Adams, will be more than happy to give us passage aboard his ship so we may track down Jacq." Her eyes sparked dangerously as she glowered at the young man. "What is your reservation with this arrangement?"

Starting at first, Miata then chewed discontentedly on his blade of grass and, returning her glance with equal ferocity, said, "If Jacq were here, she would be listenin' to me."

"Well, Jacq is not here and I am not Jacq!" retorted Alex, a bitter bite in her voice that made it obvious she was quite annoyed with Miata for bringing her missing sister up in the conversation at all. *What kind of lowlife uses such a sensitive topic in an argument?*

"Of that, I be plenty aware," the reformed thief spat back hotly.

Alex's eyes narrowed. "Come along, Mr. Dunne!" Turning her nose skyward, Jacq's sister marched off towards the dock, dragging her Mr. Dunne along behind her.

Pushing off of the building he was leaning against, he followed Alex and Nicholas Dunne towards Captain Adams' sloop–a ship sought after by pirates for its speed and small crew requirements. He trailed them, not retracting his grumbling expression as he kicked at rocks in the cobblestone streets. All around them, the villagers were busy with their daily lives–walking here and there, leading their cart-pulling donkeys down the roads with some of them constantly braying out their annoyance with having to do such drab chores. Everyone smiled at the trio, unaware of the ranting and raving that was taking place inside of Miata's head as he nonchalantly placed one foot in front of the other in the direction of the Port Gilgallad harbor.

As they approached a smaller vessel at the dock, a large man with a bushy, coal-colored beard covering half of his face and equally black hair, thick and matted, shrouding his skull, turned from talking to another man and began striding towards them. At seeing him, Miata's palms began to sweat and he felt like he was hit with a breeze from the cold north.

Nicholas and Alex, however, smiled becomingly as he grinned at them heartily, a golden tooth gleaming snidely from his large, seemingly friendly mouth.

Miata suddenly realized that he was having difficulty breathing.

"Nicholas, lad!" the big man greeted in a voice that matched his size. "What have ya been about, says I?" As he spoke, he wrapped his thick arms around the younger man's thin body in a sturdy embrace.

"Captain Adams!" Nicholas, suddenly sounding rather small, returned cordially, though he could barely breathe.

Placing him back on the ground, Captain Adams tilted his head to listen to the young man's words.

"These," he coughed, recovering from having the wind squeezed out of him, "are mates of mine who'd greatly appreciate it if you could give them passage on your ship." He smiled as he tried to keep the fact that he was struggling for air as unnoticeable as possible.

"Be that so?" the man returned boisterously, turning with his liquor tainted breath to Alex. His middle-aged gray eyes sparkled like the sea when dusted with moonlight on a cloudless night. "Ya know they say a woman aboard a ship be bearin' bad luck…"

"Is that so?" She laughed, shrugging in acknowledgement as her face squinched up and she forced herself to remain standing rather than fall backwards at the overpowering smell of strong rum on his breath. "I did not bring poor luck on the last ship I was aboard," she countered cheerfully, smiling even though she couldn't help but admit she was rather intimidated by this man, who stood well over a sound six feet in height.

Despite his sudden nerve-racked condition, Miata found that he could not help but smile at Alex's attempt to seem strong to such an intimidating man. Then his blood ran cold again as the captain's eye fell on him. Forcing the corners of his mouth up rather pitifully, he gave a respectful nod in Captain Adams' direction. *By the powers! I pray that he be not recognizin' me face! Alex would gully me fer sure!* He could not help but fidget slightly at the man's unceasing presence and stare.

"Well, lad," Captain Adams laughed heartily, "be not shy 'round Captain Adams, especially if ye be sailin' aboard me

ship!" Taking an assertive step forward, he gripped the young man's hand, which had turned into the consistency of putty, and bellowed into his face. "And what be yer name, lad?"

"They be callin' me Miata since I be rememberin'," he answered sheepishly, finding that he could not swallow the expanding rock that had formed around his Adam's apple. *This be most awful! Why the devil be he pretendin' he be not knowin'? Perhaps me face has changed to be hidin' me identity from him! Aye! It could be!* Taking the sum of his entire will power, Miata smiled boldly and casually asked, "And ye be Captain Adams o' what ship?"

"Haha!" the man laughed jovially, patting him on the back with a hand so heavy Miata lurched forward and his face contorted as if he'd been hit in the back with a large sack of flour. "I be Captain o' *Anne's Triumph*! Where be ye bound, mates?" he questioned, finally turning back to Nicholas Dunne. Miata breathed a deep sigh of relief, wondering if he was going to pass out as he did so.

"It seems Miss Luray's," he gestured formally towards Alex, "sister was taken captive by Captain Ming." He paused deliberately. "We are requesting that we leave to find them by high tide tomorrow."

Captain Adams began smoothing his beard, looking contemplatively at the small group in front of him.

Glancing nervously at Alex, Nicholas cleared his throat and added, "If Captain Ming has any treasure on his ship when we catch him, you may plunder as you wish."

Tilting his shaggy head first to one side, then to the next, Captain Adams sized up the three. "Captain Ming, be it?" he questioned quietly.

Alex took a deep breath and answered, "Yes."

Nicholas and Miata both nodded in agreement.

Adams continued petting his lengthy, woolly beard with the steady, even strokes one uses to pet a large house cat. His nostrils flared, allowing him to be enticed by the tantalizing smell of the sea's salty breath. The sun bathed his back in warmth. What had he to lose? He had no immediate plans at the moment. He and his men had been ashore for several days…

"I do have money," Alex spoke up quite suddenly, surprising them all. "If you wish to be paid for your part in performing the service of rescue…" She offered in a politeness that bordered on desperation, her eyes begging relentlessly and her tone promising guilt if he did not oblige.

Stepping in, Nicholas added, "And I would pay a part of your fee if you were of a mind to charge a lady to search for her sister." He eyed the man evenly, waiting for his response.

Miata observed the silent haggling with interest, watching Nicholas' nonverbal–what was that? Begging?

Without saying a word to them, Captain Adams turned on his heel and strode in the direction of his ship.

Alex turned panicky eyes to Nicholas, who continued to watch the large captain's retreating back as if his stare would force the man to agree.

However, Miata breathed a sigh of relief. *'Tis fer the better,* he thought coolly, turning to walk back towards the inn.

"Away with ye, crew o' *Anne's Triumph*!" Captain Adams' voice called out loudly and unmistakably into the air. "Round up the men! Prepare our ship to be settin' sail with the mornin' tide! Ye best be sober in the morn!"

Choruses of "Aye, aye!" filled the air like the spray of the waves beating on the side of the vessel at every declaration the captain made.

Alex's eyes grew wide with excitement as she turned giddily to look between Nicholas and Miata, who were looking rather proud and sick, respectively. "He is going to assist us?!"

'At's the way, Nicholas thought to himself in relief. Nodding, he grinned broadly at Alex's hardly contained joy at the news.

Noooooo! Miata's brain screamed as he steadied himself on a nearby donkey.

"He-haw!" the donkey blared at him, putting its long ears back in annoyance at the added weight and stomping its back hoof.

Dodging the hoof, Miata stepped away from the donkey and retorted, "Silence yerself, ya bilge rat!"

Captain Ming, dressed no longer in white, was still just as flamboyant aboard his ship as he was on land. He wore a long red coat with rich black and gold embroidery over a blood red shirt and a pair of black trousers that reached halfway down his calves like those of Jean-Paul's. Black leather buckle shoes shod his feet and striped stockings covered his legs between his trousers and shoes. Two baldrics were strapped atop everything else, crossing over his chest and allowing a scabbard sheathed cutlass to hang at both sides. He also donned a rather large black hat with a bold purple feather protruding from it. Around his waist he also had a wide belt with flintlocks and daggers decorating its circumference.

Jacq, now wearing an oversized cream colored blouse securely fastened shut with the strings at the top and a slightly ragged pair of mid-calf length trousers, stood before him with her new hairdo. Almost immediately, she noticed her golden

locket hanging from the chain about his tan neck. Her hazel eyes smoldered quietly as she waited for him to speak, but he simply remained silent, observing her calmly through his slanted Eastern eyes.

The longer she stared at it, the more her irritation festered and bubbled into a hot feeling of injustice. "That's mine," she finally said in a murmur, surprising herself slightly at the fact she had spoken aloud.

Other than his small mouth tugging up in the corner with smug amusement, his face remained unchanged. "I know."

"Are you going to give it back?" she asked in a growl, feeling her face flush slightly.

"Nay," he replied shortly.

Swallowing timidly, she prepared to ask another question, but he interrupted her.

"Sit," he commanded, motioning to a chair at a rough table off to one side of the room.

At her hesitation, a large man with skin the color of the darkened ship's wood came forward from the shadows he had blended into so well. His striking blue-eyed stare convinced her wordlessly to march straight to the chair and seat herself.

As she sat, Captain Ming walked to the other end of the table, seating himself neatly at the head. "Eat," he ordered coolly in his monosyllabic fashion, plucking some fruit off his table for himself.

Casting wary glances towards the large, dark, barefoot man, Jacq couldn't help but notice him wearing a strange beaded necklace and matching armband around his bicep. Further inspection revealed his worn vest and trousers shared an embroidery pattern she had never seen before. Afraid he would notice her curios gaze, she made herself focus on collecting food that looked mildly appealing to her. As she gazed about the table, dripping in apples, grapes, biscuits, chicken, turkey, wine, and various other foods, she suddenly felt a sharp pain deep within her gut. The more she smelled the food and eyed it, the hungrier she became. Snatching up first one thing, and then another, she began to devour piece after piece of food that touched her fingertips and looked good to her eye. The sweet smell of smoked turkey…the round plumpness of the juicy green grapes…the hot, seasoned scent of the sauce in which she was to dip the biscuits enticed her to eat and eat…and then she stopped abruptly, staring up at the captain.

Both Captain Ming and the swarthy man in his employ were watching her in silence. Ming was munching silently on a few grapes that he had pulled to his plate and sipping on the wine he had poured into his gem-studded golden goblet from the bottle on his end of the table. "She is most hungry," he noted to his bodyguard, chortling in depraved amusement.

"Are you going to kill me?" she asked pointedly, her mouth full of food. Gulping down part of what was in her mouth, she asked herself, *Why would you ask that? If they weren't going to, you just gave them a great idea!* Rolling the rest of her food around with her tongue, she continued to chew more slowly now, keeping an eye on them as she ate.

"Bahari," Ming spoke to the other man, "pour her wine."

Her stomach knotted as the muscle-bound man walked silently to her side and obligingly poured wine into her empty goblet. She could see his muscles ripple as he lifted the bottle from the tabletop and turned it to let some of the liquid drain into her cup. As he finished, she gave him a soft, apprehensive smile and whispered, "Thank you," as he set the bottle down and turned away.

Pausing, he reverted his eyes, shining like blue topaz set in an ebony statue, back to her and muttered in a voice so deep Jacq swore she felt it vibrate her chair, "Welcome, Shakina." Then he pivoted back around and returned to his place behind Captain Ming.

Did he curse at me or was he being nice? Jacq picked up her goblet precariously, keeping her eyes wide open and staring ceaselessly at the small man at the other end of the table, who was returning the gaze with an equal amount of evenness. "So," she began again, "what do you want from me?"

Rolling his eyes, the Easterner intertwined his bejeweled fingers and returned, "Why does it concern you so much that I would feed you?" Continuing to eyeball her as if she was being completely ridiculous, he plucked a couple of the delectable grapes and tossed them into his mouth one at a time.

Taking a sip of wine, Jacq shrugged and replied, "You are a pirate, after all. You buccaneers are not exactly known for your hospitality."

"Haha!" he laughed, slapping the tabletop to express his amusement. "She will make a *fine* pirate!" he said to Bahari in his strange accent, as if he had won a bet on the matter.

"You want me to be a pirate?" Jacq laughed, shaking her head in disbelief. However, despite her great dislike for the pirate lifestyle, she found herself ever so slightly interested. Whether the simple fact of being chosen or the call of the sea, she was not sure which was more at fault. Pushing aside any interest she had, she focused on her resolve to find out what was going on so she could make a plan to get off this ship.

"Aye." He leaned back in his chair, folding his hands over his belly.

His brief, direct answer caught her off guard. "Aboard your ship?"

"Aye."

"Under your charge?" Her face formed an incredulous expression.

"Aye." He lifted his chin. She had never seen a man look so pleased and so arrogant.

Scoffing, she scratched at her head. "And if I say no?"

"Where will ya go, lass? We're out to sea already." He grinned a little, his teeth glinting in the low light.

Sitting back, her brow furrowing in contorted knots of confusion, Jacq sighed heavily. "I don't understand. Who kidnaps someone to be on their crew?"

"A pirate o' course…" he returned with a sort of cackle as punctuation. "I heard o' Black Fred an' Gold Jem's trove. Then I heard o' Brown Bill Burgess settin' out to get the bloody booty for hisself." At this, he leaned forward while a strange smile pulled the corners of his mouth up as if it were naught but a puppet on strings. "An' then I heard o' a lass by name o' Jacq Luray, bloody leavin' all o' 'em stranded on an island without thar bloody treasure." A chuckle, almost sinister, gurgled in his throat as he took another swig of wine. "An' then I says to meself, I says, 'Cap'n Ming, ya will have the sea bowin' at yer presence if ya be gettin' that lass to be fightin' in yer crew.'" With that, he put down his goblet with a sharp *thud* and turned his dark eyes to stare deep into her soul. "What do ya say to that, Jacq?"

Finding herself at a loss for words, Jacq suddenly realized that her palms were clammy–but not with worry…She was… trembling? With…excitement? *No! This cannot be! I am no pirate!* Shaking her head, she struggled to focus on Captain Ming and recall all the horrible things Jean-Pierre had told her about him. "No. I want my locket back."

His eyes darkened, but were still shrouded in a sinister sort of mirth. "What? It be mine!"

"What?" She balked at his claim. "No…It's mine!"

"Nay, lass. Mine! I stole it fair and square!" As if to solidify his statement, Ming pulled a foreign, wavy bladed dagger from his belt and stabbed into the table next to him.

"What?" she asked, exasperated almost to the point of speechlessness. "That is rubbish! There is no fair and square way to steal!" She laughed, amazed at the ideology and insane mentality that these fiendish thieves had developed for themselves. *I stole it fair and square! Ha! What in Port Royal is that supposed to mean?* Then, eyeing the dagger that was still wobbling slightly from being forced into the table, she inquired, "Are you threatening me?"

He glanced between her and the dagger a moment, then focused on her. "There be a fair way to be stealin' under my charge," he coaxed, captivating her wide-eyed gape. "Ya see, lass, when yer not one o' me crew nor aboard me ship, yer free game, lassy. Now, if ya are one o' them what sails under the flag o' the *Wind Hawke*, there be consequences for anyone who be sailin' under our colors and stealin' from ya. But, I still can't be givin' ya back the locket, Jacq. Ya be needin' to work fer it…showin' favoritism ne'er be good aboard ship, 'specially if I be showin' it to a lass…" Cocking his head to patiently wait for her response, she could feel him compelling her to agree to this outrageous arrangement by the very demeanor of the silence that surrounded them.

"My necklace in exchange for being one of your crew?" Jacq asked, befuddled.

Ming just continued staring at her, his silence serving as confirmation.

The girl's eyes narrowed. *Just for the necklace...* she argued inwardly, looking hard at the leftovers that cluttered her plate. She could feel his quiet stare knowingly studying her face for a sign of a decision. *How could I become one of them just for an heirloom?* Her brow furrowed. *How can I let him keep it?* Fidgeting from one side of the chair to the other, Jacq kept herself from meeting the stare of the captain. *It will be just for a bit... Only long enough to get back my necklace, even if I have to steal it. I'll form a plan and escape. I'll find a way.* Alex would be furious. *Alex...* Looking up so abruptly that she startled both Captain Ming and Bahari, Jacq sighed.

Ming looked pleased.

"I cannot," she breathed, shaking her head in defeat.

"What? Why not? Yer perfect for it!" Ming argued, clenching the armrests of his chair in annoyance at her persistence to keep on the straight and narrow.

Shaking her head, seemingly as if in shame, Jacq then retorted sharply, her eyes narrowing into slits of irritation that were equal to that of the captain, "I *am not* a pirate."

"Haha! No?" he questioned, his voice lingering in a hiss. The tone was intended to entice her subconscious into being curious as to what he could possibly mean by such an absurd statement. "Yer the closest thing to bein' one without bein' one then..." This comment he made in a low, almost threatening tone of voice that made Jacq's spine straighten and her eyes blaze. The captain smiled.

"I am not! On what account?" she asked in a fierce retort, her eyes boring holes right through his fraudulent high-class appearance. Her mouth fell into a thin-lined frown and her nostrils flared slightly as she waited for an explanation.

"Aahh...but ya are, lass. Ya killed Black Tom on Martinique

Isle, ya marooned Burgess' crew, an' now yer the owner of buried treasure, are ya not?" She opened her mouth to argue, but he pressed on. "Ya were raised by pirates for a portion o' yer life…Yer in love with the sea, and ya be wantin' adventure more than most…" He let his voice fade away, watching her mind spin, and hoping it would drown in temptation.

"And what of my sister? Many of those same things apply to her!" she asked, feeling a maddening need to defend herself.

"But not all," he continued in a low voice. "Ya know, with twins, there always be a good twin, an' there always be a bad twin. Alex be not the bad twin…" He stared at her unremittingly, demanding that she look at him…look him in the eye…

Her breathing becoming heavier, Jacq swallowed an iron lump in her throat. *Why am I so upset about this? It is what he wants…me to be upset about such things and unable to think clearly. But I am not the bad twin…neither of us are…* She could feel beads of perspiration springing forth onto her skin as if she was apprehensive about being caught doing something terrible. Then, in a moment, she felt cold all over. *I did kill Tom…but it was to save Miata and Alex…*

A rush of guilt came cascading down over her persona as she sat contemplating what the captain had just said. It was a guilt she had fought with before and conquered! How could he bring it back like this now? Did that one act really change who she was and redefine her forever? Tears pricked at the backs of her eyes…but what for? She hadn't done anything wrong. Alex would be furious about her hemming and hawing over what to do. However, thinking of her sister only hardened her resolve to find a way out of this. Plus, Ming had a point… She was trapped at sea on a boat full of buccaneers. She lifted her eyes and met his gaze.

Chapter 3

Leaning on the graying railing of Captain Adams' *Anne's Triumph*, Alex squinted at the vanishing town of Port Gilgallad on the horizon behind them. Since they had left early that morning, the landmass which housed the tiny fishing village was beginning to dip below the seemingly endless curvature of the Earth's glassy Atlantic Ocean. "Miata," Alex said in a sigh, glancing at the young man who was resting against his forearms on the rail a short distance from her left, "do you think that she is all right aboard that pirate ship?" The salty sea spray sprang up towards them, lapping at the dull colored planks that formed *Anne's Triumph*'s bow.

"M'lady, it is difficult to say what awful things thieving scoundrels such as they would do to a maiden such as yourself. I can only pray that your beloved sister has the courage to be aboard such a vessel of iniquity," Nicholas Dunne said with empathy, coming between her and Miata to stand beside her in his potent gentlemanly fashion.

Straightening then leaning against the rail with his hip, Miata cleared his throat as he crossed his arms over his lean chest. "Beggin' yer pardon, sir," he spoke up, tilting his head as

he eyed the slightly overdressed and under-titled seaman, "but Alex were askin' me the question." Then, deliberately moving his gaze to find Alex's, which had turned wide-eyed to stare at him in shock, Miata replied, "I be thinkin' Jacq be fine aboard that ship o' fools. They be not knowin' what they be pickin' up when they be catchin' her." He assured her via an impish smile with a twinkle in his eye.

Somehow, Alex couldn't help but feel comfort in his expression. There was only one other person she knew that smiled like that...The best part about having Miata along for this unfortunate venture was that sometimes he made her feel as though Jacq was with them.

"Pardon me," Nicholas said, almost choking and nodding an apology. "I had not intended on interrupting your conversation," he continued in the politest tone of voice Miata had heard to date. "Please excuse me." Bowing slightly in the direction of Alex, he then turned and walked off towards the helmsman.

"Miata!" she said through clenched teeth as soon as the gentleman was far enough off that he could not hear them. "What is wrong with you? Mr. Dunne is a man of society and sophistication! You, of all people, have no right to speak to him in such a way!"

"Me o' all people?" he repeated in disbelief.

Adjusting her lacy gloves, Alex touched at her done up hair and scowled at him, scolding him with her eyes as she waited for a response.

Keeping an even, unaltered gaze straight into those big hazel eyes, Miata returned in a rather monotone voice, "I be not likin' him, Alex."

"What?" Alex scoffed, her eyebrows rising as she folded her arms in retort and expectation of a really, really good

explanation. "And why do you think I should trust your instincts when it comes to kinds of people? You *were* in with Tom Thomas on the Sea Dragon...You *were*...probably still *are*...a thief...What about you should make me even consider trusting you?" She sneered. *I shall never understand what either of my sisters see in this ruffian! What in Port Royal about him compels them to make an exception on his account? They are such higher class!* Continuing to glare at him, she took one small step forward and whispered, "And what is it about Captain Adams that makes your blood run cold?"

As Miata stood still, returning the gaze he had held while she had spewed her spiteful words of despise, a dull cloud came over his face. A hollowness he had not felt in several months formed in the very center of his being. *She really be thinkin' I be not worth the salt to keep me...How can it be that Jacq be related to such a cruel lass as this?* Grinding his teeth together to hold back the indignation welling in his throat, he straightened to a height Alex had not recalled seeing him stand at before. Then he calmly, in the softest voice she had ever heard him use, replied, "There be times when ye just be havin' to trust yerself to believe, no matter if it may be seemin' wrong."

Then, shrinking somewhat again, he furthered in an even lower tone of voice, "Besides, Jacq be trustin' me. Be ye better than her? Ye be so high an' mighty to be judgin' others? Be ye so righteous? I be one to be thinkin' only the good Lord be deservin' o' that right." Taking one more second to observe her, his head and throat throbbing with the pain that comes from restraining a tidal wave of angry words, the thief then turned silent as a shadow and disappeared among the crew members, leaving Alex alone to stare at *Anne's* wake.

As she watched him vanish soundlessly into the din of

the busy crew, a sharp pain gripped at her gut. *How dare he speak to me so! He is not but a thief!* Suddenly, she felt her eyes misting over in a manner that caused her vision to become rather blurry though no tears wet her cheeks. *But what if he is right?* She stared, blatantly troubled, back in the direction of the village that they had left behind them. "There has to be a reason that Jacq trusts him so," she murmured to herself. Realizing her forehead was beginning to ache, she forced the muscles in her face to relax. When she did, her heartbeat slowed as well. "Why did I become so upset about this?" she whispered in confusion, searching the sea sprayed air for an answer. "Lord God," she said in a ragged voice, feeling her throat contracting as she spoke barely audible to her own ears, "forgive me…and keep my sister…" Covering her face with her dainty, lacy hand, Alex doubled over on the rail as small sobs shook her body.

"There now, m'lady," Nicholas' voice soothed her suddenly as he set one hand on her back and rested the other on her arm. "There, there. I shall take care of you, just as Mr. Monroe would…" As the words slipped from his mouth, his eyes grew wide, and his breathing became much shallower.

"What?" Alex asked in a gasp, lifting her head, which had become buried momentarily in his chest and pushing off of him like he had the plague. "You know James Monroe?" *What have I done?* Her heart began to pound in her ears. Miata was right! Who was she to be judging others? She had what seemed to be a really promising relationship with a good, kind, strong man and here she was practically throwing herself at this handsome gentleman just because he was going out of his way to help her out?

"W-Why, yes, m'lady. We…We were good mates."

Nicholas smiled down at her, hoping that this familiarity would be a positive in his regard.

Were? How could Jim lose a friend? Unless some unfortunate… Pushing her fears aside, she smiled and wiped her tears from her cheeks. Clearing her throat, she cheerfully inquired, "And how is he?"

"Oh…" the man began, smiling sheepishly at her question. "Well, he's…" Looking skyward as he tried to think of a way to break the truth, Nicholas found that he could not put together a sentence that sounded proper to get the kind of results that he wanted.

Alex watched him, her emotions clouding her usually logical mind. "He is well, is he not?"

Clearing his throat, Dunne continued stalling as he attempted to string words together. "He's…Well, he was…"

Alex's soul shuddered and her breath caught in her throat. *No…No, no…*she thought fearfully. "Is he…"

Nicholas stared at her in tense silence.

She searched his face for some sort of clue, but was coming up empty from his veiled expression. "He is not…"

Unable to handle the intensity of her gaze, Dunne pulled his eyes to the deck. How could he say this?

"Is he…" her chest pulled in a pained breath of air, "…dead?" Covering her mouth, she turned away from Nicholas as tears began rolling down her cheeks. "Everyone is deserting me!" she cried bitterly, clutching at the cloak that hung about her shoulders.

Blinking in surprise at the young woman's conclusion, he came up beside her, placing his arm across her small shoulders. "There, there, m'lady." A bewildered smile breached his mouth. "I was not expecting you to come to that conclusion. Most

strong ladies such as yourself never believe their men die."

"I knew things would go bad," she sobbed, turning into his solid chest and soaking the front of his coat all the way through to his shirt, "right from the beginning. There was no way I could have kept him…And with all the bad luck going on around me, how could I expect this not to happen?"

"What be happenin' here?" Miata asked, coming up behind them.

As Nicholas Dunne whirled about, Alex and Miata both saw the wary look that embedded itself into his eyes as he scanned his surroundings. However, whatever it was apparently was not there, for he recomposed himself rather quickly and answered Miata with as much proper poise as if he had never been ruffled. "Miss Luray just discovered some dreadful news regarding Mr. James Monroe. I was…consoling her."

Eyeing the puddle on the man's shirt with skepticism, Miata shrugged and returned, "Well, Captain Adams be lookin' to have a word with ye."

"Oh! Many thanks for finding me," he returned, smiling. Then, bowing for Alex, he excused himself. "Let me know if you need anything, m'lady." Then he turned tail and trotted across the ship to find the captain.

Not saying another word, Miata turned to leave Alex to herself once again. He did not get very far, however, as he stopped at feeling her hand on his arm. Casting a glance over his shoulder, he gave her a weak smile, for she was staring at him, her eyes wider than he had ever seen and imploring him to stay and speak with her. "What be ye wantin'?" he questioned lightly, as if she had never spoken hurtful words in his direction.

"Miata," she started, whimpering pitifully, "do you think

it is true? Do you think Jim is...dead?" Her face paled as she considered the horrible possibility.

"Dead?" He scoffed. "He were a sturdy man an' good with a sword when last I saw him," Miata pointed out. "But, it be not matterin' what I be thinkin', only what ye be thinkin' about the matter."

Alex's face hollowed in surprise at his almost perfectly literate and respectful response.

Seeing through her expression, he shrugged sheepishly and acknowledged simply, "Jacq be teachin' me that." Sighing heavily, the affect of their past conversation began to resurface in his eyes; he rotated dejectedly in order that he might dismiss himself from her presence.

"Wait!" she called after him in a sulky inflection, dropping her hands to her sides.

He paused, not turning to face her.

"But this changes nothing between us!" As she grumbled her conditional sentence, she pointed menacingly at him.

His eyebrow arching involuntarily, Miata pivoted back around, his mouth twisting into a rather amused little smile as he folded his arms contemplatively over his chest. "And what be ye meanin' by that?"

"I-I did not mean for my words to be so harsh," she admitted glumly. "I...I am..." She took a breath. "I am sorry. I hope you can find it in you to...to...forgive me." Though her words were well choked on, Alex smiled honestly to help express that she was, in fact, speaking truthfully.

A warm glow radiated out from Miata's eyes and the smile that overtook his face. "Very well, Alex," he agreed, doing his best to hide his delight at her apology. "Ye be forgiven!" Giving a small bow to mock Nicholas Dunne, the ex-thief whirled about, his giant smile of victory unfurling, and marched off towards the kitchen below deck.

"So, you've got the bloody captain fooled into believing you'll join our crew, have you?" Jean-Pierre inquired, admiring a piece of old, fraying rope that had been discarded by one of the careless deckhands.

"What makes you so certain I shan't?" Jacq asked, taking a deep intake of the fresh, cool air from where she sat, perched atop a barrel. A slight breeze swept across the deck, loosening some of her pulled-back hair as it did. She smiled; the morning sun brightened.

He scoffed, shaking his head, squinting in the unhindered light. "You're not a bloody pirate!"

Laughing, she shrugged. "Well, what else have I to do while trapped aboard this ship?" she questioned, listening closely to the creaking of the ship and allowing herself to admire her craftsmanship.

She was a beautifully constructed vessel. The pirates had invested much time and effort into plastering the *Wind Hawke* with so much tar it appeared charred to anyone who was not within a few yards of her. She was an East Indiaman–a prideful find for any seafaring individual, but especially those who chose to commandeer rather than purchase. Her sails were smoky gray from being on board the well tarred ship, but it matched the look of the ship. The overall appearance of the vessel was that it had been through some strange fire that did not destroy it all together but, instead, simply seared every inch of it.

"It is nicer up here than in the brig – that is for certain,"

he agreed. Then, tilting his head in a contemplative manner, his eyebrows bunching together and his mouth curving up at one corner, he asked, "So, you made an accord with ol' Ming?"

"Of sorts." She laughed, giving him her full attention.

Rolling his eyes, he shook his head and commented, "Ming wants me to make sure you know how to use one of these." As he spoke, he tossed her a sheathed cutlass he'd been holding in his left hand.

Catching it with ease, a devious smile pulled her lips taught. "What? This?" Jacq laughed, looking down at the sword as if she was unsure as to what it was all together. Yet, her eyes sparkled as she admired the rather attractive piece of weaponry. It looked as if it was from the captain's very own personal collection.

"Aye," he acknowledged, beginning to circle her slowly. "Though I don't understand why he's so determined to make a pirate out of you. Is there nothing you can think of about yourself that would fuel this peculiar obsession of his?"

"Of that," she returned, shrugging soberly, "I have yet to learn. I have only agreed to this arrangement so that I may retrieve an object of value that he stole from me."

Snorting skeptically, Jean-Pierre eyed her a moment longer then, gesturing to the sword in her hands, he invited, "Shall we?"

Standing on the barrel, Jacq drew her cutlass in a slow, even motion that allowed the sound of the blade leaving its scabbard to drag out. Then, pointing it rather deliberately at Jean-Pierre's sword, she smiled a tilted grin and challenged, "Come at me, mate..." Rotating to follow his leisurely stroll around her, she began twisting the sword around with circular movements of her wrist.

His face breaking flawlessly into a broad admittance of devilish amusement, Jean-Pierre took two steps back and drew his cutlass in the same easy movement. Carefully, as though enticing her in some sensual way, he slid his blade along hers, making a metallic sibilant sound that either makes one's blood run cold in fear or hot with awareness of the potential danger at hand.

Jacq's eyes glittered as she, keeping her gaze fastened wholly on him, hopped daintily off the keg. She felt a shiver shimmy up and down her spine…but it was not from fear that she shuddered.

Likewise, Jean-Pierre eyed her ceaselessly, and, though his throat wished to burst forth in laughter, he somehow restrained, finding himself reveling in the tense stillness that was otherwise in the air about them. "Ladies first," he said, taunting her with his expression.

Taking a deliberate step forward, her cutlass blade hissing along his, Jacq tossed his aside and took a small lunge at him. Effortlessly, he parried her uninterested thrust and continued circling her as a predator does its prey. Listening to him walk stealthily around her, Jacq found that her subconscious was muttering to itself again. *Do not trust him…no matter how nice he may seem. He is just like the rest of them–scoundrels at their best.* Turning just in time to catch a swipe he aimed at her, Jacq found that her breath was catching slightly as her heart began to beat rapidly in her chest. "And just what am I?" she whispered in a voice too low to be heard by the buccaneer.

Nearby crewmen began to tilt their scruffy heads to try and get a glimpse of the two orbiting each other. They were each taking turns sidestepping and making playful swings at each other, assessing the other's prowess. Noticing the men out

of the corner of his eye, Jean-Pierre attempted to look more serious. "Who taught you swordplay?" he asked, sidestepping and parrying to avoid being struck by her sword. The sailors whose ears had picked up the metallic exchange between Jacq and Jean-Pierre moved a little closer.

"The credit does not all go to one man, but the man who taught me the basics also taught me to shoot," she replied, their blades clanging noisily back and forth between them. Out of the corner of her eye, she saw the peeping seamen beginning to point and whisper.

"Black Tom would agree with me, I wager, that whoever the man was did a fine job instructing you," he retorted, pushing her back so hard that she almost fell over the barrel and several locks of her shortened hair–pulled back and fastened with a leather strap–fell forward into her face.

At this, Jacq's eyes sparked venomously, and she snarled, "I'll shoot you as well if you ask me to, but spoil not the name of Captain Taylor! He was the bravest man I have ever met, and I pray that is only because I have yet to meet my father!" Shoving her cutlass into her scabbard with such force that it made a *tink* so loud that it echoed throughout the vessel, Jacq tossed her stray hair out of her face. Turning away, she almost ran into a hunched and shrunken older man hidden beneath an old brown cowl. Starting slightly, Jacq heard herself intake of air sharply as she stared at him.

He was hardly taller than she, though the look in his dark, glazed eyes suggested he had once been a grand sailor himself. His skin, tanned to a color darker than almost every other seaman aboard was wrinkled by time and toil. Jacq could see right through his mildly callous appearance. He was broken. Shoulders bent from the weight of countless obnoxious young men and guilt, he managed a sorrowful smile made about one third of wood. Her heart caved in as he reached out an old tattered hand to touch her young face. "May you someday repent, child," his old croaky voice whispered. "The pirate's life is not for you. And 'twould be an awful shame for you to join the likes of these in eternal damnation." Then, silent as a shadow, he pivoted away from her and hobbled down into the lower decks of the ship.

"Who is that, Jean-Pierre?" she inquired at a volume barely above that of a whisper. She could feel her heart beating in a dull, thudding fashion, and her very soul seemed to ache as if from a deep sadness. *For a strange old man?* she questioned herself, staring after him, looking mesmerized.

"That is the cook," Jean-Pierre returned, sounding either indifferent or disgusted–Jacq wasn't sure which. Glancing about him, his very gaze scattered the gawking sailors. "Ming keeps him because he believes that a teacher of the Holy Scriptures is the best kind of man to have preparing our food."

"Perhaps..." she agreed, still transfixed at where he'd disappeared. "Perhaps."

"Did you say Captain Taylor?" Jean-Pierre verified, taking a step closer to Jacq. His voice suggested he was entirely unaware of her hypnotized condition as she stared after the old teacher.

"Aye," she responded distantly. Something about that old man tugged at her heart. He couldn't possibly think she was a willing participant onboard, could he? Jacq looked down at her attire. She had to admit, it was a very convincing charade. *What am I doing? Playing a pirate or playing a fool?*

"Lass? Oi, lass!" Jean-Pierre called, strolling up beside her.

"What's his name?" she asked, still sounding faraway.

"Whose?" He glanced around for who she might be meaning.

Jacq turned an incredulous expression towards him. "The cook, of course."

"Oh. His name is…Well, I think it's George Brandon or some such thing. Everyone aboard just calls him Father," Jean-Pierre admitted.

Nodding thoughtfully, Jacq smiled softly and handed him the cutlass. "Thank you." Turning away from him, the young woman began to walk towards the gateway to the lower decks in a trancelike state.

"Oi! Jacqo?" Jean-Pierre called after her.

She twirled around to face him, her face not hiding the fact her interest in their conversation was waning. "Aye?"

Grinning sheepishly at noticing her loss of interest, Jean-Pierre inquired, "How long did you know your Captain Taylor?"

"Ten years," she replied calmly, her voice faltering in its attempt to be casual. She blinked a little then forced a strained smile onto her pretty but saddened face. "He was a good man." With that, she turned away once again, but this time, Jean-Pierre watched in silence as she vanished from his view.

"Captain Taylor…" He sighed, following her example of gawking, transfixed, in the direction of the old man. Jean-Pierre buried himself in thought for a few moments, his brow contorting randomly as he stood. "Good swordsmanship," he muttered under his breath, breaking his own hypnotic condition. Pivoting about, he all but ran into Bahari, Ming's brawny bodyguard. "Aah!" the Frenchman gasped, tapping the hilt of his sword to make himself feel safer.

"Captain wants to know about Shakina," Bahari's deep,

monotone voice commanded emotionlessly.

"Shakina? Oh, Jacqo…Of course." Nodding and grinning, Jean-Pierre took a step back from the large, swarthy man. "Uh, she seems to have good swordsmanship. I think she could handle any sword the captain decides to give her," he reported, nodding in confirmation that he was finished.

"Is that all?" he asked.

"Aye," Jean-Pierre assured, nodding wholeheartedly.

Not speaking another word, the man swiveled slowly about and trudged back to Ming's quarters.

After the door was shut securely behind him, Jean-Pierre exhaled a large amount of air he hadn't been fully aware of holding trapped in his lungs as he muttered, "Why does he do that to me?"

Below, Jacq had timidly found her way to the kitchen where the old man sat quietly peeling potatoes. Entering noiselessly, she approached his bent side, sitting as silently as she had walked. She watched him, slaving away for ungrateful, thieving oafs who would never thank him for his work. *How does he do this?* she wondered.

"I wasn't always this way you know," his aging voice cracked.

"What way?" she returned, startled at his random comment.

Pausing his potato peeling, it was then that he turned his languid, watery eyes to look at her. "Look at you. You are beautiful, young, and yet here you are, aboard a ship full of murders and thieves. Many would think it unfair or a tragedy…"

Letting out a ragged sigh, Jacq hung her head and whispered, "I am a murderer myself." Her heart beat loudly in her ears. *Did I just say that aloud?*

"Are you?" he countered, not at all reacting surprised with this statement of revelation. "In whose eyes?"

"It matters not. If I killed someone, then I killed someone. You, of all people, should believe that as well," she retorted, reeling back slightly at his response.

"That, child, is rubbish." He cackled, sending chills down her spine. "You are the only one that knows, other than our good Lord, if you murdered that man." As he spoke, so matter-of-factly, he returned to peeling his potatoes.

Blinking as she pondered these things, Jacq tilted her head to stare at him and asked just above a whisper, "Do you suppose I could ever be forgiven for what I've done?" She had not realized until that moment she had yet to fully reconcile the shooting of Tom Thomas several months ago. Though it was in defense of people she loved, a small part of her had pulled that trigger in anger, and it ate at her. Sometimes, on the dreariest of nights, his face, shocked and injured, would still haunt her.

"Aye, child," the cook replied easily, turning and smiling empathetically in her direction. "The unpardonable sin is never seeking forgiveness for your transgressions. Only then can you never be forgiven," he explained softly.

Smiling, Jacq found her throat swelling with intense relief at this notion. *I shall confess this very night!...and every night hereafter until I am off this vessel...* "How did you end up aboard this ship?" she inquired, picking up one of the unskinned potatoes and turning it over in her hands.

"I was taken captive," he acknowledged, chuckling slightly at the memory. "My ship was attacked, and Fai Ono had me spared because he was afraid of killing a man who studied the

Holy Scriptures…so he put me to work instead."

"Fai Ono?" she repeated skeptically. "Captain Ming is Fai Ono?"

"Aye. Your Captain Ming? That is his real name, you know." The man cackled in amusement.

"No wonder he goes by Captain Ming!" She giggled along with George. "What kind of proper pirate could be feared with a name such as Fai or Ono?"

"Aye. But what he wants with you, I have yet to figure out. What about you commands the attention of a blood thirsty captain when killing you is not his intent?" he inquired.

She shrugged.

"You should be asking yourself the same question," he advised dryly, picking up another potato. "Now, get along; I have much to do. Ming won't be pleased if his newest addition is spending her time below deck with the old cook." He smiled faintly, urging her to not stay for too long a time.

"Aye, Father…" she agreed, setting down the potato, "but permit me one last question?"

Smiling, he nodded.

"When they attack ships, do you fight alongside?"

"Nay, lass." He chuckled in his awkward, cackling way. "I pray."

Chapter 4

"And we are doing this because...?" Alex sighed, watching Miata's expression fall as he buried his face in his hands.

"Alex," he reiterated, "ye have to be willin' to be trustin' me. Just don't be gettin' too close to yer friend, Mr. Dunne. I be not trustin' him." Lifting his kind blue eyes to stare helplessly at her, he added, "Ye be needin' to be findin' out why he be so eager to be helpin' us."

Finally nodding, Alex murmured, "I suppose you could be right. He could be just a gentleman, though. Did that thought never enter your devilish mind?"

Rolling his eyes, Miata hopped to his feet and, casually wandering to the wall, he let his head fall to meet it, producing a loud, echoing *thud*.

Alex jumped. "Miata!"

"How can ye be so willin' to be trustin' a stranger and not be willin' to be trustin' what I be sayin' to ye? I be wantin' to find our Jacq. Ye be knowin' me intent, yet ye be not willin' to trust me word o'er the word o' some high-falootin' scalawag what wanders into yer life!"

"Mr. Dunne is not a scalawag!" Alex retorted with a snap.

"He is kind and considerate and has manners!"

"But how be ye knowin' the reasons he be havin' fer takin' us to find Jacq?" he pleaded with her, sitting down at the table across from her again.

Heaving a frustrated sigh, Alex shook her golden head and admitted, "I know not his reasons, but is it not possible that he is just a gentleman and wanting to help a lady in distress?"

"It be possible, lass," Miata acknowledge. "But, it be not likely." He smiled doubtfully in her direction. "It be rare fer a man to be doin' favors an' not be havin' somethin' to be gainin' from his efforts." He ran his eye up and down her attractive figure.

At his glance, her cheeks flamed. "Very well," she said, folding her arms over her stomach and forcing herself to return to her even glare at Miata. "So, what exactly are you suggesting I do?"

"Ye needn't be changin' yer behavior," he said, "but ye be needin' to be listenin' to what he be sayin' an' why an' when."

"So you want me to doubt and question everything he has said and will say to me?"

Miata shrugged sheepishly. "Ye be makin' it sound as if ye be doin' him wrong, but I say yer just bein' cautious. If we were a might more cautious o' our company afore, ol' Tom ne'er would have been shot."

Her face getting hot with crossness at such a suggestion, Alex was quiet a moment before inquiring, "And what is it about Captain Adams that makes you so nervous? I asked you once before, but you never gave me an answer."

Gulping sheepishly, Miata confided, "Cap'n Adams be havin' a run in with me afore." He smiled.

She stared at him, partly in shock, partly wishing him to continue.

"If me memory be servin' me proper, Cap'n Adams were once under the charge o' Cap'n Ming, he who has Jacq now. Some time ago, Cap'n Adams, who were not cap'n then, be comin' to an inn I were doin' business at, an' I ne'er seen a man as drunk as Cap'n Adams were that day. Seems Cap'n Ming had a disagreement with him an' he were lucky to be alive."

"Are you saying Captain Adams used to work for Captain Ming? The same Captain Ming who is holding Jacq captive right now?" Alex frowned.

"I be thinkin' so, mate," he answered reluctantly. "It be part o' my reasons fer distrustin' yer Mr. Dunne. But, aside from that, I be worried ol' Cap'n Adams be recognizin' the runt who stole from him that night o' drunken thunder."

"You stole from an intoxicated pirate?" Alex reiterated, her expression twisting in disgust.

Shrugging, Miata returned, "I done worse."

"Oh, believe me, *I* know..." Rolling her eyes, Alex shook her head and covered her face with her hands. "What did I ever do to deserve this?"

At this, there was a sharp rap on the door that allowed Miata and Alex privacy. "Who be it?" Miata shouted as Alex called, "Come in!"

Opening the door with mild trepidation due to the mixed instructions, Nicholas Dunne smiled and cleared his throat. "Excuse me. I hope I'm not interrupting anything..."

"No!" Alex smiled before Miata could say anything, taking a step away from him towards Nicholas.

Miata's eyes widened at this deliberate action. *Alex...!*

"Oh! Well, then, Miss Luray..." bowing, he offered her his

hand. "Might I interest you in a look at the stars?" His smile tantalized her heart the way the smell of a hot meal entices the stomach of a weary traveler.

"I would be delighted!" she accepted, standing and taking his arm. As she walked out the door, she turned to cast a glance at a befuddled Miata, who sat in vexation at the little table.

His mouth hung partially open, and he could feel his heart pounding in every inch of his body. Was she serious!!?? This could not be! All his efforts to articulate his legitimate concerns dashed to bits by the charming smile of this pompous oaf! As he watched her send him a look over her shoulder, his heart started to sink in ultimate defeat.

She winked.

He blinked. And as she shut the door behind Nicholas and her, Miata suddenly felt a wave of relief come crashing over him. "*Ha!*" He laughed and cheered, jumping to his feet. However, as he did so, he knocked the chair over, tripping over the legs and spilling himself wincingly all over the floor.

Holding her hand daintily in his own, Nicholas Dunne crossed the nearly empty decks to stand at the stern of the ship and gaze both at the ship's wake and up at the twinkling beauties too far above their heads to touch. "Do you study any of the sciences?" he asked her quietly.

"Sciences?" Alex giggled, taken aback and flattered that he would think such a thing of her. "I have not been able to study them as much as I would prefer, but I hope that someday I will get the chance to indulge myself with studying," she replied delicately.

Grinning at her, Nicholas turned his full attention to her. "Just when I think you can't get any more fascinating..."

She felt her cheeks get hot. His very presence, Alex

realized, made her feel as if she had really done something right. The way he looked at her…the way he talked to her…*I truly feel as if I am someone worth knowing when he looks at me*, she found herself admitting as he gazed intensely at her like he could see into her soul.

"They are nothing in comparison to your beauty," he said to her in a low tone. "Someday science will find out all about each one of those, but they will never be able to discover what makes you as lovely as you are." His eyes twinkled kindly in the moonlight. His light brown hair seemed to glow as if he was christened with a halo to show his innermost spirit.

What am I doing? she asked herself irritably. Dragging her eyes away from his constant stare, Alex felt her insides turning in circles. Decisions, decisions! Why must they always be so taxing on one's mind?

"Is there something the matter?" he questioned her, his voice displaying utmost concern.

Forcing a smile onto her face, Alex returned her gaze to him, shrugging indifferently. "Nothing is the matter…" she insisted, giggling at the simple fact that he had asked.

Suddenly she heard Miata whispering in her mind, *But how be ye knowin' the reasons he be havin' fer takin' us to find Jacq?* Her brow furrowing slightly at this, Alex tilted her head and inquired, "So, good sir, pray tell a lady why you are so willing to help a person you do not know search for someone you cannot verify to be missing?"

"Hahaha," Nicholas laughed in obvious amusement. "You see, dear lady, if there is one thing Nicholas Dunne should be known for, it is his gut instinct…not to gloat, mind you. However, I must admit that I have found myself quite useful when trying to decide whether or not something is worth

doing or someone is worth helping out. You, Miss Luray, are definitely worth my time and effort to lend a helping hand," he said comfortably, bowing in her general direction.

"Is that so, Mr. Dunne?" she replied, watching him carefully as she kept her eye steadily staring back into his.

Laughing nonchalantly, Nicholas nodded politely in her direction explaining, "There are some things in life that one just learns to trust, you know? For instance, sailors trust the stars for navigational guidance. You trust your heart on the fate of James Monroe."

At this, her heart skipped several beats, and she clenched her jaw. Every time he spoke James' name, a part of her became agitated and antsy.

Oblivious to her mildly loathsome glance, Nicholas continued, "I trust my intuition about whether or not you are someone I can trust." Searching her eyes for a doorway to her heart, he gently touched her cheek as if wiping away invisible tears that were streaming down her face. "I hope you find that I am someone you can trust."

Smiling skeptically, Alex caught a glimmer in his eye she had not noticed before. *He feels he can trust me! How wonderful is that?* her insides crooned. *Do not be a ninny! He is hiding something...* her other half chided. *Maybe Miata was right after all.* Shaking her head and blinking, Alex suddenly felt rather embarrassed when she realized that the whole time she had been raving internally, he had been continuing on about some element of science that he found quite fascinating.

"Are you all right?" he questioned, touching her forehead as if to search for fever.

"Yes, I am fine," she replied. "I was just feeling a bit... faint..." As she spoke, Alex could not help but feel a strange

sense of delight creep up in her mind at her clever little feat of disinformation.

"Oh! Let me take you to your room then, Miss Luray. It would be quite awful for you to faint on deck on my behalf," he assured her. Then, taking her arm tenderly in his, he led her carefully down below to her room.

Once they had reached the room, he opened the door for her and, smiling ever so courteously said, "And if you should need anything at all, please do not hesitate to ask."

"Thank you, Mr. Dunne." She nodded.

"Have a good night, Miss Luray."

Closing the door almost all of the way, Alex watched the young man walk casually down the corridor and up the stairs to the deck above. *So gentlemanly!* Her heart swooned. Then, shaking her head, she very quietly opened the door hardly enough for her to squeeze out, and tiptoed a little further down the corridor. Pausing at the door she now stood in front of, Alex sighed heavily. Reaching up, she knocked.

Opening the door just far enough he could peek out, Miata inquired, "Aye?"

"You might have been right," Alex confided in a low voice.

"What?" he retorted, sounding astounded and trying to hold back a gasp of shocked laughter.

"I said you might have been right," she repeated. "Now, are you going to leave me standing outside all night? That is impolite, you know."

"I ne'er been known fer me manners," he reminded casually, pulling the door wide.

"Maybe it is time to work on changing that." Taking an indifferent step forward, Alex made sure she was past the door and whispered, "I saw a glimmer in his eye tonight that I had not seen before. However, the reason for it is as yet unclear to me."

"Be he thinkin' ye be thinkin' somethin' be wrong?" Miata inquired, shutting the door.

"I do not believe so. He asked if there was something wrong, I told him I just felt a little faint. Then he walked me back to my room." She smiled again at the telling of her witty cover.

"Ye lied to him?" Miata asked, his eyebrows lifting in surprise and the corner of his mouth turning up in mirth.

"I did no such thing!" Alex retorted.

"Ye did so!" He grinned broadly, nudging her with his elbow. "I be meanin' no offense. I be impressed is all."

Alex felt the corners of her mouth twitch upward, despite the insulting potential of the comment.

"The captain wanted me to give these to you."

Taking a breath of the dark sea air, Jacq turned around to see Jean-Pierre holding something in his hand. Lamps from the captain's cabin transformed him into a silhouette. "What? He could not bring to give it to me himself?" Jacq asked teasingly, taking one more glance at the black, glassy sea, sprinkled with stars. Pulling her legs in from between the rungs of the ship's railing, the girl rose to her feet.

"Well, perhaps he thought it would be less obvious this way," he suggested, shrugging his shoulders in admittance that he did not know why he was requested to perform the delivery.

"Or perhaps he thought that, for some strange reason, I would be more receptive of a gift from you," Jacq suggested, holding her hand out for the present. "And on that account, he

would probably be correct."

Smiling, Jean-Pierre placed the gift he was carrying into her extended hand.

Jacq curiously pulled at the cloth covering that masked the identity of the gift. Finding the strings that tied it shut, she carefully tugged apart the knot and revealed to herself a set of swords unlike any she had ever seen before. "What are these?" she asked breathlessly, letting the fabric drop thoughtlessly onto the deck and examining every inch of the sheaths in the dimmed light.

"Why," laughed the Frenchman, his lip curling slightly as he tossed his head in the direction of the gift, "those are blades of the East. They are made light so that one may easily wield one in each hand."

"Truly?" As she ran her fingers over the smooth surface of the sheaths, she felt herself drifting away from the reality she was standing in. Inside her chest, she could feel her heart beating heavily with awe inspired wonder. The young woman soon found her fingers tracing the intricate carvings of the handle. Wrapping her fingers around it to hold it securely in her hand, she suddenly felt as though it became one with her arm. It seemed that the very metal began to run through her veins, hot with her blood. *What is this?* she thought to herself. *What is this sensation?* Realizing she was getting lost, she mentally cleared her throat. In an instant she was back in reality, standing beside Jean-Pierre. "What are they?"

"Twin katana blades I think; they are swords from Japan, one of the Islands of the East," he went on to explain. "I guess the bloody captain thought you might do well with a pair of swords." He folded his arms over his chest, studying them from the short distance he was away.

"Fascinating," she breathed, running her tongue along her slightly chapped lower lip as she continued to inspect the blades.

"And what have we here, Pike Legard?" an unfamiliar and not entirely friendly voice interrupted boldly.

"Oi, Red Handed Jesse!" Jean-Pierre called out in just as perky a tone as he had when he talked to everyone else.

"Yer bein' friendly with the lass, eh, says I?" He chuckled, coming up beside Jacq and looking nosily over her shoulder. "And what have ye there, lass? A set of swords says I..."

Jacq backed away from him slightly, attempting to smile at him. However, she found it rather difficult. "Aye, a set of swords it is," she returned coolly.

"Aah...An' ye must be the lass the cap'n be decidin' to be bringin' aboard. Me name's Jesse Smith, but ye be callin' me Red Handed Jesse. An', from I what I be hearin', the lads be callin' ye Shakina, says I," he noted in an upfront fashion that gave Jacq chills straight to her marrow.

She eyed the short brute a moment. "Shakina seems as fine a name as any," she replied as detached as possible.

"Ah! So be it, Shakina." Red Handed Jesse nodded, smiling such a ragged smile as Jacq had hardly seen before. His teeth, the ones he had, were small and singled out on his dark colored gums. It was easy to see, even in the dim lighting that Red Handed Jesse was a stout blond man, shorter than Jean-Pierre, with green eyes of poison. His demeanor alone was dreadfully cold and contumelious.

"Pike Legard!" he said in such a loud voice that Jacq's heart skipped. "What be ye thinkin' the purpose o' the cap'n holdin' this pigeon fer so long be?" He took a deliberate step forward, invading the space Jacq had provided herself with as a barrier from him.

"Of that, Red Handed Jesse, I know not. Now, back off the lass afore she cuts ya to pieces with her new arms," he spoke up, taking a step forward in her defense.

"Pigeon suits ye good, says I," Jesse said in a menacing mutter, turning to ogle Jacq. "I'll be seein' ya around, Pigeon, says I." Winking, he then sauntered off, plucking a half empty rum bottle out of the hand of a drunken sailor who had already drifted off for the night. Putting the bottle to his lips, he wandered down to the deck below.

Turning to Jacq, Jean-Pierre cleared his throat. "Why didn't you stand up for yourself, Jacqo?"

"I wanted to stay on his good side," she retorted.

Putting his hand on her shoulder, he smiled and whispered, "He does not have a good side." Then, casually walking to the rail, he lifted his eyes to the heavens. "Aren't they beautiful?" He sighed.

Coming up beside him, still holding the blades in her hand, Jacq inquired meekly, "The stars?"

"They are diamonds in the sky, lass." He chuckled, nudging her gently with his arm. "There they sit…just waitin' for the takin' by the likes o' them who discover the path first."

Glancing up at the stars again, Jacq then casually returned her gaze to the pirate at her side. A soft smile curved the corner of her mouth upward.

"Oi!" He laughed, nudging her again. "What is that?"

"What is what?"

"On your face…right there…" Reaching up, he grazed her lip with the rough edge of his tar and sun darkened thumb.

Jacq felt her face involuntarily smile further, a pain swelling in her cheek from holding the expression so taut. "I'm not sure," she admitted. "I had all but forgotten what such a thing is."

A pleasantly quiet moment ensued, wafting between them like the delicious smell of freshly baked sweet bread on a cold afternoon. He smiled again. "Well, it is very pretty indeed, lass."

Heat rose in her chest at his compliment. *Now wait just a minute there, lassy!!* part of Jacq's mind ordered indignantly.

What? the other half countered innocently.

You are flirting with this piratical scoundrel!!

I most certainly am not!!

Aye, you are too!! What good do you think this is going to bring you? To what end? What fortune?

He is less of a pirate than others aboard this wretched ship!

Less of a pirate? More civilized and good-natured, perhaps, but that is no excuse! Remember, scoundrels at their best.

Oh? What would you have me do then? Sit around and not gather friends in case I someday need them?

Friends and lovers are two entirely different castes...You know this!

What are you talking about?? You are not insinuating that I am even slightly interested in this hooligan, are you? A strange silence enveloped her thoughts.

"Are you all right, Jacqo?" Jean-Pierre inquired, touching her arm softly.

"Fine, thanks..." she agreed, smiling in embarrassment as if her thoughts were but signs on her forehead. "I...I-I think I am going to turn in for the night." She forced herself to smile again, nodding awkwardly in his direction.

Nodding, obviously oblivious to her predicament, he patted her on the shoulder and laughed aloud. "Very well! Good, lass! I'll be seeing you in the morning, Jacqo. You rest well now, ya hear? Ya never know when thar will be trove for the taking on the horizon!"

At this, Jacq's heart fell, long and hard, into her stomach, almost making her ill. Bobbing her head in agreement, she turned away to find that she had a painful choking feeling in her throat as though she was trying to swallow a rock and it had gotten lodged halfway. *Trove...* Both halves of her agreed on this. What a terrifying proposition! "What are you doing, Jacq?" she asked herself as she passed the entrance to the deck below. "Who are you?" she whispered, pausing to stare down at the hole. *What have I become?* Sighing heavily as she wedged her new pieces under her arm, she kicked at the boards that made up the deck and forced herself to trudge down the stairs.

Once below, she drearily dragged herself down the corridor to the kitchen where she knew George Brandon was most likely still cleaning up after supper. As she shuffled in, his aging eyes glanced up and slightly started when he saw her. "By the powers," he murmured, "you look as though you have lost something terribly important to you."

"I fear," she admitted, picking up a towel that sat near him and a dish that he had not dried, "that I shall become one of them..." Carefully running the towel over the metal bowl, Jacq found it easy to glance between the cook and the shiny surface of the cookware.

"Nonsense, child!" He chuckled softly. "But if you do not wish to be on this vessel, then I do wonder very much indeed why the Captain went through such pains to find you and bring you aboard..."

"It is curious. He sent Jean-Pierre to give me these," she admitted, pulling out the swords she had stowed, "and I do not know why." As she handed them to the old cook, she

found her eye scanning the intricate designs of the sheaths and acknowledging to herself that they were indeed beautiful.

Staring rather flabbergasted at the gifts, George tilted his head and inquired in a tone that matched his facial expression, "What does he have in store for you?"

Jacq turned a sad, uncertain gaze to him.

"These are from his personal armory. Such gifts he does not give lightly. The last person he bestowed such generosity on, if that is what you wish to call it, became his first mate."

Shrugging, Jacq shook her head. "It does not make sense. I do not know why he wishes me to be here and become a pirate. How did you avoid becoming a pirate all these years?"

Laughing sullenly, George wagged his head slowly from side to side. "That, my child, I did not succeed in."

She watched him, with her glazed expression, for an explanation.

"I did my share of piracy, but there came a day that I decided I would no longer commit such blatant heresy. And, I suppose, that is why I do not complain about the job I do now. It is, as you might say, a reaping of the harvest I had once sewn." At this comment, he seemed to travel back many, many years ago to a time that he wished had not happened as it had and to circumstances he wished he could forget.

"I do not wish to steal and kill so that I might steal," she acknowledged glumly. "Yet here I am, unable to change my fate."

"Your fate, my dear?" he inquired, seeing deeper into her thoughts than she realized. "Your fate is often not what it seems, especially in times of great distress. You have a hope within you that burns, though it may be low. Whatever you do on this ship, do not let that go out."

Smiling, she traced her fingers over the hilt of the sword that lay on top. "I very much wish that I were with my family." She sighed. "I mean, I have not even met them all yet, but I would very much fancy the chance to do so."

"Do not lose hope," he encouraged again. "It is what will keep you alive. Now off to bed with you afore morning greets us both." Handing her the katana blades, he took the towel and began to dry another dish he had just finished washing.

Thoughtfully picking up her swords, Jacq nodded and sighed. "Thank you for talking to me, Father." Bowing slightly in his direction, she found that it was quite easy for her to smile at him.

"Not a chore at all, my child," he insisted, a strange warm feeling creeping into his bones that he had not felt in a very long time. "Perhaps we shall speak again?" he inquired with a semi-interested chirp to his voice.

"Perhaps," she answered, giving him another smile before she turned and trudged up the stairs for the night.

"Jacq!" an old voice called as her door squeaked.

Groaning, Jacq rolled over in her hammock. Then, squinting through the early morning light that was bursting in through the door, she could make out the bent figure of George Brandon, the old cook, peeking around the edge of the door. "Aye?" she yawned, blinking away morning tears that sat at the corners of her eyes.

"Many apologies, lass," he whispered in his low, old voice. "But I was wondering if you wouldn't mind giving me some of your time." Nodding, Jacq stretched as she crawled out of bed, gesturing politely for him to please come inside.

Tottering in, George inquired, "Are you interested in art, Jacq?"

Shrugging, Jacq returned skeptically, shutting the door behind him, "Aye. I suppose I am. What kind of art?"

"Well," he began, reaching into his jacket, "I have been working on a sort of song for a few years now, and I cannot think of an ending. I wrote the first stanza and the chorus before I was taken captive on this vessel...and that was a very, very long time ago." He produced a folded piece of parchment that he carefully peeled open. Then, first clearing his throat, he began in a polished voice she had not anticipated him having in a tune that was far sadder than any she had heard in a long, long while,

> *I am weak but Thou art strong;*
> *Jesus keep me from all wrong;*
> *I'll be satisfied as long*
> *As I walk, let me walk close to Thee*
> Pause.
> *Just a closer walk with Thee,*
> *Grant it, Jesus, is my plea,*
> *Daily walking close to Thee,*
> *Let it be, dear Lord, let it be.*

"That is the chorus," he informed her, smiling with a strange twinkle in the sad cheerlessness of his eye. "There are two more verses."

Blinking in astonishment, Jacq smiled and obligingly motioned in his direction as she leaned against the wall. "Please continue."

Smiling, he shrugged shyly and continued,

Through this world of toil and snares,
If I falter, Lord, who cares?
Who with me my burden shares?
None but thee, dear Lord, none but Thee.
Pause.
Just a closer walk with Thee,
Grant it, Jesus, is my plea,
Daily walking close to Thee,
Let it be, dear Lord, let it be.
Pause.
When my feeble life is o'er,
Time for me will be no more;

Then, stopping awkwardly, he sighed and admitted, "I have not been able to think of the last two lines. I have been trying for the past few months to find them, but I have been unsuccessful thus far."

"You will find them," she told him, confident and touched that he would share with her.

"I wish you to hold onto this for me. Keep it safe," he requested.

Jacq's brow furrowing, she shrugged and returned, "Why? Why are you giving it to me? Why don't you just keep it until you can get away, then you can turn it in as a…a…hymn or something."

"Because," he explained in his old, chipper tone, "I do not think such scribble can possibly become a hymn of any kind… but it is one of my most prized possessions, and I would very much wish you to have it. I have no children of my own, but if I was ever blessed with a daughter, I would wish her to be much like you." His old eyes shimmered with gallant nobility that seemed to suit him far more than the old, ratty clothes he wore and the thankless job he performed. As he gazed into her eyes, he chuckled. "I daresay, my child, you shall find him."

Jacq's heart leapt to her throat and clung to her uvula, choking her. "What?" she gasped, finding her knees weak and her heart pounding with fierce rapidity.

Smiling sweetly, George lightly touched her cheek with his calloused left hand as he scooped her right hand into his. "My child," he confided, "I am old. I say little and see much. You will return to those you love before it is too late, of that I have no doubts." Then, glancing down at her hand, he gently pressed the parchment into her palm. "Now, please keep this for an old man."

Swallowing the rocklike feeling that had formed in the back of her throat, Jacq nodded resolutely and returned, "So shall it be! I shall keep this for you, but only if you agree to take it to the church when you have a chance."

His face blossoming with his wooden grin, he gripped the hand he had pressed the leaflet into and chuckled. "Then we have an accord!"

The salty water slapped angrily at the boat's bow, impatiently pushing and pulling at the vessel as if the sea wished for it to be off of the water in a hasty fashion. Alex's eyelids slid back, her eyes feeling inflamed with the grogginess of an early morning preceded by a sleepless night. Blinking several times, she stretched and dragged herself from her hammock bed. The ship's sway began to lessen as she slipped out of her night gown and into her daywear.

I wonder where we are putting into port. Yawning, she reached for the wall, closing her eyes a second. "Wait…!" She stopped suddenly, her eyes flying open. "Putting into port? What possible reason could we have for doing that?!" Scrambling to ensure she was presentably dressed, she then flung the door open and raced out into the corridor, only to run headlong into Miata. Colliding full force, the two fell in opposite directions onto the floor.

"What are you doing??" she demanded, rising breathlessly to her feet and madly straightening her clothes.

"What be I doin'?" Miata returned, trying to catch his breath from her shoulder knocking the wind out of him as he

stood. "What be you doin'?" He nodded his head jerkily in her direction.

"Well, I want to know why we are putting into port!" she retorted brusquely.

"I be wantin' to be knowin' the same, Alex!" he said in an irritated tone, finishing tucking in his shirt rather forcibly as he glared at her.

"I am surprised you do not already know what is going on!" she said at an elevated volume, charging ahead of him towards the stairs that led up to the salty air.

"What be ye sayin', Alex?" he called after her from between his teeth, catching up with her quite easily. "I be nothin' but loyal to our Jacq!"

"Sure you are! Just as you have always been, is that not right?" she returned as they spilled out onto the deck.

Pulling her back down the stairs far enough that she could not be seen by those atop, he whispered venomously into her ear. "Yer sister be trustin' me. If that ain't enough, I be wishin' ye luck when ye be throwin' in yer bet with a man who be mates with a lot o' pirates. Instead o' questionin' me, perhaps ye should be questionin' yer newfound mate."

Ripping her arm free from his grasp, Alex replied in a hiss, "Do not touch me, *mate*." Curling her lip in disgust, she stalked up the remaining stairs to the deck. There, she was rather surprised to see Nicholas Dunne watching the head of the flight of stairs rather curiously. Tilting her head sweetly to one side, she smiled and greeted, "Good morning, Mr. Dunne."

"Good morning," he returned, wiping the look immediately from his face.

"I was wondering," she said coolly, "why we are putting into port. Have we found the ship that took my sister hostage?"

"Nay, my lady," he acknowledged, "I am afraid we cannot chase pirates if we have no idea where they went. So, we are putting to port in order that we might find information giving us some kind of clue as to where those cutthroats might have taken your beloved sister." He smiled eloquently, seeming as genuine as any girl hopes for, and bowed to dismiss himself. However, he paused in the middle of his about facing and, turning back to Alex, inquired, "Would you care to join me for supper this evening in one of Penzance's elite inns?"

Blinking, Alex smiled awkwardly and agreed, "Oh...Of course!"

"I do so enjoy your company," he said in sincerity with a hint of shyness. "Walk with me...?" At his invitation he, ever so gentlemanly, extended his arm to her.

Feeling her face light up with a dainty shade of scarlet, Alex shrugged sheepishly and nodded. "Well, all right."Taking his arm, the two then very casually wandered away from the opening to the deck below.

Miata, peeking out at them between the floor of the deck and the rail, shook his head and sighed uneasily. "Penzance..." Straightening, he then sauntered out from below and over to the rail. "Who be I knowin' in Penzance?" His brow furrowing, he drummed his fingers on the rail and drawled, "Hubert Bixby? Nah, he were put behind bars a year ago..." Running his finger along his chin, he continued, "Maynard Fischer, rest his soul, been pushin' up daisies in France fer a few months now. Me mate, Jefferson Reinard...Gunther Caractacus! He be livin' in Penzance last I be hearin'! An' he always be knowin' the information I be needin'."

"What are you planning now, Miata?" Alex questioned simply as she approached his side.

"I be thinkin' ye be takin' a walk," he answered, mimicking Dunne's polished, high society voice.

"I *was*," she retorted indignantly, "but I was thinking about it and realized that I should apologize for my behavior earlier. I know we are on the same side and for me to treat you so is quite unladylike and remarkably unfriendly."

His brow wrinkling, Miata crept a little closer to her and whispered, "What be bringin' ye to these conclusions, Alex?"

Sighing rather dejectedly, Alex shrugged. "Everyone aboard this ship knew we were going to be stopping in Penzance except the two of us."

"Ye be believin' me that I be not knowin'?" Miata verified, smiling at this new turn of events.

"Yes." Alex sighed. "You have not lied about anything so far, and Jacq is the best friend I do believe you have ever had. So, because of these things, I have decided to try and put a little more faith in what you say." She offered up a smile.

Blinking several times, Miata found that he was completely, utterly dumbfounded and that fumbling for words was nearly useless. After numerous attempts to form his tongue and voice into words, he finally found himself saying in a coy tone, "Well…Thank ye…"

At this concise, yet so faultless response, Alex felt her heart warm slightly. *Perhaps*, she thought mindfully, *there is hope for him*. Then, shaking her head to rid herself of the fuzzy feelings growing in her brain, Alex repeated, "So, what are you planning now, Miata?" She glanced to where Penzance was steadily growing on the horizon.

"Well, one thing be in our favor." A wickedly handsome grin turned up the corners of his mouth. "There be a turning o' the tides."

Holding one of her new katana blades in each hand, Jacq closed her eyes and let them hang loosely at her sides. *Ya know, with twins, there always be a good twin, an' there always be a bad twin...* she heard Ming whisper in the darkest corners of her mind. Her mouth tensing into a straight, disapproving line, Jacq gripped the hilts of her swords tighter.

"It does not have to be that way," she said in a growl, her teeth clenched together. Twisting her wrists to twirl about the katana blades, Jacq spun about her room, daring any of the furniture to advance towards her. "We are not just as everyone else," she seethed at the boards that created the walls surrounding her. "They say there is an exception to every statute..." Then, turning quickly to face the part of room that contained a small window, she hurled the sword through the air. As it stuck in the wall, Jacq smiled. "Finally!" she said proudly. However, seconds later, the sword began to droop, becoming dislodged and clattering onto the floor. "Argh!" she pouted in dismay, trudging toward the fallen weapon. "I get so close..."

"Jacqo!" a voice yelled from beyond her room.

She eyed her door as she leaned over to retrieve the blade.

"Jacqo, Jacq!" the voice continued, coming closer and closer.

Stashing the swords in a corner of her room, she casually sat on her hammock, awaiting the entrance of the speaker into her room.

"Jacqo!" Jean-Pierre called again as he cracked her door and peered inside. "Tell me, are you feeling fresh, lass?" he inquired giddily.

"Why?" she asked distrustfully, her mere diction conveying her feelings.

"Because we are!" Flinging the door wide, he raced in, pulling her out of her room and directly to the rail of the ship. "Do you see her, lass?" Pointing at a spec out across the waters, he whispered, "There. On the horizon."

"What kind of ship is it?"

"It is Sea Legs Bill's ship, lass," Ming acknowledged, stepping up beside them. "She is one of the fattest fish of the sea, the *Eos Demeter*." His chest swelled with pride at the prospect of catching such a prize vessel, dripping with loot that only the inner demons of his mind could imagine. His dark eyes sparkled, and his smug smile twitched with pleasure. "Prepare to attack, lads!" Then, turning directly to Jean-Pierre, he added, "Oi, keep an eye on her."

"Aye, aye, Captain!" he agreed readily, smiling broadly at Jacq.

"Wait…What?" she asked in disorientation, whirling about to find herself eye to eye with the Frenchman.

"Get your blades, Jacqo," he whispered elatedly, cupping her face in his hands and leaning so close he could have kissed her. "There be treasure on our horizon!" Then, releasing her, he turned to the rest of the ship and shouted, "Gentlemen of Fortune!"

The entire ship turned their ears at this salutation. "Aye!"

"We are to add to our spoils the sweet plunder of *Eos Demeter*!"

Jacq watched in amazement as the whole crew cheered in unison.

"So what are ya standing there for? Away with ye, me hearties! The chase is on!" He pointed a long finger out in the direction of the hapless ship.

Cheering again, the crew burst out in a song with a chipper tune Jacq had not heard since the Midway Zebra. She listened to them shouting their notes boldly as they unfurled the sails and went about prepping themselves for their soon coming engagement. As they sang their song brazenly into the air, she recalled only a few times hearing Jemima singing it as she cleaned. Then, suddenly, for some strange reason, she felt at home. And as Jean-Pierre escorted her to her room to extract her weaponry, she found herself humming along with the rest of them.

What be better than rum I wonder?
Maybe stringin' me foes asunder?
Or sittin' on a good day's plunder,
An' me weight be in gold by t'under!

"Ye know this song, Pigeon, says I," a cold voice hissed in her ear, sending shivers down her spine and making the hair on the back of her neck rise in haste. The smell of the voice's owner wafted into her nose, causing her teeth to clench involuntarily, in part to keep her from retching where she stood.

"Aye," she replied, turning to face Red Handed Jesse as she exited her quarters and stood near the railing of the ship.

"Ye be fightin' b'tween Pike an' me, Pigeon, says I," he continued, smiling his smile so deceitful and twisted with seemingly years of evil. "Ye be safe next to me, says I. I been doin' this fer upwards o' five years, says I," he boasted.

"Five years," she echoed, the very idea making her want to retch again.

"An' I still be havin' all me timbers," he added after a second

of glowing pride about his previous statement.

"That is such a reassuring reason to fight beside you," Jacq said to him in sarcastic compliment. Glancing down at the blades in her hands, she then looked about her. So many men that were rank with a filth that penetrated far beyond the surface of their unwashed clothes and unkempt hairdos… There were no two ways about it. She was not home. She was stranded on a ship full of disgusting thieves. Turning, she found that Jean-Pierre was approaching her, an insanely happy tilt to his smile. Then, as he came to a stop beside her, she moved her gaze to the sea.

There it sat, basking so innocently in the sunlight. A vessel of beauty and grandeur filled with precious belongings that one man had stolen from another. Each crewman eyed it as if he had some right to its riches that was as yet unaccredited on his behalf. The blue water around it splashed high up on the sides as it raced to get away from the unavoidable. As Jacq stood observing the ship captained by a man born as William Drake and inevitably going to die as Sea Legs Bill, she could hear Jean-Pierre clear his throat and say, "The captain wanted me to give you these."

Turning, she saw him holding in his hands two flintlocks. Chuckling, Jacq shook her head retorting, "Are you serious? Where shall I hold them? My hands are full. And to what end? I do not intend to injure a soul."

Watching her awkwardly, Jean-Pierre sighed and pleaded, "Jacq, please take them…for your safety. You may not intend on slighting any of those men, but there is likely naught but a bullet that would stop them from hurting you. Nary a man aboard that vessel will wish you alive as much as I."

Glancing at him with a squint that could have been

mistaken for a glare, Jacq sighed. "As you wish." Snatching the two firearms, she tucked them into her trousers. *And why do you wish me to be alive?* She internally challenged him. As she looked into his eyes, she wondered, *Wait…is that genuine concern? For my safety? What manner of pirate is this? Quit being so kind!* She watched him stand uncomfortably a few seconds more before she said, "Thank you."

Smiling at this, he gently patted her cheek and replied, "You're welcome, Jacqo."

"So, let me make sure I understand this correctly," Alex sighed, looking hard into Miata's eyes. "You want to bring one of your thieving friends into this situation to help us out and give us directions?"

He nodded.

"And this is your brilliant plan?"

He looked a little sheepish and nodded again.

Sighing, she tugged on one of the loose locks of hair beside her face. "I have not yet met my father and I am standing here hoping that when I shall meet him, I shall not be embarrassed by having half of my associates previously involved in the occupation of piracy."

"At least ye be havin' the hope o' meetin' him," Miata commented in an unusually melancholy inflection, casting his glance momentarily away from her. "I be not havin' any idea at all what be of me own father an' mother."

"I am sorry," Alex returned, conflicted over if she should console him or take his comment as an attempt to cheer her up. She went for the latter. "So, tell me of your friends. How do you know you can trust them?"

"Me mates? Well, fer one, we be goin' far back as mates, an' fer two, they be honest thieves," he explained very matter-of-factly, nodding his head in an affirmative way.

"Honest thieves?" She laughed in disbelief, leaning forward so that she could look him in the eye.

"Oh, aye," he replied very pointedly, not seeing what was humorous to her. "Quite." He tilted his head in sheer curiosity as to the meaning of her laughter.

"I am sorry. I do not mean to make fun, but what kind of nonsense is this honest thief idea?" she asked in a laughing whisper, hoping she would not arouse attention.

"It be not nonsense!" He scoffed. "There be a difference between a thief what lies and a thief what doesn't!"

"And what is that?" She chuckled, wishing for something profound that would ease her mind some.

"Well, I told ye. One be tellin' lies and the other ain't," he concluded in a rather confused tone of voice. Eyeing her, he crossed his arms nonchalantly across his chest.

"Well, this is great...This is just great." She sighed, drumming the railing a moment with her fingers. "We are going to be using thieves to find thieves in the midst of thieves. Why can you not manage to operate things in an honest fashion? Why, for the love of England, Miata?"

"Nay, Alex, fer the love o' Jacq," he retorted, eyeing her rather evenly. "Have ye any better ideas?"

She was silent a few moments, desperately trying to come up with something, but with no success. "No..." She sighed dully and stared out at the ocean. The sea air tossed her hair slightly, tugging at her skirts as if in encouragement. "Well, if this is what we are to do, you continue editing your masterful plan. I am going to rest a bit while we finish putting into port, if that is good by you."

“O’ course,” he replied, nodding amiably.

Smiling, she curtsied mildly then sauntered down below to where she was staying, still trying to think of any possible alternatives.

After she was safely below deck, Miata turned to the ocean and mimicked in an overly exaggerated high pitch, “You continue editing your *masterful* plan. I do not mean to make fun, but what kind of *nonsense* is this honest thief idea?” Whirling back to where he could see the entry to the lower decks, he muttered in a mocking tone, “Oh, thank ye kindly, Alex. Yer belief in me rezorsefulness be heart wrenchin’ly sweet.” Smiling sarcastically in her general direction, he turned and began to pace along the rail.

The cool air of the sea seemed to get much colder the closer the *Wind Hawke* got to *Eos Demeter*. It seemed as if the saltiness of it was burrowing into the pores of the skins that stood waiting to catch the fattened prize trying so desperately to elude them. Jacq watched as barrels and crates went bobbing past to disappear in the frothy wake their East Indiaman was making. The men aboard the ships were hastily trying to prepare themselves for whatever misfortune might come their way. She could see, against the taut blue sky, the crewmen serving under Sea Legs Bill scurrying and hustling about, readying weapons and still throwing objects of all sorts and sizes over the railing of the ship. She felt a strange twinge in her heart. The staunchness of the condition of the men aboard *Eos Demeter* seemed to be fueling the attitudes of those aboard the *Wind Hawke*. The more frantically the others rushed about, the broader the grins became, the bolder the singers grew, and the faster the *Wind Hawke* swam to catch *Eos Demeter*.

"Jacq," the afflicted young woman heard a hushed voice call.

Whirling about, she saw George Brandon peering around the corner of the doorway that led to the deck below. "Mr. Brandon!" Jacq said, glancing about and hurrying to where he stood, clutching the doorpost. "Go below and stay there. Please, please do not come back up here until it is over."

"Jacqueline!" he restated her name, concern rising in his voice.

"George," she looked over her shoulder, "I intend to kill no one. Please just stay safe below."

"Lis'en to her, Father, says I," Jesse agreed in a harsh, raspy voice, coming up behind Jacq and giving the crumpled man a small shove.

"Leave him be!" Jacq snapped at Jesse. "He's harmless!"

"He be impedin' our mission, Pigeon, says I," Jesse retorted, eyeing her with a surly stare.

"Jesse, there will be no picking fights amidst our own crew, or five lashes be owed you," Jean-Pierre's voice shouted abruptly, interrupting the budding scuffle. "Jacqo, get back to the rail," he added sternly. Then, sighing, he turned to the cook. "And, Father, get below unless you plan on helping gather the plunder."

"But…" He cast a worried sidelong glance in the girl's direction.

Following the old man's distressed gaze, Jean-Pierre stopped and whispered, "I will keep a watchful eye on her, sir. No harm shall come to her if I can help it."

Nodding, the old man peeked at her one last time as she looked after him before tottering down the stairs to the kitchen. He took in her loose locks blowing about in the wind, now hardly longer than her shoulders. Her eyes, which spoke of happy memories and wondrous dreams, were filled with the sorrow of the moment at hand. She stood, two pistols tucked into her trousers, a sword gripped so tightly her knuckles were white in each hand, and her heart beating so violently the old man thought he might have seen it pulsating in her throat. "If I can help it," he repeated Jean-Pierre in a doubtful tone. "Never have I known words to seem so shallow." Just before he turned away, she turned towards him, and her lips, taut with concentration, formed a brief smile. In that instance, amidst the din of the hollow men about them, whose hearts were hardened to the beauty of life, George Brandon remembered for a moment what was good in this world.

As he disappeared below, Jacq returned her watch to what lay ahead.

"Ye be carin' too much fer an ol' useless man, Pigeon, says I," Jesse commented in a cold tone.

Not giving him the courtesy of looking his direction, Jacq returned between clenched teeth, "If you knew the value of people, Mr. Smith, you would understand my allegiances."

"Be that a threat, Pigeon, says I?" he inquired, squaring up to her offensively. His cold green eyes were rank with his wont immoral disposition and lack of any want to change whatsoever.

"Mr. Smith!" growled Jean-Pierre, pushing aside Jacq and forcing himself forward. "There will be no fighting aboard this vessel amongst her own crew," he paused rather pointedly, "or five lashes be owed you. I won't be warning you again." Turning away, he looked Jacq quite deliberately in the eye and added, "And don't be provoking one another either."

A playfully devilish smile pulled at the corner of Jacq's mouth.

Jean-Pierre tilted his head, glaring at her with a light in his eye that shone part in amusement and part in severity. "Be careful, Jacqo," he said quietly as he slid past her to stand again to her right.

Her mouth tilting in muted agreement, Jacq withheld her thoughts and permitted her gaze to venture menacingly in the direction of Jesse Smith. Her eyes, filled with annoyance at his impudent insolence and lack of reverence for a man such as Father Brandon, were hot with want of being rid of his company. Though her body made no such declaration in its movement and gestures, she felt the great desire burning deep within the recesses of her soul. His very presence worsened the state of her already dreadful environment. Tearing her gaze away from him, she recoiled slightly at the sudden recollection that they were almost upon *Eos Demeter*.

As she looked away, Jesse cast his glance sideways at her, sneering.

"Scotch!" Jean-Pierre yelled into the air, throwing back his head. He turned his eye then, glinting in anticipation, at *Eos Demeter*, who was almost by their side now. Her weighted body began to slow slightly in the water as her sails were beginning to sag. Shouts leapt from her rails – measures the sailors were to use to counter attack the *Wind Hawke*.

A burly reddish-blond haired man turned intense green eyes toward Jean-Pierre in response to his call. "Aye, Pike?" he asked, his voice thick with Scottish accent. His close-cut beard seemed to glow as the sun shone on it, like his chin had been dipped in gold.

"Prepare your men to board her," Jean-Pierre ordered

coolly, glancing up at Ming. The captain nodded solemnly, keeping a watchful eye on the nearing ship. Turning back, Jean-Pierre continued, "Jean-Paul!"

His brother stopped his preparations and moved to meet his brother's gaze. "Aye?"

"Ready the guns, lad!"

Nodding, Jean-Paul returned to what he was doing, shouting orders out at the men around him as he stumbled with his awkward gait.

The squeak of cannons being rolled into place filled the air; Jacq felt as though she were breathing in the noise. Her heart began to pound heavily in her ears and all the voices around her blurred into an indistinguishable din. *This is it...* Jacq could feel her stomach turning over with anxiety. Suddenly the large ship in front of them, loaded with plundered gold, all but stopped. Their cannons crept out of their gun ports in the side of the ship, and as the *Wind Hawke* pulled up alongside *Eos Demeter*. Jacq thought her heart stopped for a moment as Captain Ming yelled, "Fire!"

"How can you be sure this fellow will be of aid to us?" Alex inquired, skeptically.

"He be our only hope. An' he always be knowin' who to be askin' if he be not knowin' hisself. That always were most helpful in an' o' itself," Miata assured her, taking her hand gently in his and patting it with care. Sighing, he turned back to look at the dock they would soon be entering.

Gruff looking men trudged around carrying parcels of varying sizes. Hunched over fishermen pulled and pushed carts around, some smiling, others grimacing. Apprenticed

boys scurried about, doing their masters' bidding, glad to be having business down at the dock.

"All right, lads!" Captain Adams' voice called in a bellow. "To shore with ye! Be back here afore long. We sail with the mornin' tide!"

"Aye, aye!" and "Yes, Sir!" rose up in a hearty chorus throughout the ship.

Nicholas Dunne sidled up beside Alex and asked quietly, "Are you still to dine with me this evening?"

Smiling coyly, Alex found herself at a loss for words. "I… Uh…I…" She glanced at Miata who was doing a perfect job of looking the other way as if he didn't realize she was struggling. "Of course I will," she finally said, nodding with an awkwardness that Nicholas misread as Alex being in awe at his gentlemanly pursuance of her. Noticing this, she forced a small smile, curtsying lightly in hopes that he would never suspect her reactions were otherwise motivated. "However, Miata and I wanted to look around Penzance as we have never been here before. Where and when shall I meet you this evening?" As she spoke, she suddenly felt her stomach begin to twist around, tying itself into knots. *How can I enjoy dinner when Jacq could be…?* Her mind didn't finish the thought and her gaze turned towards the ocean.

"Oh. With Miata? I could be your guide if you wish," Dunne offered, sending Miata a smug smile. "Where did you want to go?"

Alex opened her mouth to respond, but before she could utter a word, Miata casually replied, "We were hopin' to be crossin' paths with an ol' mate o' mine. I hear he be workin' at a tavern in town by name o' Thirsty Thaddeus."

"Yes, yes…" Nicholas nodded. "Thirsty Thaddeus Tavern

is on the main road through town. It is preferred by Penzance's working men of society. Though, I daresay, I have never seen a lady enter Thirsty Thaddeus," he noted, glancing at Alex.

Tilting her head slightly at this, Alex inquired, "Are they forbidden in the tavern? Or do the women of Penzance simply never have a reason to enter?"

Nicholas glanced at Miata, surprised at Alex's questions.

Looking between them, Alex continued, "Have I said something wrong?"

"You have a way of surprising me," answered Nicholas in a flattering inflection, "that I have yet to adjust to. I am sure that an accompanied lady such as yourself, although you will draw every eye, will not be looked down upon." His eyes sparkled with intrigue as he gazed at the young woman.

"Right now I have little concern for what the men in the tavern of Penzance might say," Alex informed him soberly. "My sister's life is far more valuable to me than the whispers of men I do not know in a town I never intend on setting foot in again." Turning to Miata, she concluded, "This friend of yours, he will not mind my presence?"

Shrugging, Miata admitted coolly, "If nothing else, ye will be forgiven yer forwardness because of yer beauty." Miata smiled. This bolder Alex was not to be trifled with, and he was rather enjoying her. *Maybe*, he chuckled inwardly, *Alex be growin' fonder of me...*

Her cheeks heating up in an attractive, rosy glow at Miata's compliment, Alex smiled and returned, "Thank you." An awkward moment ensued in the air around the three before Alex cleared her throat. "Please excuse me a moment...I left something below." Gathering her skirts, she walked briskly to the entrance of the lower deck. As she passed between the two young men, zigzagging her way through the crew completing the final preparations for docking at the harbor, she breathed a heavy sigh. *Was I just flattered by something Miata said? To the point of coloring my cheeks? Am I starting to see a goodness in Miata that I did not believe existed at all…a goodness that I believed to be in my sisters' imagination?* Shaking her head as she trudged down the stairs, she paused a moment before opening her door, and in the silence, she heard soft voices down the hall.

"Yar, mate…Cap'n Adams be lookin' forward to meetin' up wit da man dat almos' killed him when he marooned him, says I. He be harborin' naught but curses upon dat Cap'n Ming."

Alex's ears rang with the names. "Heavens…Miata told the truth," she whispered. Breathing shallowly, Alex began sliding further down the hall, straining her ear to catch any additional conversation.

"Yar, Bart…I says that afore we set sail from Port Gilgallad! I said dat Cap'n Ming don't be knowin' what be comin' after him, takin' da wind from his sails. Too bad da Cap'n took da pardon from da t'rone."

Trying to lean casually against the wall to enhance her eavesdropping, Alex toyed thoughtfully with the chain that held the locket beneath her blouse. "A pardon," she whispered, sighing with relief that he was no longer supposed to be a pirate. "Miata might be relieved to know that." A faint smile creased her face as she thought about him a moment and continued to listen to the conversation.

"Why be dat a bad ting? It be meanin' he can be takin' revenge on Cap'n Ming and den be gettin' a reward fo it…no harm in dat, matey…No harm in dat a' all, says I!"

The two broke off into a jerky laughter that cracked Alex's

concentration and returned her to reality. Scooting quickly to her door, she let herself into the room, her thoughts turning quite abruptly to Nicholas Dunne. "Does he know of Captain Adams' past?" Blinking, she hurriedly grabbed her parasol, although she was uncertain that was what she had come to retrieve. *What am I supposed to do? Tell him? Jacq would have an opinion...* Sighing pensively, she marched off to join the men waiting on deck for her.

The smell of burning wood and hot cannon balls reached in and tore at Jacq's nose as she blinked, her ears ringing with the roar of the volley. As she attempted to gather her semi-scattered wits, she thought she heard instructional exclamations roaring from the lungs of Sea Legs Bill. Shaking her head, she glanced around at Jean-Pierre and the others aboard. They were shouting and scurrying about, but to her still recovering ears, they were naught but the low din of a conversation above the noise of a crashing wave. Flicking her swords slightly, Jacq turned in time to see *Eos Demeter* turning with a sneering lilt in their direction.

"Jean-Pierre!" she yelled, but she was immediately concerned as she felt her voice more than she heard it. "Jean-Pierre! Pike! *Eos Demeter*!"

Glancing at Jacq, he turned to see the ship then began bellowing out more orders, flailing his swords threateningly in the air. "Away with ye, lubbers! You're going to have forty lashes owed you if you don't hasten this pace!"

The gunners were hastily running under the cursing of the Legard brothers, trying to avoid being seen at all, let alone caught not performing well enough. "Hurry up, ya bloody

jackals! Do ya understand me? Are ya deaf?" Jean-Paul asked, snorting and throwing other colorful, piratical expletives into the gunner crew.

"Brace!" Ming's voice interjected forcefully from close behind where Jacq was still standing, almost paralyzed at what she knew she was about to endure.

A moment of silence ensued. Some would say it was long, some would say it was short; Jacq knew it would never have been long enough to postpone what followed. The terrible *ka-wack!* of the cannon fire and the eerie hiss of the assailing ammunition made her spine tingle and her heart pound in her ears as Sea Legs Bill's ship rebuked Ming's for her actions. As the smoke rose from the mouths of *Eos Demeter*'s guns, *Wind Hawke* shuddered at her fury. Then, as wails rose from below, the ships collided, scratching and scraping. Jacq wobbled, fiercely trying to keep her balance. She saw Scotch and his company, ropes in hand, bound readily to the rails, awaiting the go-ahead to launch their end of the attack upon the prey at hand.

Stepping up beside her, Ming nodded, adding an order in Scotch's direction, "An' convince his minstrel to join us."

At this, Jacq's heart stopped, her brow twisting morosely into a grievous conglomeration of lines as her throat tensed to the point she thought it would shatter if anyone touched her. *George! All those wails from below deck! What if…?* Sheathing her swords, she turned, stumbling over a barrel that had rolled out of place.

"Jacqo!" Jean-Pierre called after her, turning at the sound of the barrel in time to see her hurriedly stumbling toward the hatch to go below. "Jacqo, where are you going?"

Seeing her ignore his calls, Jesse started after her.

"Mr. Smith! You mind those rails, ya bilge rat! Miss Luray's under my charge!"

Jesse turned bitter eyes to face Jean-Pierre, who had managed to come up on him much faster than he'd anticipated. The shorter pirate all but growled. "Pigeon be not mindin' yer orders, Pike, says I. That be callin' fer some kind o' punishment, no, says I?" He leaned in as close as he could to Jean-Pierre's face.

"You listen to me, Red Handed Jesse, and you listen well. That lass is under my charge. Only the captain and I can be owin' her any kind of punishment. Is that clear?"

Jesse glowered, his body at the brink of shaking with anger.

"Now, mind those rails," Jean-Pierre ordered in a level, restrained tone. "I am going to retrieve our Jacqo."

Below deck, Jacq had slid, tripped, stumbled, and ran all the way to the kitchen where, when she turned the corner, she saw beams crowding the room. Pots and pans were strewn about, and a smoky haze hid the ceiling from her. Her chin trembling, she called out, "George! George Brandon?" A weak coughing sound caught her ear to the right of the room. "No, no, no…" she whispered, climbing inside, her arm scraping against some splintered pieces of wood.

"Oh, Jacqueline," he whispered in a voice that was even more choked up than usual, "my dear, dear child."

At hearing his voice, she turned to find him, partially hidden by a beam and other debris. "Oh!" She gasped tearfully, her dirt covered hand rushing to cover her mouth. Shaking, she reached out and touched his old, leathery cheek. "No…you have much else to do. You cannot go just yet." She sniffed, trying to sound lighthearted.

"Jacq…" his old voice whispered.

"You just have to hang on until I can get you out of here," she ordered him, looking around at the mess that was piled on top of him. "You have to see me out of this mess."

"Jacq…" he whispered again, a strange smile crawling onto his face.

She stopped, understanding, but not accepting, the look in his eyes. "Aye?"

"Stop fussing about me," he said softly. She opened her mouth to retort, but he interrupted. "It is finally over, Jacq. My body is broken. The only tomorrow it will see will be in Davy Jones' locker…but it will be alone, for I will not be there. The good Lord, grace be to Him for forgiving me, will be guiding me to His shore. After years of this torturous penance, I shall be free." Silence stole the air for a moment, but then George Brandon's eyes shone in a way Jacq would never forget and he said in a low voice, "Dear child! I know the last two lines… Write them down, will you?"

"What?" Confusion took hold of her face.

"For my sonnet. The last two lines…"

"Ha," Jacq laughed in awe, wiping away the start of a tear. "Of course…Tell them to me. I shan't forget."

"Guide me gently, safely o'er…To Thy kingdom shore, to Thy shore." He smiled, more pleased with himself than she had ever seen. "That should do it, eh?"

"Aye." She sniffed, smiling.

"Eh…is that a tear…rolling down your face?" he questioned her, his luminous eyes darkening slightly. Her jaw dropped to answer, but he started before she could, "Now, Jacq, I want you, if you can, to get off of this wretched boat with these God-forsaking swine. They have left Him behind, and when they square with that someday, you don't want any part of it…"

"Those other pirates did this to you," she said in a halting whimper. "Do you not think they should pay for their wrong doings?"

"And who would make them pay? Hmmm?" Jacq looked away at this question. "My dear girl," he said, "do not allow yourself to be embittered by the death of an old man. If you care to know, I was dead long before I met you…"

At this, Jacq turned back to look at him, her eyes welling with tears, and her brow contorting sporadically like a child trying to figure out how to flex a singled out muscle in his body.

"Yes," he continued, a distant smile growing on his face, "you brought me back to life so that I might be able to die in peace. I owe you more than you will ever know." His eyes darkened all the more, and his voice quieted to a pitch she had to strain a might to hear. "Now, don't forget…

When my feeble life is o'er,
Time for me will be no more;
Guide me gently, safely o'er
To Thy kingdom shore, to Thy shore."

"I shan't," she said, nodding.

"Jacq!" he whispered, his eyes closing for long lengths of time. "I can see it! The shoreline…!"

Biting her lip to try and keep her voice from trembling, she asked softly, "Is it lovely, Father?" Timidly, she reached out and grasped his hand.

"Oh yes, quite lovely, dear Jacqueline," he murmured, his mouth smiling and his eyes closing contentedly like a satisfied cat, "…quite lovely…quite lovely indeed."

At this, his breath left him, and his spirit was gone. Putting her head to the floor beside him, Jacq could not stop the tears from rocking her body and flooding the boards she was kneeling on. Everything around her faded into nothing. No sound. No smell. No sight. All she could feel, was the raw spot in her heart where she felt as if someone had so rudely reached in and cut it open, allowing her soul to bleed out onto the floor in front of her. "Alex," she said in a muffled whimper, "come find me..."

Standing silently in the doorway, his sword drawn but hanging in his clutched hand, Jean-Pierre sighed, disheartened. Then, quite suddenly, he noticed the very clear and staunch smell of...rain? The boat began to sway in the waves with an upset that he had never encountered so suddenly. Turning, he peeked up the stairwell and noticed the sky was no longer there, but hidden behind a curtain of enraged, waterlogged clouds. They swirled darkly about, spitting that which they held down upon the pirates fighting over someone else's goods. He trotted up the stairs, glancing about at the crew, already drenched from the downpour.

Ming, standing near the rail preparing to board *Eos Demeter* with a band of men, looked about, sneering skyward. Then, seeing Jean-Pierre peeking out of the hatch, he hollered, "Pike! What is goin' on?" Leaning forward, he grasped the rail in a manner one would take as a suggestion of how angry he was when in reality, he was clutching the rail so that the mighty winds that were careening about would not sweep him off to sea.

"I do not know, Captain!" Jean-Pierre replied honestly, his statement echoed by a deep, rolling thunder. "I've never seen anything like this before!" He gestured at the unmerciful sky, his sword still drawn.

"It be as if the heavens themselves are comin' down upon us!" he shouted angrily. Then, scanning the deck, his eyebrow raised and he inquired crossly, "Where is the lass?"

"She's below...The Father died in the cannon fire from *Eos Demeter*!" Jean-Pierre returned. "I'll retrieve in her a moment!"

"Blast," muttered Ming. "We will have to find a new cook." The men with him chuckled callously at his comment. "Bring her. She boards with us."

"Aye, aye, Captain!" Jean-Pierre agreed, his innermost heart feeling a little downtrodden at this. Turning to go down the stairs, he realized that the waves were calming and the wind was dying down. As he took a few steps in confusion, he looked forward to see Jacq emerging from the rubble that used to be the kitchen. "Captain says you're boarding with us." He watched as she wiped a tear from her red, puffy face, and he noticed the rain had lessened to a drizzle.

Sniffing, Jacq took a deep breath and retorted, "Ming may find that coercing me into joining his band of pirates was not the wisest of choices he ever made."

Smirking, Jean-Pierre shrugged and admitted, "I could have told him that, Jacqo." As he finished his sentence, a stream of light shone around them, causing him to turn and peer out at the sky, which was beautiful blue with not a cloud in sight. "What th-" he started. "Jacqo, the weather...It has behaved so strangely! Such a sudden storm I have never seen before, and now gone...As if bad weather had never clouded the skies!"

Shrugging, Jacq returned, "I've seen the weather act up like that before plenty of times. Not that it happens frequently or anything, but I would never consider it an anomaly." As she

spoke, her mannerisms were quite calm and collected, looking at the pirate with an expression that suggested he was being silly. However, on the inside, she was smirking. *Ha! If only you knew the terrible sadness that was stretched across the skies...the tears I cried for a man you don't even care about...* "I would not worry about it," she added after a choked moment of silence. Nonchalantly, she pushed past him, trudging up the stairs, each step hitting her heart, pounding in her ears. Oh, how she wanted to be furious...Every motion that took her upwards, brought her closer to the noise that had just murdered her friend. The actions set in motion by Ming were being carried out still, and as she reached the top of the stairs, the cool salt wind greeting her, she saw him. The sight of Captain Ming–the man at the top of her list of people she wished would die—her skin crawled, sending a small shiver down her spine.

"Nice o' ye to join us, Jacq," Ming commented loosely.

Stopping in her tracks, her eyes slanted slightly into a glare. Tossing her hair over her shoulder, she eyed him evenly and replied, "Nice of you to wait for me."

Having followed her up the stairs, Jean-Pierre was not quite to the deck yet as she spoke her sentence. Looking up, he took in her stance, feet shoulder width apart, weight sitting on her left hip. Her swords swayed readily at her waist as she stood with her arms crossed. He smiled slightly, and muttered, "By the powers...The bloody captain is making himself the perfect weapon...and it backfires."

After staring at her a moment, finding he had nothing to reply to her with, Ming looked past her to Jean-Pierre and ordered, "Pike! We've not got all day! Move along!" Taking one more look at Jacq, he thought to himself, *Are those tears?* Then, disregarding it and grabbing a rope, Ming swung to the besieged *Eos Demeter*.

Friendly villagers smiled at Alex as she walked, accompanied by Nicholas on her left and Miata on her right, down the cobblestone street towards Thirsty Thaddeus Tavern. She found that many things in this town reminded her of *Port de Couler de Bateaux* and, consequently, Jacq. Every time her sister's name entered her head, it was followed by a painful twisting she found to be almost anxiety inducing. An elderly woman noticed them and smiled, waving cautiously in their direction. The three managed courteous return gestures as they meandered past where she stood in front of a bake shop, holding a basket of freshly baked goods on her arm. "My," Alex said, breathing in the sweet scent of the bakery as it intermingled with the sweet hay smells of a well kept stable a small distance down the street, "what a lovely town."

"Yes," Nicholas replied before Miata, who was taking in his surroundings very carefully, even had a chance to respond, "it is a lovely town, Miss Luray. Lovely as they come some would say. The local government was talking about building a university." He paused a moment, turning smitten eyes her direction. "This would be a fine place to make a home," he said delicately.

"I be quite certain," Miata piped up as Alex's walking and breathing slowed in shock at Dunne's pointed comment, "that Alex be wantin' to be meetin' her father afore she be decidin' where she be wantin' to be settlin' down for a permanent amount o' time." He glanced casually in Alex's direction, seeking her approval for this protective remark.

Smiling, Alex nodded. "Yes, yes…I am afraid that Miata is right," she said, looking up at Nicholas Dunne, who was looking between the two of them with mounting concern. "I do very much wish to meet my father before I make any such life decisions."

"Of course, of course!" he agreed flawlessly, understanding her reasoning with ease. "I beg your forgiveness for not thinking of that before I asked such a question! Where was my head?" He laughed, shaking his head. "I daresay, sometimes my mouth gets ahead of my mind…And…" He paused uncomfortably. "And…I just manage to make an utter fool of myself." Laughing a little more awkwardly, he shrugged and added, "It must be your beauty. Not only does it take my breath away from me, but also my mind." Smiling bashfully, he scuffed his shoes on the cobblestone. *She must think I'm a complete fool now!* he complained internally, forcing himself to breathe. He paused in his tracks, one hand on his hip, the other nervously running through his light hair as he madly tried to think of something to say that could possibly erase the imbecilic way he had just behaved, but nothing was coming to mind.

Miata, casting his glance over his shoulder to try and be discreet, rolled his eyes and shook his head at the fumbling fellow to Alex's left. However, in doing this, he again noticed the elderly lady, basket still in hand, standing not too short a distance away, watching him rather curiously. She was slightly hunched over, her skin well wrinkled with age and hard work. Her eyes were a sad green that held in many happy memories she was ready to share with whomever she could. A few light gray strands of hair fell about her face and out from the bun that was done up on the top of her head. His blue eyes sharpened in her direction as he paused slightly to get a better glimpse at her. Seeing this, she grabbed the hood of her old brown cloak with one hand, pulling it up over her head. She turned away from his gaze, fidgeting uncertainly at the shop she was standing in front of.

Alex, rather aghast at all that had just taken place with Nicholas Dunne, touched Miata's arm to signal him to wait a moment. This regaining his attentions, he turned from staring after the old woman to the matter at hand...a very disgruntled Mr. Dunne standing off to the side, trying desperately to think of some way to make a comeback. Clearing her throat, Alex interrupted, "Excuse me, Mr. Dunne...Please understand that your slip of words is not insulting to me at all. However, considering the task I have at hand, I simply cannot spend too much time on frivolous flattery while my sister's fate potentially rests in my hands." Reaching out, she barely touched his elbow.

"But it was in the worst of taste," he insisted, whirling about, bending on one knee, and taking her hand in his. "Please, accept my sincerest apologies so that I may move forward, knowing that I have not offended you?"

Surprised by this dramatic change, Alex speechlessly looked between his face and her hand, carefully sandwiched between his. "I…Of course I forgive you, Mr. Dunne," she returned haltingly, "though there is nothing to forgive." Mustering a well-mannered smile, she inwardly choked on laughter. *What odd behavior…*

This be rubbish… Miata snorted internally. *But it were in the woooooorst of taste*, he mocked in his mind, casting foul glances at Nicholas Dunne. However, being sufficiently hidden by Alex's parasol, he remained unseen by either one of them. *Just nonsense!* Folding his arms over his chest, he squinted back to where the woman had been mulling about. However, much to his curiosity's utter dismay, she was no longer there. "This Penzance be a strange place."

Suddenly, Alex whipped around to Miata, who smiled eloquently as though he had been behaving as a perfect gentleman. Pointing her lacy finger straight at his nose, she commented in a mutter, "I do not believe it for a second."

"Believe what?" He laughed, holding his hands out for want of an answer.

"You know perfectly well what I mean," Alex retorted, smiling somewhat playfully in his direction.

"What do you mean, m'lady?" Nicholas inquired, curious.

"Nothing by you, Mr. Dunne," she assured, turning back to him and smiling innocently.

"But by me ye be meanin' somethin'?" Miata retorted, pointing to himself.

Glaring good-naturedly at him, Alex repeated, "You know perfectly well what I mean." Her lips pursed and a smile picked up the corner of her mouth.

"Miss Luray, I am confused," Nicholas admitted. "You mean nothing by me, but something by him that he does not know?"

"Do not let this one fool you, Mr. Dunne," Alex returned. "He knows very well what I mean."

"Excuse me..." a little rickety voice interrupted. All three turned to find the little old woman in the brown cloak standing timidly in front of them, basket still on her arm, hood on her shoulders, and an inquisitive glimmer shining in her eye. "Am I interrupting anything?"

"No, no, no! Not at all!" Alex laughed, stepping forward. "How can we help you?"

Turning then, to Miata, she cleared her throat and inquired, "What's your name, lad?"

Shifting his weight a little uneasily, as both Nicholas and Alex looked at him, rather shocked, he cleared his throat a little and laughed uneasily as he moved about. "W-Well..."

The old lady straightened slightly and walked closer to him, peering deep into his eyes.

You better not have stolen anything when I was not paying attention! Alex thought angrily, waiting for the woman to state her interest.

"Th-They be callin' me Miata," he finally said in a shy, hushed tone.

"Miata," she repeated, mumbling it under her breath as if processing his name. "Tell me, lad, what is your father's name?" she questioned, a bony hand coming out from beneath her cloak to point at him.

"I-I be not knowin' me father," he acknowledged, feeling as though the entire world was suddenly staring impolitely at him, listening to every beat his heart made.

Watching the conversation unfold, Alex felt an empathy for him. In some ways, he was an orphan – just like she and Jacq.

“That is a shame.” She sighed, her hand disappearing behind her cloak again. “You look just like him. Well, except your eyes. I suppose you must have gotten those from your mother.”

Miata blinked. “Me mother?”

Coming forward, Alex questioned, “Excuse me, but, do I understand you to mean that you knew his parents?”

“Well, his father anyway. His mother had died before I met him. Say, are you two together?” the old lady piped up cheerfully, her old eyes sparkling a little.

“No,” Alex answered, astounded at the question and drowned out by the very loud and earnest voice of Nicholas Dunne. Casting him a rather irritated glance over her shoulder, Alex continued alone, “No, we are just friends.”

“Pity,” the old lady muttered. “He’s a good lad. Always was.” She gave him a small smile.

Miata blinked again, utterly speechless and dumbfounded.

“How do you know him?” Alex inquired on Miata’s behalf.

“Aye,” Miata finally spoke. “How be it ye be knowin’ me an’ I be not?”

“Oh, heavens! Where are my manners? Well…” She cleared her throat. “I am Sister Mary Katherine. I was the nun at the orphanage when his father brought him to us. Such a beautiful baby boy,” she recalled, looking him up and down.

Miata smiled sheepishly.

“Anyway, he asked us to care for him because his mother had just died and Mr. O’Keeffe could not bear to take care of the child at that time, so we agreed to take him,” she gestured to Miata, “for a year while Mr. O’Keeffe got himself pulled back together. He was not yet four months old then.”

"He never be comin' back to get me, though," Miata noted bitterly.

"It happens that way to a lot of children," Nicholas responded in a tone one uses when a child's first toy breaks.

"Hush up there, young fella!" the old woman snapped, pointing her bony finger at him menacingly, making Nicholas jump. "Now," she continued, turning placidly back to Miata, "your father meant to come back. I could see it in his eyes when he brought you to us, clinging onto you as if you were the only thing in the world he had left. But, I believe he died just a few months after he brought you to us...Heart break most likely." She paused in a moment of sad remembrance. "Anyway, when you were old enough, the older boys at the orphanage began daring you to steal things for them...and pretty soon, before we knew it, despite our best efforts," she chuckled, "you were the best in the house...a natural they might say."

At this, Miata turned rather blushingly to glance at Alex who just stared up at him.

"Either way," she continued in her little voice, "when you reached the age where there weren't many older boys and you didn't take orders from them anymore, you would steal for the small, hungry boys...a regular Robin Hood you might say. Teehee," she giggled lightly.

"So, you've been a thief your entire life?" Alex asked in amazement.

Moving his eyes to meet hers, he shrugged sullenly. "Longer than I be knowin' me father anyway..." Turning back to the nun, he inquired, "What were the name o' me father, Sister Mary Katherine?"

A deep sadness crept over Alex's heart and she put her hand on Miata's arm as Sister Mary Katherine thought and

then answered, "Kee...Keegan. Yes, yes...That was it. Keegan O'Keeffe. It was a cold second of December that he brought you in. Your mother, Lolita I believe her name was, had died in October, less than two months after your birth. I was never sure what your first name was. He was in an awful hurry and quite distraught when he brought you in, but it sounded like he was saying Miata, so that's what we called you." She paused for a moment, looking far back into recesses of her mind, dusty from time. "And then you left." She looked up at him with languid eyes.

His jaw dropped slightly, but Miata found he could not think of anything to say. He was torn between apologizing and interrogating the frail looking woman.

However, before he could make a decision, she perked up and said, "Oh! I must be off!" Touching his cheek with her thin hand, she smiled, "But come see me any time, dear lad!" Then, turning, she began hobbling away.

"What? Where be ye off to?" Miata asked, watching her trot past him.

"To deliver these baked goods," she answered, hurrying down the street. "I completely forgot I had them when I saw you! Come see me again soon! I still live near the orphanage!" she called over her shoulder as she hastened back down the street from the direction of the harbor.

Giving Miata's arm a small squeeze, Alex smiled and stared after the elderly nun. "You have a name," she said.

A short laugh escaped him as he also watched Sister Mary Katherine disappear. "Aye."

"If Jacq were here, she would be so happy for you," Alex added, moving her eyes to stare at the sea in the distance.

Nodding, Miata agreed, "Aye. She would." His heart

was barely beating, but each pulse that it made could be felt soundly throughout his entire body. The little thief who hadn't a family now had a name…Miata O'Keeffe, son of Keegan and Lolita O'Keeffe. His throat tensed up, feeling as though it might close on him altogether. His mouth and lips went dry; his palms felt moist and clammy.

Turning to Alex, he said in hoarse voice just above a whisper, "I be havin' a name."

She laughed, nodding. "Yes."

Grinning, he sighed, a strange feeling of satisfaction that he had never felt before creeping over him. *I think I shall be askin' Mr. Dunne to be callin' me Mr. O'Keeffe!* Heaving a delighted exhalation of air, he bent and put his arms around Alex in a warm hug, appreciative of her sweet support despite their turbulent history.

Nicholas Dunne, who, until Miata's arms were wrapped around Alex, had been engrossed in brewing about her hand resting on Miata's arm, snapped back to reality. Clearing his throat, trying to behave ever so appropriately, he noted, "Oh! Thirsty Thaddeus is just up the street a small distance. Shall we continue on?" He smiled good-naturedly as the two turned to look at him. "If we are to leave on the morning tide, then we should gather our information as quickly as possible."

"Of course!" Alex agreed as she and Miata broke apart. "Let us go!"

Turning to lead the way, Nicholas buried a snarl towards Miata as he noticed the lanky man had a joyous new lilt to his walk. *Upon His Majesty's head*, Nicholas thought bitterly as he caught Alex's coy smile towards Miata, *Miss Luray cannot possibly choose him over me. He is no gentleman at all! Hardly a man at times I would say! For heaven's sake…he just found out his name!* Casting a sideways glance in Mr. O'Keeffe's direction, he huffed inwardly. Then, looking up, he found they were nearly on the doorstep of their destination.

"Oi!" he called out cheerfully. "Here we are! Thirsty Thaddeus Tavern!" Turning kindly to Alex, he inquired as he extended his arm, "Shall I escort you, m'lady?"

"Oh... Yes, you may," Alex agreed, taking his arm delicately, closing her parasol as she did so.

Glancing rather smugly in Miata's direction as Alex's lace-coated hand came to rest on his arm, Nicholas was rather disappointed to see that the other young man didn't even notice.

Pushing open the door, the three entered into a clean, though slightly smoky, conversation filled atmosphere. Wig clad gentlemen in their smashing coats and spotless knickers absorbed the left of the room, pompously sizing each other up through their spectacles while they drank their opulent liquors and talked of science, politics, philosophy, and other such social caste expected subjects. Meanwhile, crowding the right side of the room, were sophisticated men of the working class, sea captains and the like. Some were puffing on pipes, others gesticulating in amusement at the wigged fellows on the other side of the room. Although to the untrained eye they seemed very much the same, Alex knew exactly why these two groups of men thought themselves so different from one another. She made a very distinctive show in behaving as the perfect lady, walking smartly and not allowing her gaze to wander anywhere but directly in front of her. She knew she was doing a proper job of it too as much of the chatter quieted as they crossed the floor.

She took in the bar they were approaching at which three

men were working. Two of them were slightly portly and balding while the third man was younger and leaner, obviously doing more of the work and eating less of the food. His young, chiseled face broadened into a smile upon seeing Miata enter. Glancing between the bug-eyed, slightly uncomely looking men standing on either side of him, his dark eyes twinkled as he greeted eloquently in a very soft voice, "Good day to you!" Eyeing Alex a moment, he nodded then turned to Miata, inquiring, "What business brings you here, old friend? I trust you are well?" As he spoke, he extended his hand.

Taking it heartily, Miata returned, "Greetin's be to ye, mate! We be well, thank ye kindly." Releasing his hand, he gestured towards the other members of his party. "This be Miss Alexandria Thorpe Luray and our acquaintance, Mr. Nicholas Dunne."

Nicholas smiled painfully at this diminishing introduction.

However, turning back without even the slightest of hesitations, Miata continued, "We be needin' some information, Gunther. Can ye be helpin' us out a might?"

Leaning forward, Gunther stared levelly into Miata's sparkling blue eyes. "What kind of information?" A mischievous smile tugged at the corner of his mouth.

Putting his weight on the bar, Miata returned in a lowered voice, "We be needin' information on the whereabouts o' a ship captained by a man what calls hi'self Ming."

Gunther's left eye twitched slightly in the corner.

"He be takin' captive a good mate o' mine, Gunther," Miata pressed, holding his gaze and nodding towards Alex with his head, "an' her sister."

"Your friend and her sister?" he inquired, casually gesturing first to Miata and then towards Alex.

"She be one in the same, mate," Miata confirmed, smiling devilishly.

Alex, who was very surprised at Gunther's speech and mannerisms, found her eyes moving back and forth between the two conversationalists. She could not help but feel intrigued. She could tell there was more haggling going on than they were saying – and the way Miata leaned forward so confidently and spoke so persuasively surprised her. *For such a timorous person*, she thought, *he has a lot of hidden talents.*

"Captain Ming, you say?" Gunther queried, glancing slightly off towards the door. "There was a chap in here not but a few days ago. He was a self-proclaimed crewman for Captain Ming. He got in a bit of a scuffle with someone the both of us know, and that someone might be willing to tell you what he knows…for a price."

Miata's eyebrow arched at this. "A price, eh? Who be this person both of us be knowin'?"

Smiling, Gunther pointed towards the far front corner of the left side of the room. The trio followed his gesture to the back of a broad shouldered man with a shaggy mess of nearly straight dark brown hair hanging loosely about his head. "Crevan."

Miata turned back to Gunther with a smirk tugged up high on one side. "Crevan? By Jove!" He laughed, slapping the bar. "When be Murtaugh gracin' Penzance with his presence?"

"Who? Who?" Alex chimed in, her curiosity, after Miata's reaction, suddenly peaked.

"His name be Michael Murtaugh, though he be more commonly known as Crevan." Miata sighed, his eyes returning to stare at the man's back. "He were supposed to be joinin' the Irish to fight the English. Or were it the other way around?"

Alex stared at him, her eyes asking him to continue.

"Anyway, he be against the fightin', fearin' it would be killin' innocents. So he left, shunned by his fellows an' near banished by his country. Least ways, that's what he be tellin' us all the years we be knowin' him." He paused a moment, as if calling to mind past conversations. "Always the very same story, with the very same sadness."

Sighing, Alex let her gaze also trail back to Crevan. "What makes you believe he would be willing to help us?"

Clearing his throat, Miata shrugged. "Just a hunch."

Alex's brow furrowed at this, and she opened her mouth to ask where this hunch was coming from.

However, having already turned back to Gunther, Miata asked, "So, why be yer fellow workers stayin' quiet while we be takin' up all yer time?"

Exhaling dejectedly, Gunther acknowledged, "They work the corners, selling to the gentlemen of the tavern. I get strangers and extra gentlemen who need help when we are busiest."

"Tsk, tsk, tsk," Miata sounded, shaking his head at this. "Well, be considerin' this me thanks, mate. I be back again someday to be seein' ye." As he spoke, Miata produced some coins out of a small drawstring bag he kept beneath his belt, dropping the coins rather loudly into Gunther's left palm.

Smiling rather dumbfounded, Gunther looked back up at Miata. "You don't need to be giving me this, mate. We are too old of friends for this."

"Gunther," Miata returned, grasping his other hand and squeezing it assuredly, "we been mates long enough for nothin' o' the sort, an' that be why I be givin' it to ye."

As Miata released his grip and turned, Alex curtsied in Gunther's direction, thanking him wordlessly for all his help.

Then, she scurried back to catch up with Miata, practically dragging Nicholas with her. "So, he was a thief?" she whispered, glancing over her shoulder where Gunther stood, glancing between their backs and his co-workers' irritated faces.

Chuckling softly, Miata turned a smiling face to look at her. "An honest one…" he answered simply, and then continued walking towards Crevan.

Falling in step behind him, Alex smirked to herself. Then, she turned to find Nicholas Dunne all but glaring uneasily in the direction of the man that Miata was almost beside. She paused her slowed walking and inquired with sincere concern, "Is there something wrong, Mr. Dunne? You look as though something is troubling you."

"Tish tosh!" Nicholas quietly replied, snapping out of his trancelike state of cynical observation. "That's nonsense, m'lady," he said, looking gently into her eyes. "I merely hope that this," he gestured towards Miata, who was now laughing and heartily embracing Crevan, searching for a word, "chap… knows what he's doing. I mean, a man who forsakes his duty to his country is rarely a man worth trusting you might say," he noted defensively, shifting his weight around.

Cocking her head to the left so it was easier for her to stare up at him, Alex's mouth twitched slightly at the corner, threatening to elongate into a rather amused expression. "What you say is perhaps true," she returned, watching him nod smilingly in approval, "if, in fact, he is the same man who abandoned his duties years ago."

"Pardon, m'lady," Nicholas replied with a chuckle, glancing up in the direction where Miata and Crevan were conversing in hushed tones, "but am I to understand that you feel it is safe to trust this man with whom you have no history? And whose

history speaks foully of him?" His voice was deeply contorted with shock.

Alex's brow furrowed in intrigue. "Mr. Dunne, by those standards, I should not trust you either."

Clearing his throat, Nicholas straightened and said, "Miss Luray, I should hope my conduct speaks well of my character."

"As do I," Alex returned. "As to your question, however, I would not say it would be safe to trust this Crevan fellow. Nevertheless, if trust him I must, then trust him I shall." She glanced first at Crevan then up at Nicholas, who was looking down upon her with seemingly very little understanding. "My dear Mr. Dunne," she said with a sigh, tugging on his arm gently, "please try to remember that my sister's value is more important to me than the potential repercussions of the company I shall keep to find her and bring her back. And, though I would be hard pressed to admit it to him, I find that I do not believe Miata would intentionally put my life in danger."

Putting his hand empathetically over hers, he nodded. "Very well, m'lady. As you wish." Grinning amiably, Nicholas then proceeded to lead them forward to meet the now approaching young men.

"Miss Alexandria Thorpe Luray," Miata introduced politely, "this be me mate, Murtaugh."

She curtsied.

"Murtaugh," Miata continued, smiling unabashedly, "be willin' to be tellin' us all that he be knowin'..."

Alex's eyes lit up with delight.

"...in exchange for passage on the ship o' Capt'n Adams."

Naturally... Exhaling heavily, Alex blinked.

"How do you feel?" Jean-Pierre asked, his eyes shining just as brightly as the hoops that now hung from his ear lobes.

Wagging her head slowly back and forth, Jacq grinned as the hoops that hung from her ears tapped her jaw, but she winced as they tugged just a little painfully on the new piercings. "I feel well," she said casually.

"Haha!" he laughed loudly, patting her on the back. "What fortune we gathered today! Though," they turned and looked at their ship, which was pulled up on the beach upon which they sat, "our carpenter is probably cursing us as if there is no tomorrow while he's repairing that ship." Cracks and holes brazenly splintered across the right hand side of the vessel could be seen even from where they sat, in the dark. And, as if that wasn't reminder enough, the smell of tar wafted strongly from its direction.

"How long will we be here?" Jacq questioned, sighing heavily at the memory of the encounter. She could still hear the shouting in her ears, a monstrous, clanging sound. The eyes of George Brandon, a strange, murky mixture of happiness and sadness still haunted her mind's eye. She could still smell the burning heat of cannons singeing the walls of her nostrils and feel the angry collision of the ships knock her off of her feet, sending her hurdling to the deck. Then, to top it off, she could still taste the bitter hunger of the greedy men on all sides of her – an astringent, metallic flavor of which she feared she would never free her mouth of the aftertaste.

"A couple nights would be my guess," Jean-Pierre returned, picking up the bottle of rum he'd gotten for himself and taking a long, thirsty drink out of it. "You can expect no less. The lads will want to trade their plunder for pleasures…of every kind." He grinned mischievously, thinking thoughts Jacq was glad he did not speak, and took another drink from his bottle.

A couple days? she thought, feeling even more nauseous. *How will I ever escape? Perhaps if I could find a small boat…*

Becoming aware of her silence, Jean-Pierre gave her a little push on the shoulder saying, "Come on, Jacqo! Relax! Have some fun!"

"Aye," she agreed, a halfhearted smile forming over her lips. As she glanced again at the ship, she noticed some of the men still unloading the debris carry a crumpled body to a rowboat which then began to head out to the sea…*George Brandon.*

"Aye," Jean-Pierre started as if answering an unasked question. Wiping his mouth with the forearm of his sleeve, he nodded towards the scene and continued, "Father George Brandon. A fine cook. Worthy of a fine eulogy, I imagine. But, as with all pirates," Jacq turned to look at him, pain swelling in her eyes, "he gets buried at sea, in Davy Jones' Locker. Not a word to be spoken about how he lived or even a small utterance as to how he died."

"How utterly dreary," she remarked, returning her sober stare to the quickly vanishing procession.

Taking another swig, Jean-Pierre turned to smile again at Jacq. "You are a pretty lass," he noted, "I give ya that much." Then, rather abruptly, his eye caught movement behind them and he turned, calling out, "Oi! Is that Elizabeth *Norington*?"

As he scrambled to his feet, Jacq pivoted to find herself staring at a younger than middle-aged blond woman, large ringlets of hair piled high atop her head and little confinements at the top of her dress to hold back her bosom.

"Jacqo, this here is Elizabeth Norington. One of the finest women of the Isles of Scilly." Laughing and wrapping his arm boldly about her waist, he turned back to Jacq and winked. "Good evening, Jacqo. I'll be seein' ya on the morrow!" Then, grabbing up Miss Elizabeth Norington like a fresh loaf out of the baker's shop, Jean-Pierre trudged off for the night.

Giggling as he marched off with her draped all over him, Elizabeth swooned, "I thought I was *the* finest of women on the Isles of Scilly?"

Jean-Pierre mumbled an inaudible reply at which she giggled all the more.

Blinking in shock, Jacq realized that although she knew he was a pirate, she had not really explored in totality just what exactly that meant in its entirety. The shrill giggles of the port's barmaid floozy echoed rhythmically in her mind, bouncing off her brain's cell walls as if they were made of rubber. Yet, his words, *'worthy of a fine eulogy, I imagine,'* were still ringing fresh in her ears.

As she sat, her mind, she suddenly realized, felt disconnected from her body, as though it was wandering the coastline unattended. Staring listlessly towards where the ocean rolled to meet the sands, she noticed a small choking feeling deep within her throat; her eyes began to water slightly. Although she was completely alone, she felt suffocated in the emptiness. "This," she said in murmur to the sky, "is loneliness."

Watching the sky blacken, she felt the pent up tears beginning to slide from her eyes and stream, ever so soundlessly, down her cheek. She could hear the cursing of the carpenter as the waves picked up, annoying him as they splashed, reaching up for him with their cold, frothy fingers and began rocking the ship more vigorously. With slightly trembling fingertips, she extended her hand up, touching the dangling jewelry that now hung from her ears. "What am I doing?" she asked herself in the very lowest of whispers, breathing in the cooling air around her. Pulling her knees up to her chest, she wrapped her arms about her bent legs, resting her chin on her kneecaps.

It was then, in the quiet stillness of the solitude where she sat upon the sandy shore that she saw, so vividly she wanted to reach out, the face of Captain Daniel Taylor in her mind. He smiled so gently, as he always did – his dark eyes compelling her to listen. "Pray, Jacq. No matter what happens, promise me that wherever you go – you shall always be who you are."

Her gaze, rather trancelike as tears still slid from her eyes, didn't move from staring off into the nothingness of the dark night. "But, who am I?"

She wanted him to answer her, but he was already gone. The silence squeezed her heart mercilessly, as though bleeding her out all over the sands beneath her.

Closing her eyes to the world, she pleaded in a tearful prayer, "God…Forgive me my transgressions. Hear my plea for help. Rescue me from this darkness." As she breathed the last words, she heard stumbling footsteps approaching. As she took a deep breath, the clouds moved away and the ocean calmed as she dried the tears from her face. Gathering her thoughts and emotions, she turned to see which drunkard it was that was so obviously drawing near.

"Pigeon, says I," Red Handed Jesse said in an intoxicated slur, his stench worse than it was when they were onboard the *Wind Hawke*. "What be ya doin' out here all alone, says I?" he inquired, stopping a few paces away from her. His swagger had considerably increased, and he was carrying his alcohol with him in his right hand.

Rescue from this hideous beast would be nice too, she thought, part of her humored by the situation. Getting nonchalantly to her feet, Jacq shrugged and answered, "Gathering my thoughts. We had a rather eventful day, you might say." Smiling distastefully in his general direction, she then glanced past where he stood to where the pirate haven rose up from the ground – one of the busiest, noisiest, smelliest, dirtiest, least populated places Jacq recalled ever having been. Rowdy men and promiscuous women were slopped ubiquitously all throughout the town, behaving in manners that ranged from calling enticingly to each other to shooting at one another.

"But, alone on the beach, says I?" he repeated.

"It was a little noisy for that over there," she noted, gesturing towards the buildings.

"I be wary o' ya, Pigeon, says I," he trailed on. "Ya be havin' a strange way about ya, says I…" He squinted at her through his vision inhibiting, inebriated haze. "An' I don't fancy the way ya speak to me, says I." As he babbled, he tapped the hilt of his sword in offense at the mere thought of it.

"Careful, Mr. Smith," Jacq warned cautiously, "you are not feeling as well as you think you are." She shifted her weight slightly, getting a soothing sensation as her weapons lightly tapped her legs.

"I be feelin' better than ya think, says I!" he retorted, shaking his mostly empty bottle at her. "Ya think yar soooooo high an' mighty cuz Cap'n Ming be wantin' ya in 'is crew, says I! Well, Pigeon, ya think too high o' yaself, says I…" Blundering a few short steps toward her, he drew his sword, brandishing it in every direction like an intoxicated conductor.

Taking a few short steps back from his flailing arm and weapon, Jacq ground her teeth together, glaring at the short

and stout curmudgeon of a buccaneer. "You listen to me, Mr. Smith," she spoke, her voice rising slightly. "You have drank too much for such talk. Your rum is affecting your mind. Now, put the sword down before you hurt someone." Self-reassuring, she put her right hand on the hilt of her katana.

"The only person I might be hurtin' is you, Pigeon, says I," he responded, sputtering and swaying where he stood. "An' that wouldn't be ta bad o' a thing, would it, says I." His eyes suddenly began to glow an evil, poisonous green hue that seemed to sizzle in the cool night air. Holding the flask up to his lips, he tipped his head back and let the numbing liquid flood his system, entering every minute crevice of his already venomous being. Then, in one motion, dropping the bottle from his lips and into the sand beside him, Red Handed Jesse pointed his cutlass directly at Jacq and commanded in a growl, "Dafend yarself..."

Her upper lip twitching at the corner, Jacq grimaced and drew her swords. Showing off her sober agility, she flicked her blades around in the air, the light from the town catching on their clean surfaces and making them glint in the dark. Planting her feet in the sandy earth, she found that a strange strength seemed to take hold of her, her heart rate increasing as she settled into her stance. Twisting her foot and taking a slow, deep breath, she found she could not help but smile at his circumstantial misfortune. "Nay, Mr. Smith," she purred in a low tone, the annoyance with him for all the foul things she had heard or seen him do suddenly welling up inside of her, "you are the one that needs to defend yourself."

Blinking awkwardly, the graceless pirate straightened a little and tried to focus on her fuzzy image – if he could figure out which one was her. However, drunkenness does not always rob one of his or her pride as it should, so he gallantly clomped forward, swinging his blade in a manner that horribly missed his target and jabbed right into a mid-sized clump of grass protruding from the beach. Then, turning his glassy eyes towards the young woman, who had backed up a little further in disgust, he sneered. "Ya think yar soooooo smart, Pigeon, says I. Think yar soooooo quick, says I!" With an unusually high amount of effort, he hoisted his blade out of the sand, making him stumble backwards. Then, holding it straight out in front of him, he charged at Jacq.

Stepping just slightly to the side, Jacq, in the same smooth motion, simply held up her right sword out past her left arm. She heard Red Handed Jesse curse as he fumbled past her and a part of her smiled at his expense. "Don't be a fool, Mr. Smith," she suggested again, coolly wiping the tip of her blade on the grassy mass he had so accurately stabbed previously. Looking up, she saw Red Handed Jesse totter around to glare angrily at her as he held his hand over his left cheek and a few small streams of blood trickled out between his fingers and strayed down his hand.

"Ya will be sorry fer that, Pigeon, says I!" he said with a snarl, wiping his hand on his pants leg. Lifting his sword with much deliberation, he let out a short war cry whoop, but was interrupted by a solid *thunk*.

Jacq watched in confused curiosity as he wobbled slightly, tottered forward not quite a step, and then fell to the ground in front of her, hands outstretched. Staring at him, a moment, she looked up to see a large, dark mass emerge from the shadows of the nearby trees. "Ah!" she gasped, stepping back abruptly in alarm and readying her swords in defense. However, as the mass paused and she realized it was a person, she squinted and asked, "Bahari?"

"Shakina." He smiled kindly at her, tossing a rock back into the trees.

"Bahari!" She dropped her swords to her sides. "Now, why'd you have to go and do that?" She gestured to the still form of Red Handed Jesse. "He might have killed himself." Sheathing her swords, she watched as Bahari, chuckling deeply, bent to turn Jesse onto his side, thus preventing him from suffocating in the sand. "What if he wakes up later and is even angrier with me? Then what will happen?"

"I have done this to him many times," Bahari said, straightening from stooping over the repulsive rogue. "He has yet to comprehend what has taken place."

Folding her arms, Jacq tilted her head. "Many times?"

The large, muscular man nodded confidently.

"Haha!" Jacq laughed, shaking her head. Quite suddenly, however, she stopped and turned a rather intrigued stare at Jesse Smith's secret assailant. "But why?"

Grinning again, he held his hand out to the north side of the pirate refuge, almost completely opposite of the direction Jean-Pierre had trudged off to. "Come with me, Shakina."

Glancing about her, Jacq shrugged. It wasn't like her alternative options were looking so great and, for some reason she couldn't quite identify, she did not feel threatened by this intimidating man. So, heaving a sigh, she began walking northward beside Bahari. Kicking at the sand a little nervously as she trudged beside the burly, quiet man, she cleared her throat and inquired, "Why do you call me Shakina? What does it mean?"

"In my country," he answered, in his deep, slow, rhythmic voice, "it means beautiful one. It is what I wanted to name my daughter if I would have had one, but I only had sons, and that is no name for a son." He smiled pleasantly at her, though a glint of sadness shone in his eye.

"You have a family?" she asked, staring at him with intense inquisitiveness. *If you do*, she continued internally, *what are you doing out here?*

"I *had* a family," he said, sighing dismally, his brow furrowing. "I was told that if I joined this ship, they would not be taken as slaves. So, now I am a slave instead."

"I'm sorry to...*wah!*..." Stopping immediately in mid stride, Bahari turned to find Jacq picking herself up off the ground, slapping at the sand that now cluttered the front of her blouse and pants. "Heh heh," she giggled self-consciously. "I...Uh...I tripped."

"Are you unharmed?" he asked quite seriously, his voice filled with concern.

"Aye." Jacq laughed, nodding. "I'm not that frail," she said dismissively, grinning broadly and continuing to dust herself off. "And, what I was trying to say was that I'm sorry to hear of your hardships. I have yet to meet my father. I was actually on my way to meet him for the first time when Ming hunted me down and kidnapped me." A sardonic smile played onto her face as she paused a moment, staring off into the black.

"I am sorry," Bahari said after a few moments of watching her gaze into the night.

At his voice, she shook her head and shrugged. "Oh..." Not wanting to press her luck and misjudge his loyalties, she steered the conversation back to him. "So, you are from Africa?"

"Aye," he returned, beginning to move forward again. Then, also redirecting their discussion, he glanced at her and noted, "You are sad this night."

"Aye," she acknowledged, nodding with a downtrodden air. "It grieves me deeply that George Brandon died today."

"I too will miss Father Brandon," Bahari sympathized. "He was always kind to me. It hurt me greatly to learn of his death this day."

"How is it that you speak English so well as you do?" she inquired, changing the subject back again, quickly realizing she did not wish to speak any more of the deceased old man.

"Three years with Captain and Father," he said in a dull tone. "But, also the kind Esperanza, who we go to see now. They have taught me all I know." At her name, a small smile tugged at his cheek.

"Who is Esperanza?" Jacq asked, staring up at him a moment. *What a beautiful name*, she thought, baffled. *How could someone with such a glorious name be out here on such a wretched island?*

Motioning out in front of them, Bahari pointed out a small, rather rickety looking structure nestled amongst a few trees and hidden by a large rock just a few strides away; it was not much more than a shack. Watching her reaction, which fell somewhere between shock and curiosity, Bahari chuckled. "Come." Then, crossing the distance to the front door, knocked three times, cleared his throat, and then whispered, "*Nunca luchar con un cerdo.*"

"*Ambos se ensucian*," a heavily accented feminine voice replied.

"*Y el cerdo le gusta*," Bahari returned, leaving Jacq confused.

However, at his last statement, the door opened. A warm, sweet cascade of air greeted their noses with a trim, pale skinned, dark haired woman standing in the entry way. Her moderately conservative dress and uniquely patterned shawl were a little ragged, but still somehow looked mysteriously attractive. Much of her long hair fell behind her, but what did not was done up ornately on her head with sparkling accessories. Her bare feet were clean with rings on the toes, and her upper arms each had a gold band with a spiraling design wrapped around them. Nodding at Bahari and Jacq, she smiled and stepped aside, sweeping her hand out to gesture them welcome. "*Hola*," she said in her breathy Spanish accent, smiling grandly at each of them individually as her dark eyes sparkled.

As Jacq passed through the doorway, it did not take her long to realize that the inside of the surprisingly cozy little abode was not much more heavily decorated or much fancier than the outside. Furniture was sparse and sat along the walls of the front room of the two room building. A small, rough table with a cheery oil lamp on it and four humble stools around it stood off to the left of the door. Behind the open door was a tall set of shelves that contained her dishes, some food, and kitchenware. Beyond the other end of the table, almost in the far corner of the room, stood a fireplace with a blanket laid out in front of it.

Walking further in, Jacq noticed, almost centered on the floor, was some kind of a rug of the like she had never before laid eyes on with a bold, colorful pattern. To the right of it was a large collection of sea chests and shelves lined with books, some various kinds of artwork Jacq found to be rather intriguing, a couple more oil lamps, and other knickknacks and bedding type items. There was a door directly across from the one they had entered and another by the fireplace.

"Come in, come in!" she said, smiling brightly at them, her richly colored lips wide with joy to have their company.

"Please make yourselves at home." Then, turning to Bahari, she inquired, her voice low and her R's rolling like a purr, "What is her name?"

"I call her Shakina; she calls herself Jacq," he replied shortly in his semi-choppy manner of speech, taking a seat on the corner of the blanket in front of the fire.

"Jacq," Esperanza repeated thoughtfully, watching the man set himself down cross legged and straight backed on the floor. Then, turning to Jacq, her mouth flowered into a smile again. "What are you doing so far from home, *señorita*?" Looking her up and down, the woman continued, "You do not look like a *bucanero* to me."

"A *bucanero*?" Jacq echoed, tilting her head slightly at this.

"*Sí*, a *bucanero*. A…Uh…A buccaneer…A pirate," she translated obligingly. "You do not look like one."

"Are you an expert on what a pirate should and shouldn't look like?" Jacq replied cagily, studying the woman's mannerisms and dress.

Shrugging slightly, Esperanza continued wearing a kind of smirk Jacq couldn't read. "I would not say that perhaps, but I would say that I know when a good soul," her gaze moved briefly to Bahari, "is in a world it was not meant to be in." Curtsying, her skirt spreading farther than any Jacq had ever seen before, she then sat delicately on the stool closest to her, keeping an even eye on Jacq. "You were happy once, *sí, señorita*? Happier than you are now anyway…?"

"Aye," Jacq returned, smiling dolefully. Then, sighing and looking a moment at Bahari, who was sitting, eyes closed, soaking up the heat of the fire, she realized suddenly that the woman had not introduced herself. Turning sharply back to the foreign lady, Jacq inquired in a low voice, "Who are you?"

"My name," she responded, heaving a sigh of her own, "is Esperanza. Most people on this island call me Espa because Esperanza seems too difficult for them to remember. I am from *España* years ago, but I was too free for my parents, and they were afraid I would become a Gypsy." Looking away from Jacq, at the unimpressive walls she called home, she sighed again. "In order that I would not bring shame to my family, I left *España* with intent to go somewhere that my want of freedom would not be considered shameful. A man offered me free passage on his ship to take me to a place where desires were unhindered by laws and not considered shameful." Returning her eyes to Jacq, she smiled as if in amusement at her own story. "So, here I am, in a place where I can do and be whatever I want."

"Do you fancy your freedom?" Jacq inquired, her curiosity in this woman having increased tenfold. She crossed over from where she'd been hovering by the shelves and sat on the stool beside Esperanza, noticing that deep within her eyes was a dark, endless emptiness.

"My freedom? *Sí.* My loneliness? No." Her dark eyes became slightly overcast as she thought about it a moment or two. "I would exchange my freedom for happiness and companionship. All I do is dance in town three or four times a week, and that gives me enough money to live, though not in a mansion, comfortably. I make a point of trying to help others who come here, not knowing what they have gotten themselves into…like Bahari," she gestured to the man who now seemed to be asleep sitting up. "I saw him for the first time two years ago. He was carving a doll out of a piece of driftwood, for one of his little *niños*, and when I saw him, I knew he was not a *bucanero*…not really. He has killed many men in his life, over half of which was before that *demonio* Ming conned him into joining his crew to save his family. Trying to help such people is my only source of happiness."

"What else do you know of Ming?" Jacq inquired, her interests suddenly making a dramatic shift in focus. "They say he is one of the vilest pirates to sail the seas."

"Ming? Nobody is sure how long he has been a *bucanero*," she said, shrugging uncaringly about his very existence, "but they say he has one of the blackest hearts on the sea and will be one of the most notorious captains before long. He has a curved dagger from his homeland that is said to be cursed with *demonios* that obey his commands. It is also known that he was apprehended and held prisoner for a short while by a then Captain Bartholomew Luray."

At this, Jacq's heart nearly leapt into her throat and gagged her.

"They say that his *demonios* are what helped him escape. They say he swore to take vengeance on the good captain by turning one of his own children into a *bucanero*." Pausing, she blinked almost speechlessly at Jacq's changed state of being. "My, *señorita*, you look pale. Have you fallen ill?" Reaching over, she grabbed a large red handkerchief from off her shelf and stuffed it in Jacq's hand.

"Nay." Jacq shook her head, forcing a smile while her stomach was turning knots inside of her. Her throat was swelling, making it difficult to swallow, and her palms were suddenly sweaty as the rest of her began to feel cold and prickly. She gripped the kerchief and clenched her teeth. *Captain Ming was captured by my father?...He swore revenge upon my father by turning one of his own children to piracy...? Heavens! That's me!* Staring at the floor as if it were falling apart beneath her feet, she forced herself to breathe.

"Jacq?" Esperanza asked, eyeing her knowingly. "Do you know this man? This Captain Bartholomew Luray?"

In an instant, shock gave way to spiteful vengeance. "Nay, Esperanza," she said, a mischievous grin pulling the corners of her mouth tight, "but I intend to."

"They say he is a very good man." Smiling in amusement, Esperanza continued, "You know, *señorita* Jacq, Ming has had much bad luck with good people. First Captain Bartholomew, then there is rumor one of the crewmen he had marooned is now a pardoned captain of his own ship, and then there was that young man he was trying to get aboard his ship. Nobody is really sure if the *muchacho* joined with him or not, but I can tell you," her eyes glittered with a fascinated sparkle, "Skippy Rackham was one of the most sought after and the most attractive *bucaneros* to ever set foot in the Isles of Scilly. Captains and *muchachas* alike fought for his attentions."

"Skippy Rackham?" Jacq repeated, her mind spinning circles about all this information. She gulped a large rock she'd hardly noticed in her throat. The very same Dante "Skippy" Rackham who'd had her smitten with that wickedly handsome smile of his?

"*Sí*," Esperanza sighed fondly. "He was a fine *bucanero*, but a finer man, I would say. Rumor has it that he is no longer in the business, as you might say, any more. I have heard that he joined up with an honorable captain and now does an honest day's work aboard an honest ship." Heaving a breath, she smiled again to herself. "I am glad that he will not die a *bandito*, but I do miss our conversations."

"Your conversations?" Jacq repeated, her already racing mind beginning to sky rocket with such an idea. She was

suddenly afraid...so very afraid. *Did he tell me the truth about his past? Is there someone...a special someone...here...?* She shook her head, loose locks falling to her face.

"Oh, *sí*," Esperanza willingly continued, as though she were trailing Jacq along with strings and breadcrumbs, gently guiding her through the conversation to exactly where she wanted her to go. "He is a much better man than Jean-Pierre." Her painted lips curled slightly at his name. "Skippy had many *muchachas* after him, but he never really seemed to care much about them. Sure, he flirted with them, but I never think many got past that. I think, personally, it is because they did not have enough to offer. After all, who truly wants a spent *muchacha, sí*? It would be like," she paused a moment, looking around the softly glowing walls of the tiny living space, "like giving someone an already opened and used gift. Is the gift still valuable? *Sí*...But, there are other gifts out there," her eyes moved momentarily to the door before returning to continue to steadily gaze at Jacq, "that are worth so much more.

"Jean-Pierre, on the other hand, is a gift opener. He opens them and toys with them and then puts them back for later though they do not belong to him. True," she nodded at this, "he does have his favorites, but that will not stop him from taking advantage others." Cautiously reaching out her hand and covering Jacq's, which was resting on her knee, she added, "Be careful, *señorita*. I am surprised he has not already made any advances on you." Stretching out her hand, Esperanza brushed the hair that had fallen across Jacq's face. "There must be something very special about you, or something very secret."

Jacq's thoughts raced rapidly to the comment Esperanza had made only a few moments ago regarding Ming's sworn

oath of retaliation. "I think you have given me more answers," Jacq said, astounded, "tonight than I have received in my entire life. For that, I wish I could repay you." She sighed.

"You repay me with your smile," Esperanza replied in a sad inflection. "I deserve nothing more. I only wish I could give aid to more people like you."

Jacq opened her mouth to retort, but Esperanza quickly pressed her finger to the younger woman's lips.

"Shh..." she ordered gently, shaking her head. "You cannot argue with me over this." Smiling, she pulled back her hand. "But, it would please me if you slept here while your shipmates remain. That Red Handed Jesse can be a very temperamental fool when he has had too much to drink."

An appreciative smile crawled easily onto Jacq's face. "He is a temperamental fool when he has had nothing to drink."

Esperanza laughed.

Chapter 7

"So, ye be knowin' the whereabouts o' Captain Ming, but ye be wantin' to give the infermation in exchange fer me lettin' ye be a part o' me crew?" Captain Adams asked in his booming voice as he sat across the table from Crevan.

The group had left Thirsty Thaddeus to go find Adams, eventually locating him at a lesser tavern near the harbor called The Silver Bottle Alehouse. Most of the men that came in and out of The Silver Bottle were fishermen and other townsfolk who worked hard for their livings but did not have a lot of extra money to spend. The two brothers who owned and ran the tavern were retired fishermen themselves and, recalling the hardships of their trade, catered to them.

Alex held her breath as she watched Crevan, in silence, lean forward, his eye unwavering from the captain's. His high cheekbones and his hushed blue eyes were cool and collected as he allowed the aura of his presence to fill the room, wordlessly trying to convince the captain that it was worth his while. Then, with a suave, confident smile tugging his mouth apart, he answered in a charming Irish brogue, "Aye, Sir."

Bursting into laughter, Captain Edward Adams slapped

him on the back and thrust out his hand. "Very well, lad!"

Turning to Miata who was sitting beside her at a table near where Adams and Crevan were discussing his now confirmed passage on *Anne's Triumph*, she commented in a low tone, "Though I find it strange he wishes passage aboard the ship, I am grateful for his keenness to be of assistance."

Shrugging, Miata sighed, a larger than life smile conquering his face. "Aye, but, Murtaugh...He be a right good mate." Stretching his arms upwards, he laced his fingers together and brought his hands behind his head as he hunkered down a little lower in the chair to relax.

At this, Nicholas Dunne, who was sitting across the small, round table from Alex, deliberately cleared his throat. "M'lady..." He smiled engagingly.

Looking at him over her shoulder, she smiled. "Yes, Mr. Dunne?"

"Shall we go to supper soon? The evening is carrying on without us. I am rather famished myself, and I would wager that you are quite hungry as well?" Inclining forward, he rested one arm on the table, lightly tapping his fingers on the surface.

Nodding in admittance, Alex sighed, glancing at Miata. "I could use a bite to eat. Where is it we are going? I wish for Miata to know in case anything develops. I am very interested to know what this fellow Crevan has to say regarding my sister's whereabouts." She glanced at the grinning Irishman then turned back to Nicholas. "I am quite certain you understand this."

Nicholas gulped.

"I do find it curious how a man may seem so terrible and dishonest to one person and be a saint for another." A sadness descended upon her countenance like a light fog. *Jacq would laugh at me for it.*

"Haha..." Nicholas laughed, forcing a smile. "Yes, yes. Funny how that is, isn't it, m'lady?" Then, pushing up, he walked to her side, holding out his hand to nonverbally request her company.

"Oh!" She stood, delighted at his unwavering gentlemanliness.

Taking a deep breath, Nicholas turned to Miata and reported, "Miss Luray and I will be dining at Roaming Sailor Inn."

Alex noticed all eyes in the tavern seemed to turn in their direction, though Nicholas Dunne didn't seem to notice at all.

"It is southeast of Thirsty Thaddeus Tavern and beside a small shop by name of Claude's Linens. It is not easy to miss."

Miata too had noticed the swiveling heads at Nicholas' announcement of their supper location, and he smiled, generously replying, "That be swell, mate. I know ye be treatin' Alex with the kindest o' manners." His mouth twitched and Alex couldn't tell if his response was a genuine comment of assurance, or a command. *Conceited coxcomb...He be flauntin' his supper plans purposefully.* However, despite his internal grumblings, he turned to Alex and said in a heartfelt tone, "Be enjoyin' yer evenin', Alex. Perhaps we be able to be findin' Jacq afore long."

"W-Would you care to join us?" she asked, feeling uncomfortable, as she slid her little hand into the crook of Nicholas Dunne's arm.

Nicholas stopped breathing. *What the devil!? No! No, no, no! This is all going so wrong! So terribly wrong!!* He ground his teeth together, yet managed to maintain his composure as he stood beside Alex, a spurious smile painted on his face. *Utter nonsense! How am supposed to... Ugh!* Breathing deeply, he forced himself to continue smiling. *Calm yourself, man*, he coached, *don't let this little predicament get under your skin...*

"Nay, mate," Miata was saying, "but thank ye. Me evenin' be spent here with Murtaugh an' Cap'n Adams if he be carin' to join us."

At this, Adams raised his mug and then put it to his lips.

Looking back at Alex, he shrugged. "An' it be time fer me to be catchin' up with me ol' mate." At this, he gestured to Murtaugh.

Nicholas exhaled heavily through his nose. *What the devil is he doing!?* At this point, he paused a brief moment, letting all that was going on soak in. He knew every ear in the tavern had heard him say Roaming Sailor Inn and turned to hone in on the speaker. *Bah!...The price of being a gentleman...*Grinning as graciously as he could muster and choking on every syllable of the words he was shoving up his throat and over his tongue, Nicholas invited, "Miata!, mate, are you certain you would not fancy to join us?"

"Aye!" Miata, chuckled, good-naturedly. "I be sure o' that!" His broad, pleased expression could only have widened if the very structure of his face somehow expanded.

"And thank you for inviting me as well," Murtaugh piped up, winking at Nicholas, "but I'm in agreement with Miata here...You enjoy your evening with the pretty lass, but don't keep her out too late." An attractive grin broke out across his lightly tanned, broad jawed face.

Alex, who, along with everyone else in the tavern, had been watching the slightly abrasive discourse with great interest, glanced rapidly back and forth between Nicholas Dunne and Michael Murtaugh. However, Murtaugh's last remark had her all but hiding behind her parasol as she waited for them to finish so the evening could just move forward. In the rather short, but seemingly disturbingly long pause that followed Crevan's conclusive comment, she felt her cheeks beginning to burn. The small fire spread to her ears and the end of her nose, and before she knew it, Alex could have sworn she was going to set her dress aflame. *This is ridiculous!* she thought in annoyance. *Preposterous rubbish!* The more she blushed, the harder she had to fight from saying something.

Finally, though, Nicholas broke the ten second silence. "Well, very well. Then we bid you a fair evening." He moved his gaze one last time to where Crevan was sitting, watching him rather intently. "May you enjoy your company," he added.

That being said, he tugged softly on Alex's arm and inquired in his ever so sophisticated diction, "Shall we, m'lady? The night is getting no younger." Glancing out the small windows of the tavern, his keen eyes were quick to notice the sun was on the verge of beginning to set. *Perfect!* "If we do not hurry, we shall miss the splendid view the fine inn has of the sunset," he prompted, glad to feel her move in step beside him.

"Oh! How delightful!" she returned, her lovely smile gracing the tavern one last time before the two exited through the door. "Is it far?" However, even as she bantered back and forth with him, she wondered to herself, *Such odd behavior... Mr. Dunne does seem rather tense as of late. Could it be he is more comfortable at sea than he is on land? What a shame that would be.*

Despite his cordial demeanor as the two were making haste to the Roaming Sailor Inn in time to watch the sunset while they ate, a new terrible feeling came over Alex. Her heart sank to the soles of her feet, and the happy glimmer in her eyes diminished to almost nothing. *Oh*, she thought breathlessly, *Jacq...* Her eyes turned up to Nicholas, who was now describing the serenity of the inn and that he had heard from local townsfolk on previous visits that it was considered the best place in town to get a meal. *What am I doing? How can this perfect gentleman sweep me away with my sister still out there?*

"So, tell me," Nicholas disrupted her thoughts abruptly, "what makes you so ready to trust an Irish coward and thief on the whereabouts of your sister?" His eyes, a soft tone in the warm, waning evening light, turned sincerely to search her for an answer. He thought he noticed, for a moment, a fleck of dejection glistening in her eye, but she blinked it away too fast for him to know for certain. Then, before, he could ask, she was answering his question...

"Although Miata has his faults because, believe me, he does...His heart has always belonged to Jacq. I am certain he would do anything he could to find her." At this she paused, a pang of sadness pinching at her emotions. "As for his associate, though I do not know him, I do not believe Miata would involve anyone who would hinder our mission." She eyed him curiously a moment. "Besides," she carried on with a rather relaxed and somewhat happy lilt to her voice, "you often cannot tell everything about a person by what you see on the outside."

Glancing out towards the sea, Alex sighed. "Jacq is very fond of looking for the good in people. Of course, if you do not keep an eye out for the bad, you might be hurt by it, but I guess that if you spend all of your time looking for the bad, you will never get to see the good." Smiling pensively, her heart heavy again at the thought of her sister out there somewhere terrible, she then turned to look ahead of her and was a little surprised at what met her eyes.

A tall, elegant, rich mahogany colored structure towered above her between two seemingly sumptuous shops. A large, proud sign protruding out above the inn's doors, engraved with eloquent, stylish lettering, hung still in the mellow evening air. The large, beautifully trimmed windows in the front made the inn shine brighter than any of the other buildings in town. Rows of nice, smaller windows for the upstairs guestrooms glowed warmly, sending out a subtle invitation for any passerby. The shops all around were closing down for the evening, as the hour was getting late and the sun was nigh on setting as they drew closer to the Roaming Sailor Inn, which simply enhanced how dashing and charming the inn appeared. The sweet and savory aromas of the fine cooking within wafted out and tantalized their senses. Alex's mouth began to water and her stomach began to complain about its hollowness loudly.

Seeing her eyes grow in obvious pleasant surprise, Nicholas, who had allowed them to slow to a pause a few short strides from the doorway, nudged her with his elbow. "Is this quite all right, m'lady? Shall we go in?"

As they stood admiring the upscale beauty of the inn, it vaguely reminded her of the Midway Zebra. Again, a wave of tortured guilt came gushing over her again. *I should not be having fun while Jacq is suffering*, she thought miserably, momentarily wishing ill upon herself. *What kind of sister am I? My sister is in danger and all I can think about is enjoying the evening with some romantic gentleman…?* Miata's previous conversation and behavior suddenly came back to her, her heart sinking even lower than her feet. *Upon my word…Miata is being a better friend to Jacq than I!! How could this be happening?* Small tears began to slip from her eyes and glide unhindered down her cheeks as she stood, smelling the wonderful scents and soaking in the beautiful architecture. "I cannot dine here!" she wept, releasing her hold of Nicholas' arm and turning away from him, covering her face with her delicately gloved hands.

By the powers! He stared at her in bewilderment. *What happened now?* "M'lady? Miss Luray?" His voice was pleading and kind as he implored her to look at him with every movement as he rushed to stop her from walking away. "What has happened? What has come over you? Is there something wrong? Have I utterly offended you?" He took a deep breath as he watched her back. *There truly is no rest for the wicked!*

Composing herself, Alex managed to reduce her crying to sniffling, dabbing at her tear streaked cheeks with her fingertips.

"Miss Luray," he asked softly, "*please* tell me what is wrong."

"I cannot dine here!" she repeated, sniffling a little. "How can I enjoy such lovely company and delight in such fine food when for all I know Jacq could be starving at the hands of those barbarians!" Her shoulders started moving up and down as she stifled additional sobs.

At this, Nicholas reached out a tentative hand, barely grazing her elbow with his fingers. When she didn't pull away, he slid his hand up her arm and rested it on her shoulder. Heaving another sigh, he looked at the yellowing sky in exasperation while tears poured like waterfalls from her eyes, and her body trembled from the pent up pain she had been avoiding for the last couple days.

"Please forgive me," she said in an emotional blubber, continuing to regain composure. "I do not intend to ruin your evening. I am certain," her now puffy eyes moved again to the summoning windows, "you could find another supper partner better suited for tonight."

"Miss Luray," he returned kindly, handing her a handkerchief to dry her eyes, "there is no other person I would rather spend this night…Err…Evening with." He smiled gently, helping her to stand upright once again, her dignity returning to her tenfold as every second past. "There is no one else I have ever met that fascinates me as you do, m'lady. I-" He paused uncomfortably, watching her dab at her cheekbones and her flushed eyes.

"You what?"

Grinning, he waved away her question. "I do not believe this to be the right time to finish that sentence. I do, however, think that you are not a horrible person for wanting to sustain yourself. And, though I do not know your sister, I think she would want you to eat and keep up your strength." Alex opened her mouth in protest, but Nicholas held up his finger to request her wait, and continued, "It is not your fault, Miss Luray, that I am insisting you eat here…With me…I will take the blame for that gladly, in full. In fact, I apologize for being less considerate of your current emotions. You maintain your composure so well, I…I was insensitive and thoughtless. Please forgive me."

Heaving one last ragged breath, Alex shook her head, smiling weakly. "Your tongue must have been forged of gold, Mr. Dunne. But once again, there is nothing to forgive."

Blushing painfully, Nicholas glanced again at the horizon and shook his head, laughing. "M'lady, you are markedly gracious." Then, grinning sheepishly, he gestured towards the inn again. "Shall we eat?"

Stretching contentedly, Jacq yawned, her body feeling more rested than it had in days. As her eyes slid open, she started awake, thinking for a brief moment everything that had happened in the last couple of days had been a bad dream. However, morning sun rays peeped through the thin slats of the northern wall, spilling light in at odd angles on Esperanza's bed, which sat kitty-corner from where she lay. Beside her was a sea chest she guessed contained the dancer's money and most valuable items. The genteel Spanish woman had generously allowed her to sleep in her room, the second of the two rooms in her small shack, on a mat she kept for special guests. The room was quite small, half the size of the main room, yet somehow quaint. Even though they were, Jacq estimated, a good ten minute walk from the seafront, the cool, salty ocean air seemed to penetrate every inch of the home.

"Shakina," Bahari's voice called gently from the front room.

Yawning again and wishing it had all just been a nightmare, Jacq pushed herself up from being curled up amongst the blankets on the floor. "Aye, Bahari?" Trying desperately to rub the sleep from her eyes, she made her way to the door that separated the rooms and pushed it open.

Bahari, smiling broadly, motioned for her to sit at the table where two plates with some eggs and meat sat steaming alongside a couple mugs. "Come, Shakina," he invited, beckoning her with big, swooping gestures. "Sit and eat with me."

Smiling in awe filled surprise at what met her sleepy, watering eyes, Jacq agreeably crossed the floor to the table so that she could join him for breakfast.

He watched approvingly as she closed her eyes and privately whispered a prayer of thanks for her food before beginning to fork it into her mouth. Grinning, he bent over his own food and added, "We have much to do this day."

He made this last comment as she took a long drink of the cool, surprisingly fresh water from the cup in front of her. Gulping, she put the mug down and stared at him in bemusement. "We do?" Watching him with interest, she took another bite.

"Oh, aye," he said as though this should not have been a surprise, "a lot!" He then returned to scooping the food hungrily into his mouth.

Looking about at the otherwise quiet surroundings of the hovel the hospitable and cordial Spaniard called home, Jacq swallowed what was in her mouth and asked, "Where's Esperanza?"

"She has gone for provisions. She will be back soon," he replied easily. "What do you think of her?" His bright blue eyes searched her for an answer before she spoke.

"She is both gracious and fascinating. How did you meet her?" Jacq smiled, recalling the brief story the Spanish woman had told her last night.

"Well," Bahari began, completely unaware of Jacq's knowledge, "I was sitting behind William's Tavern, the one that is the most east. I had picked up a piece of driftwood from the surf and was making a figurine out of it for whenever I get to see my children again." Jacq's face brightened a little with a warm glow at seeing Esperanza's speculation was correct. "I have made many on these shores. She keeps them for me," he noted, his tone perking up a little, "in that chest right there." Jacq followed his finger to a dark, heavily strapped chest close

to Esperanza's bedroom door.

"How kindly of her," Jacq responded, smiling broader inwardly than her face allowed. "Now, pray tell me, what did you mean when you said we have much to do today?" Raising the cup to her lips again, Jacq bent her head back, enjoying the thirst quenching liquid splashing into her mouth and cascading down her throat.

Gesturing to his sword, which sat by the fireplace, he returned simply, "Practice."

Her spine stiffened and she gulped down the remaining liquid in her mouth. "Practice? I think I know how to swordfight rather well, thank you." Her voice, she realized, sounded a little bit indignant.

"Ah, yes, Shakina." Bahari smiled, nodding agreeably. "You may fight well with your sword, but you can fight even better with your mind. There are some things about our captain that you should know."

Jacq's eyes narrowed slightly at this. "What kinds of things, mate?" she inquired, her interests peaking. "I don't believe in that rubbish about his dagger, or whatever it is, having spirits."

"That wavy dagger of his, it is called a kris. Many men have died by it...Many men fear it greatly," Bahari warned. "But, you listen to me, Shakina. I can help make you stronger."

Bahari spoke to Jacq in low, careful tones clear through the morning and a little ways into the afternoon. The sun sailed blissfully across the sky as the conversation carried on and on, however, Jacq became curious about this pirate town she was so nearby. So, she excused herself, assuring him she would return before dark and giving him permission to come looking for her if he became concerned.

After using Esperanza's washing facilities, Jacq, pulling

her hair back, fastened it in a ponytail. She pulled out the red kerchief Esperanza had given her last night and tied it around her head as a bandana. Then, glancing down at her clothes, she sighed. During the plundering the day before, she had made a point of collecting some new clothes for herself. Yanking her dark colored boots on over her equally dark colored breeches, she shook her head. Again, the poisonous words of Ming that day in his cabin rang through her mind.

Always a bad twin...

Grinding her teeth in defiance, she slid into a rather tight jerkin that was a deep burgundy in coloration with silvery and gold hues laced into it over her loose sleeved white blouse. Belting on her swords, she took a deep breath of the mild air and pushed her way through the door of Esperanza's bedroom. Bahari was seated again on the corner of the rug nearest the hearth, soaking up whatever heat the now low burning embers had to offer. Smiling softly in his direction, she walked to the front door of the shack and stepped out onto the island again.

As she trudged the distance between Esperanza's shrouded abode and the drunk and disorderly town, Jacq kicked a little at the sand, keeping her ears open for anything unusual. However, all she heard were whispers in her mind...

Ya know, with twins, there always be a good twin, an' there always be a bad twin. Alex be not the bad twin...

Jacq whipped around, her hazel eyes, though she knew nobody was there, scanning the tall trees whose leaves were rustling slightly in the slow breeze that was wandering around above her. "There is not always a good twin and always a bad twin," she retorted in a mutter, carrying on with her steps, rather deliberate now. "I'm sure there are sets of bad twins just as well as there are sets of good twins." A shiver ran up her spine. She scowled, and continued to mumble to herself for the rest of the hike to town, purposefully ignoring the hoops tapping her jaw.

Upon reaching the outskirts of the squalid village, she was not all too surprised to see men and women laying out here and there, still recovering from the afore evening's late night activities so that they could do it again tonight. She saw several of Ming's sailors, partial bottles in hand and empty bottles all around, lounging in the warm, early afternoon sunshine. A strong odor seemed to rise from the very ground she was standing on as she wandered down the main street. She could hear music coming from the largest and least dilapidated building in the cluster of rogue constructions. It was a tall, yellowish structure with stains in strange places on its walls.

As she approached it, a scraggly looking man sitting near the corner opposite of the one she approached with two missing teeth lifted a dirty palm to wave at her. "Oi!" his scratchy voice called out.

Jacq paused, still a fair distance from the door, and turned to look at him.

"Ya new aroond hea?" he questioned.

Taking a few small steps closer to him, she nodded.

"I knew it!" He cackled, slapping his knee. "This," he jabbed towards the building he was leaning on with his thumb, "be the inn."

Smiling, Jacq casually glanced up at the large sign that hung across the door stating boldly and proudly, *The Inn*. Clearing her throat, she nodded and looked back at the scruffy vagrant. "I can see that."

"Can ya now?" He snorted, crossing his dirty arms. "Ya can spot an inn jus' loike dat, heh? Wit'out e'er steppin' inside

oi it?" He eyed her, waiting for some impressive return volley of words.

Pointing at the sign, she retorted, "It says *The Inn* right there!" Glancing up at the letters, she guessed them to be at least half her own height.

"So, now yar tellin' me yas can read?" He grabbed up a bottle that had been sitting in the sand beside him and took a long gulp of it.

Nodding, Jacq strode confidently forward and knelt to look the ruffian square in the eye. "I am, and I don't appreciate you mocking everything I say, savvy?"

The man's eyes narrowed at this.

"Perhaps you should find a better job, mate."

"Wha-what do ya mean by dat?" He stuck his chin out in confused agitation.

"It means you should learn to read, Baggett," a masculine voice chimed in. "Now, you know Innkeeper Julian doesn't fancy you hanging around out front like this...He feels it's bad for business."

"But he's my brotha!" Baggett snapped.

"Baggett..." the stranger scolded.

"His bidness cou'n't be worse if he moved it un'er water," the man complained, grumbling as he pulled and pushed himself up. He then staggered around the corner, where he slid down the wall to sit on the side of the building.

Jacq, who had not gotten up or turned around, watched in amusement as the scalawag barely relocated. However, internally, her mind was racing. *Do I recognize that voice? It can't possibly be...*

"You'll have to forgive Baggett," the voice continued. "When he's had a lot of rum, he gets a tad...Well, rummy...

But, he isn't too bad of a man, and a rather upstanding pirate, when he's sober…If he's sober."

Jacq couldn't help it, she turned to glance over her shoulder as she stood, and her breath left her.

"J-Jacq? Jacqueline Taylor?" the voice asked in astonishment. The owner of the voice was a slightly shorter than average man with thick, curling dark brown hair that swelled around his neck and fell slightly below his collar in the back. He had a dark tan, the darkest, in fact, Jacq thought she had ever seen. His keen and observant brown eyes absorbed her in her entirety. "How ever did *you* end up *here*?"

"Didn't you hear?" she retorted flippantly, shrugging and smirking with a natural air of sauciness that many women worked hard to achieve. "I'm the newest addition to Captain Ming's crew." She looked him over, dressed as flashy as ever.

He had a baldric looped diagonally around his upper body, flintlocks stowed away in it, and a rapier hanging at his side. His boots, a striking black, reached his knees and gave way to his trousers, equally dark in coloration. For a shirt, he donned a rich blue silk blouse, open partway down his front and tucked into the thick red sash he wore to hide where his pants and shirt met. A gold chain with a large gold locket hung around his neck as well as a leather necklace with a couple very pointy teeth decorating it, and, lastly, a metal cross hung around his neck by a small rope. Some of his fingers were adorned with rings, and small portions of his hair were held together in braids, starting from beneath his three-cornered hat, the only relatively beat up looking piece of apparel he seemed to have on him. He had a small amount of facial hair, which was even darker than the rest of his hair, and arms that had the appearance of thick rope.

"And my name's Luray now, Jacqueline Taylor Luray." With that, she spun around to walk away.

"Jacq! Wait!" he called after her, quickly crossing the small distance between them, and spinning her to face him by grabbing hold of her shoulder.

"For what, Audric?" She spat his name, shoving his hand off of her. "I waited for you once; it didn't work out so well for me though, did it?" Her voice was overflowing with sardonic annoyance and perhaps a small amount of outrage that he would ever think to say those words to her again. *Of all the nerve!*

"Jacq…" he pleaded, sounding rather exasperated.

"Give Miss Tabitha Trent, if that is still her name, my regards," she said in a growl. "And don't touch me again!" With that, she turned and began to stomp further down the street.

Baggett, wide-eyed, peeked around the corner at them.

"Jacq!" Audric called out again, heaving a belabored sigh. "Jacq, I'm sorry, and I'm not seeing Tabitha anymore. I've missed you, Jacq." At this, Jacq stopped in her tracks. "I've missed our conversations…Your brilliance…" Delicately, he began to move forward in her direction. "I was wrong, Jacq. I didn't want to push you away."

"You told me there are other fish in the sea, Audric," she said with a fiery inflection, whirling about and drawing her sword. She realized that her heart was racing as though she were running along the sandy beaches, though she was standing perfectly still. Maybe pulling a sword wasn't the best idea.

Stopping abruptly, he held up his hands. "I was wrong, Jacq."

"Nay, Audric," she returned in a livid tone, stepping closer

to him, her sword pointing steadily at his throat, "you were right. There are other fish in the sea." By this time, as she spoke methodically deliberate, she had reached his side, and, continuing to hold the point of her blade at him, she whispered in his ear, "What you didn't realize, before you threw me back, was that I was the best catch you'd ever get. What I didn't realize, until after you threw me back, was that I could find someone much," she breathed into his ear, "much better."

Turning his face into hers, he whispered in return, "You didn't think that then, why do you say that now? If you had really found someone, Jacq, you wouldn't be here now, with me…"

Pulling away from him, her lips tightened into a smirk. "Don't be a fool, Audric. You proved to me there is better out there when you chose Miss Trent over me for…" she paused thoughtfully, "…whore-ific reasons. Savvy?"

Keeping a level eye with her, he sighed. "A truce then? We can still be mates, can't we?" Holding out his hand, he implored her with his gaze. *What the devil happened to her since last I saw her? The last time I saw her she was…* He started slightly as he stood, hand outstretched, watching this older, wiser, and seemingly even wilder Jacq ponder his proposal. *Well, she actually fancied me last I saw her… What? Three years ago?* He cleared his throat. "I must say, though, you're lovelier than ever." At his comment, Audric Schellden smiled – a smile that could melt any woman's heart and turn her into a fawning fool at his feet.

Even now, despite her rage and pre-knowledge of this, it softened Jacq just a little. Clenching her teeth, she lowered her katana. "Don't think that your silver tongue will win you anything special from me, Audric, and keep your claptrap to yourself."

Letting his hands drop to his sides, he nodded. "Very well."

Shoving her sword back into its sheath, she breathed a heavy exhale. "So what are *you* doing here? You're too lazy to be a pirate."

Chapter 8

Night had fallen. The stars shone bright as candles at Christmas, twinkling and winking down at those who had a care to look up at them. Winds all but slowed to a halt for the evening, and as far as any watchman would have been concerned, all was well that night in the town of Penzance. Rumors of war were trickling into the town, but most of the local townsfolk were dismissing it as gossip and hearsay until official word arrived from the crown. So, they continued about their business as usual.

However, in an upper chamber of Roaming Sailor Inn, Alex sat, her hair combed and long, shining down her back. After sitting a few moments contemplatively in front of a mirror, she stood and began pacing the floor. Her parasol lay on the bed behind her alongside her gloves and an unopened package. Heaving a sigh, she glanced at the package.

Earlier, after her emotional breakdown which led to a short dinner with a somewhat put off Nicholas Dunne, she had slipped in to ask the young porter to fetch her a set of clothes from a local tailor in exchange for a handsome tip. Taking a deep breath, she opened the parcel and found she was not disappointed. Reaching inside, she pulled out a blouse, a pair of trousers, boots, and a coat. Stretching them out onto the floor, she then stood and sighed again. "Where are you, Jacq?"

Knock. Knock. Knock. "Alex?" a familiar voice called out.

Looking around, she sighed and plodded towards the door. "Who is it?" she asked in a mumble.

"It be me," Miata answered, sounding rather dignified.

Alex's eyes grew in horror upon wondering what he might be dressed as, standing in front of her door, and her mouth twisted as she frantically unbolted the lock to let him in. As she flung the door open, she was pleasantly surprised at the sight that met her eyes. Not that he was unkempt before, but she could tell by his manner and his scent that he'd dressed up a little just to come speak with her in the lauded inn. "Good evening." She smiled, forgetting the condition of her room and letting him in.

"Thank ye, Alex," he returned with a polite nod. Then, seeing the clothes, his eyebrow raised. "Alex, what be the purpose o' this?" He gesticulated towards the collection of items on the floor.

"Oh!" Alex squeaked, quite obviously a little embarrassed. "I...I..." She mouthed her words a few seconds, finding no other suitable explanation than the painful truth. "I...I am trying to think like Jacq."

Miata's brow furrowed and he glanced at the clothes again.

"I mean," Alex explained, returning to the seat in front of the mirror, "I am trying to think of what she might do to help me find her."

"It be possible she be unable to be leavin' a trail for us to follow, seein's how she's been at sea an' all," he pointed out thoughtfully.

Alex, relieved he wasn't laughing at her, sighed. "You do not suppose me mad for attempting this?"

"Nay, mate." He shrugged. "But, I be thinkin' ye be goin' about it in a rather unnecessary manner."

Alex's face contorted slightly at this.

"What I be meanin' by that, is that ye are Jacq's sister…Yer blood…Kin…Ye be not needin' this," he motioned towards the items on the floor, "to be knowin' this." He reached his fingertips out and lightly touched below her left shoulder.

Silence crept between them momentarily as she sat, dumbfounded at Miata's input. Reaching up tentatively, she touched at where his fingers had brushed against her skin.

Taking advantage of her speechlessness, Miata then added, "Besides, me mate Murtaugh be knowin' where they be headin' towards. He be havin' a scuffle with a mate aboard Cap'n Ming's vessel what calls hisself Red Handed Jesse."

"Truly? So, we are setting sail to track down pirates in the morning?" Alex asked, looking meekly at the slightly older fellow who towered almost a foot above her.

He nodded solemnly.

"I fear I shall be utterly useless," she said in lamentation, crossing her arms, "if we have to fight."

"I can be teachin' ye a wee bit o' swordplay," he offered nonchalantly.

"You?" Alex verified.

He bobbed his head up and down confidently.

"And wherever did you learn swordplay?" She stared at him, her voice hinting at great surprise at the revelation of this apparently well hidden fact.

Shrugging, he replied, "Jacq had to be practicin' with someone." He could not refrain from letting a smile full of

amusement and a little bit of self-perpetuated pride filter into his expression. He leaned back casually against the wall beside the door.

"I knew it!" Alex retorted, standing up, extending her finger in his direction, and walking towards him wagging it back and forth. "I knew it all along!"

Miata said nothing, only smiled.

Jamming her fists down onto her hips, she heaved a sigh and shrugged. "What fortune is ours, yes?" Shaking her head, she shuffled over, scooping up the items.

"I be not throwin' those away if I was ye," Miata admitted, folding his arms pensively over his chest.

"Of course not," Alex agreed, giggling. "I shall donate them to the children's home." She nodded confidently decisive at this, a grin shining onto her face.

"That be not what I be meanin'," he corrected, pushing off the wall and beginning to pace. "I be thinkin' ye should be keepin' these clothes. For one, ye may be needin' 'em in the near future, an' for another, ye may think o' somethin' if ye be seein' 'em an' thinkin' o' Jacq." Winking, he stepped to the door, took the handle, and added, "I were just wantin' to make sure ye be safe, Alex. Jacq would be wantin' it..." Opening the door, he strode outside of it and concluded, "Be goin' to sleep. Ye be needin' it for tomorrow. We be settin' sail for the Isles o' Scilly."

As he closed the door, Alex smiled.

The following morning, as Alex watched the horizons, now all of which seemed endless, she focused on the bow's sight of where the water met the sky. "I am coming, Jacq," she whispered, a small, sad smile playing onto her lips. "I shall find you." Reaching up, she began toying with the locket beneath her dress, letting her mind idle a minute as she ran her fingers over its now familiar surface. After a moment, breaking out of her dazed stare, she looked about her and noticed that Nicholas Dunne was nowhere to be seen and that Crevan and Miata were chatting congenially at the bottom of the stairs that led to the poop deck.

Turning back to look at the oncoming waters and heavens, she glanced skyward and murmured, "Mighty Creator, please keep her safe until we can find her."

"Top of the morning to you, Miss Luray!" the Irishman greeted her as he and Miata walked up to her, laughing and clapping each other on the backs.

"Oh, you may call me Alex," she said kindly, twirling about at their arrival.

"Very well." He nodded. "Miss Alex, top of the morning to you just the same! How does your day find you?"

Smiling slightly at this, Alex shrugged shyly. "I am doing well. And you?"

"Doing quite well myself, thanks," Crevan returned with a light Irish accent. Casting a glance at Miata, who was smiling and chewing on a small piece of wood, he nodded again. "I just wanted you to know that according to the drunken clod of a man I spoke with – if you could call him that, your sister was taken captive to be made a part of the crew. He seemed quite outraged about it, honestly."

"A *part* of the crew?" she repeated. "Why…Why that is preposterous! Why on Earth would someone want a girl as a part of their pirate crew so badly to seek her out and *kidnap* her? What utter nonsense! Are you sure this man…This clod as you called him…Was speaking the truth?"

Shrugging, Crevan responded, "Drunk folks are terrible

liars. In fact, they are usually quite painfully truthful and insult you with honesty. I mostly figure the rum makes them stupid so as they don't know when they should tell the truth or lie, on top of having poor manners and bad behavior."

"Oh heavens...!" Alex huffed, glancing at Miata.

"It be true, Alex," he agreed.

Her mouth turning down at the corner, Alex groaned. "I just hope we get there in time to save her."

"If she is anything like the Jacq I met a few years ago, I am certain she will give them no quarter," Crevan said in an attempt to be supportive.

"M-Met?" Alex looked puzzled. "You... You have met Jacq before?"

Shrugging nonchalantly, Crevan said, "Aye. Four years ago I was in *Port de Couler de Bateaux* helping a mate of mine. Things went south between my mate and me, and Jacq kind of got caught in the middle."

Her cheeks flushed slightly. "Oh... You are *that* Irishman?"

Suddenly looking a little uncomfortable himself, Crevan shrugged. "Aye...?"

Grinding her teeth together, she turned a fierce glare on Miata. "Miata! You knew this?"

Holding his hands up in surrender, he shook his head. "It be not matterin' to me about the history that be between them. I only be carin' that Murtaugh be willin' to be helpin' find her."

Clearing his throat, his composure fully restored, Crevan smiled down at the young woman. "Miss Alex, your sister and I, unlike my mate, parted on good terms. She is a fine lass, and I would not stand for any harm coming to her."

"So, you believe her to be well?" She breathed a sigh of relief at this.

"If she couldn't take care of herself at least a bit, I very much doubt our Cap'n Ming would have gone through the trouble of chasing her down...Twice..."

"Tish tosh, m'lady!" Nicholas spoke up, slinking in to stand beside her. "Don't let this man fool you into believing your sister is not in grave danger. Although I'm sure she is still quite all right, I very much doubt that she is in league with the blackguards who kidnapped her."

"Aye," the Irishman replied, sauntering closer to Nicholas, "she may well be in great danger. One would think, however, that you, of all people, would understand the ways of said gentlemen of fortune, aye?"

Alex stared up at them, startled by Crevan's comment and watching Nicholas' nostrils flare at this innuendo. "I would not be so presumptuous if I was you," he warned him. "Rumors and hearsay can really muddy up a gentleman's reputation."

"That they can," Crevan returned, his eyes flicking so quickly in Alex's direction she wasn't sure if he really had glanced at her or not. "And reputations can be so complicated to get clean once they're dirtied up." His eyes flashed like embers united with fresh oxygen.

A strange quiet filled the air, stifling the conversation for a few brief moments. before Crevan, who didn't seem remotely perplexed or disoriented by the conversation, bowed his head slightly and tapped the top of his brow with his fingertips as a parting gesture. "It was nice to officially meet you, Miss Alex. I hope we can speak again sometime soon." Then, as he turned to leave, Miata at his side, he gave Nicholas Dunne a wink that seemed to make every inch of the blond man's body stand on end and growl.

As Murtaugh and Miata casually strolled across the ship's

deck, Alex inquired, "Of what does Crevan speak?"

"He speaks of nothing pertaining to you or me, m'lady," Nicholas told her, watching them out of the corner of his eye. "It is just the empty prattle of a coward and a thief." He was quiet so briefly that Alex didn't even have time to open her mouth to ask the questions percolating in her mind. "Tell me," he requested as he turned back to her, "did you sleep well last night? Their beds are quite comfortable...said to be the finest guest beds in town."

"It was lovely to sleep on," Alex said with a sweet smile. "But I-"

"Ahoy! Dunne!" Captain Adams yelled from near the helm.

"Oh! Pardon me, m'lady," Nicholas said in apology, unhappy at being called away. "I shall return when I can." Bending at the waist, he then scurried across the ship to speak with captain.

"...could not fully enjoy it," she finished. As he went, Alex's eyes turned to find Miata and Murtaugh pointing and nodding as they looked towards the horizon. Glancing once more at Nicholas' retreating back, she wasted no time in hurrying over to the company of the two young men. "Miata!" she called to him in a loud whisper.

"Alex!" He grinned, his attentions turning to her agreeably. "Ye be lookin'..." he paused, the smile fading slightly from his face as he observed her ruffled demeanor, "...a might displeased."

"What is your problem," she glanced between them, "the both of you!, with gentlemen?" Pushing out her lower lip, her eyes narrowed, and she shoved her fists down onto her hips.

"Our problem," Crevan reiterated, "with gentlemen?"

She nodded.

"I really am not sure what you're talking about, Miss Alex. To which gentlemen are you referring?" He leaned quite coolly against the rail, tilting his head with great interest as to her meaning. His calm blue eyes observed her rather analytically, searching for an answer before she spoke.

Then, tossing her braided hair, she scowled. "You should know perfectly well what I mean! Nicholas Dunne has been nothing but kind to me, and I would greatly appreciate it if-"

"Wait..." Crevan laughed, peeling off the railing to keep himself from spilling onto the deck in a strange combination between laughter and shock. "Nicholas Dunne is this gentleman we have a problem with?"

Her head tilted back indignantly at his amusement with her inquisition.

"Pardon the laugh, Miss Alex," he said, continuing to chuckle, "but, *gentleman?*" He spat the word *gentleman* like a seed. "He is positively the worst gentleman you will ever meet."

"Wha-? How could you say something like that?" Alex gasped. "As if you would know!"

"Miss Alex," Murtaugh added easily, returning to leaning against the rail, "you don't know much about me."

Blinking, she looked down at her hands, straightening her violet dress. "No."

"No. Now, because you don't know much about me, you wouldn't likely know that I actually have very accurate knowledge of our Nicholas Dunne's history."

She lifted her eyes to meet his gaze. "Truly?"

"Aye, lassy. That pretty lad of yours isn't as innocent as he seems."

Alex suddenly felt more insecure than she could ever remember…Even more insecure, perhaps, than when she was left with Mrs. Bumbleridge at the Midway Zebra by Madam Thorpe all those years ago. This Nicholas Dunne…All the compliments he had given her, all the attention he had shown her…Could it all be a guise to hide something else? Laughing awkwardly, she inquired, "So, what, precisely, are you saying?"

"Not that he isn't interested in you," Crevan commented as though he could read her mind.

"But as I be sayin', Alex," Miata sidled up next to her, "ye be needin' to be findin' out if he be havin' any other intentions or interests…Other than bein' a gentleman, o' course." He smiled lightly at this, but she glared at him, a glare that was actually a mixture of amusement and defensive reactions. *Come on, Alex…We be on the same side…*Taking her hand gently in his, he looked deep into her eyes, wanting to think of a way he could tell her the suspicions Crevan had of Nicholas Dunne. However, as he stood there, he found he could think of no kind way to state it. And as she stared at him with those big, hazel eyes, he admitted to himself how lovely she was – a perfect duplicate of Jacq. Before he knew it, as she remained motionless, staring back, he felt his heart rate increase. Reaching up, he toyed with a thin tress of golden hair that was hanging alongside her face. Despite their differences, she really wasn't so bad.

Simultaneously, Alex's heart began fluttering. *Why*, she thought self-consciously, *his eyes are so blue…*Her breath was short, and she found she could not speak. When he wound his finger in her stray hair, she could not help but lean into his hand, and as his palm touched her cheek, her eyes flitted closed. In that split instant, the world seem to swirl and rush past them both, but the two were snapped back into reality when Murtaugh cleared his throat.

Bouncing apart from each other, they exchanged sheepish glances. Then, in a moment of bravery, Miata extended his hand out towards her. Her mouth twitching at the corner, she accepted his invitation, allowing him to put his arm around her and rest his chin on the top of her head. His eyes becoming overcast, he whispered, "We be findin' our Jacq, Alex…I be promisin' it…" Then, backing up and lifting her chin so he could look her in the eye, a smirk stretched his mouth. "When be ye wantin' to be practicin' that swordplay?"

"So, you're trying to tell me that you *were* a pirate, but you're not anymore?" Jacq asked, laughing. "And you don't take part in any form of piracy of any sort?" Picking up a mug, she took a drink of the water that Innkeeper Julian had, in great perplexity, given her. She sat with Audric at a table in the corner of the sordid inn's dining hall – essentially a tavern, where they had agreeably consumed a large portion of the afternoon.

Nodding, he retorted, "Is that really so hard to believe?"

She put down the mug and smirked, but didn't answer.

"Jacq! I'm offended! Here we are not having seen each other for just about three *whole* years and you don't believe what I'm saying?"

"Four years, Audric. And why should I believe you? Four years ago it didn't do me any favors. Why should it now?" She tipped the chair back, observing and assessing him.

"That was three years ago!" he retorted, his voice elevating

slightly and his hands slamming down on the table top at her persistent distrust.

"Four, Audric, and aye! Since then you've been a pirate, which you say you're not anymore, but how can you think that all these things wouldn't have any effect on how I view you?" Her question was laced with sarcasm and frosted with disbelief. "There's a funny thing you know," she continued, running her fingertip around the lip of the cup in front of her, "about history. History can be proven. The future, however, hasn't happened yet. There is not even a guarantee it will." At this, she swirled her beverage and glanced about the room.

"And what about my Irish friend, hmmm? I seem to recall the two of you getting on well enough when we all went our separate ways." He glared at her.

Jacq's lip curled a little at his remark. "Michael Murtaugh was a man of integrity. He parted ways with us to work on his trade!"

Leaning forward onto his elbows, Audric smiled enticingly. "Well, forget him. Why not take a little step of faith? Try a future with me, Jacq? We'll face tomorrow side by side. What say you to that?"

Smirking, she wagged her head back and forth, scoffing at his insistence. "Nay, Audric. Something you never learned was that a girl needs to be able to feel she can trust a man, hopefully in part by his reputation, before she can trust him with her heart."

"Then what does love have to do with it?" he asked, snorting and leaning back into the chair, folding his arms. "All you're doing is looking at my past to determine how you feel."

"Love?" Jacq laughed. Moving her eyes from his to the mug, she sighed. "Love is an important emotion, but I've

discovered that what's really important in a relationship is trust. And, when one has proven their untrustworthiness, it takes a very, very long time to prove otherwise."

"Audric, da'ling!" a feminine voice trickled into their conversation as a woman in a wide skirted orange and blue dress approached. She had a tall, full blue feather protruding from the top of her head where there was a massive pile of dark hair. Running her hands along his shoulder blades, she queried, "Audric, da'ling, what is it for you today? A bottle of rum? Or a jug of ale?"

"Brigitte!" Audric greeted, chuckling rather uncomfortably as he watched Jacq's eyebrow arch. "Why," he switched his gaze to the woman rather than Jacq, "you should know by now that I don't drink…I gave it up, remember? Except once a week I'll have a bit of rum with Nathaniel O'Grady!" He gave her his award winning smile as his insides begged, *Wench! You're going to ruin my new reputation!*

"Oh…? Oh…! Aye!" she agreed, nodding in confirmation, winking at Jacq. "He does drink a might less than he used to!" Elbowing him jokingly in the shoulder, she sighed. "So, would you care for anything from me today? Anything…at all…?"

"Nay, Brigitte," he assured her, forcing his smile. "I'm fine, but I'll be sure to let *you* know if I need anything."

As Audric sent Brigitte on her way, Jacq watched a group of men come trudging into the inn. Her nose twitched involuntarily at the pungently putrid fragrance they brought with them. She noticed Jean-Paul, his footfall and limp recognizable almost anywhere, walking in with a small band of fellow outlaws from the *Wind Hawke*. Her thoughts then drifted to the night before, and she wondered how Red Handed Jesse faired on the beach. At this, she couldn't refrain from snickering. As she was giggling to herself, she saw Jean-Pierre saunter grinningly into the establishment, and she rocked back a little harder on the legs of the chair to lift her hand in a friendly gesture. However, when she did so, she distinctly heard a *crack*, and her eyes widened, shooting a worried look to Audric for help. Unfortunately, her mouth didn't open fast enough, and she crashed to the ground in a heap of splinters and wood.

Seeing her wave out of the corner of his eye, Jean-Pierre stood on tiptoe to try and get a glimpse of her over the table. "Jacqo! Jacqo, is that you?" Tromping over, not even noticing Audric, he found her laughing on the floor amidst the debris of the chair. Shaking his head, he took her hand, now outstretched, and yanked her promptly to her feet with such force that she fell forward, almost spilling onto the table, had he not been in the line of projection.

Giggling partially from embarrassment and partly from good humor, Jacq patted him on the shoulder. "The chairs here are just as bad as the patrons."

Peeling the laughing girl off of his chest, he smiled down at her, watching her smiling and her eyes twinkling with humor. Her expressiveness slowed, however, when she realized he was staring at her. "Keep laughing, Jacqo," he requested, continuing to hold her in his arms. "You're even lovelier when you laugh."

Stopping uneasily, she suddenly realized that knowing what she had learned about him from Esperanza made him much less attractive. "Thank you, Jean-Pierre." Pushing herself away from him, she gave him a small smile. "Did you have fun with your mate last night?" As she asked, she began backing up from his body, the repulsion she felt about it shining obvious in her eyes.

Taking her chin in his hand, he smiled, and though his eyes were bloodshot and clouded over, they displayed an honest care that Jacq found she craved. "You, Jacqueline Taylor Luray, have many layers. You're as I imagine his majesty's treasure room…All kinds o' fancy gems and baubles in the front, but the most valuable and precious jewels and trinkets are stowed away in the back where nobody but him that has the key can get them."

Jacq blinked, suddenly feeling very self-conscious. "J-Jean-Pierre…I…"

"Jacq, if I were any manner o' man at all," he continued in a lowered voice, "I'd be asking for that key, but I'm not any sort o' proper gentleman…I'm a pirate, and there are things I fancy to just pick up off a table without much thought or care. But there is something special about you, Jacq. And, for what it's worth, it makes it so that key," he nodded down in the direction of her heart, "is not one of those things." Then, taking a cautious step forward, he kissed her forehead, and put his hand on her cheek. "And I never thought I'd fancy calling a lass my shipmate, but you're something else." Giving her one last smile, he turned to walk away.

However, he stopped short after he'd only gone a few steps and returned to the table. "Oi! Iron Audric Schellden!"

Audric glanced at Jacq innocently, then smiled at Jean-Pierre, insistently wagging his head back and forth.

"Aye! You've a…Uh…A specialty for using your flintlocks."

Glancing between Jean-Pierre's grinning recognition and Jacq's unimpressed forehead grooves, Audric laughed. "Wha-? That doesn't sound like me!"

"What do you mean that doesn't sound like you?" Jean-Pierre laughed at the outlandish reply, slapping him on the back. "There's nothin' to be ashamed of! Jacq here's a beautiful shot herself, ain't ya, Jacqo?"

Audric stared up at her, his eyes displaying more shock than any words he could have summoned to his mouth, which was uselessly gaping open anyway.

"'Tis what some say," Jacq said mischievously. "And it would seem," she sighed, glancing at Brigitte, "that although I've changed over the last *four* years, sadly, you have not." Moving around the table, she smiled at Jean-Pierre. "I'll see you later, mate."

Jean-Pierre turned back to Audric in surprise. "You know her?"

"Umm... Well, I-" Audric stammered, watching her weave her way to the door.

Moving through the gawking faces spewing laughter, she observed them but realized she neither knew nor cared to know what they were laughing about. Pushing her way out the front double doors of the inn, she glanced up and down the street, noticing people were still lying around and only now waking up, coming to life as the afternoon began waning into evening.

"Jacq! Jacq!" she heard Audric calling as he shoved his own way to the door, nearly falling out of it onto the ground in front her.

She eyed him a moment, as if waiting for an explanation, then twisted away and began to march off.

"Jacq! Please! Let me explain! It's not what it looks like in there!"

"Oh it's not, is it?" she retorted, swinging back around to face him. "There is nothing for you to explain, Audric. Or is it Iron Audric? Unlike you, Jean-Pierre isn't a liar – at least not

when it comes to telling me things."

"I didn't lie to you!" he shouted at her. "I…I was confused! I didn't realize all that you had to offer." Advancing towards her so they would not yell across the distance between them, he added, "I never got over you, Jacq."

"Could've fooled me," she returned with a snarl. "And the biggest reason you didn't realize what I had to offer was because you were wanting things a Miss Trent had to offer that I would not. Why should I reward you now for your stupidity then?" Turning away from him, she screamed inwardly. *Why? Why do I have to be here with him of all people? Why not Murtaugh on this forsaken island with these heartless mongrels? Ugh…I can't believe I still find him handsome! Curse that smile of his!*

Gritting his teeth, Audric took a few deliberate steps forward, grabbing Jacq by the shoulder. Whirling her around, he pinned her against the wall of the inn. "Jacq," he whispered through clenched teeth, "you are being stubborn. We can work things out. I know you don't think I've changed, but I have!" Looking deep into her eyes, he searched for some small glimmer of hope, even the tiniest hint…"Come on, Jacq… Give us a chance."

As she stood there motionless, aside from the blinking of her eyes and the rising and falling of her chest, she tried to think of something to say.

However, as Audric stared down at her, seemingly trapped beneath him, he was suddenly overwhelmed with the urge to kiss her and, without thinking, pressed his lips to hers.

"Ye be not too bad, Alex," Miata said, flopping down onto her hammock and wiping the sweat from his brow. "I be thinkin'

ye be havin' no know-how."

"I was afraid I had forgotten. After all, my fencing lessons were dreadfully long ago," she commented, leaning against the wall and glancing down at the trousers and blouse ensemble she'd had previously laid out on the floor of her room. "This was good, though. I did need refreshing." Casting a glance at Crevan, she questioned, "How are you with a sword, Mr. Murtaugh?"

Shrugging, he bit into the apple he was holding and grinned. "I've picked up a few tricks here and there, but it's not something I've ever made a practice of being good at. Is Jacq still handy with a blade?" He assumed chewing the bite of fruit as he awaited her response.

"I am not positive how good she really is compared to pirates, but she is not bad, that is certain." Brushing at the loose hair that fell forward, decorating her face, she heaved a deep sigh. "What do you say, Miata? How is Jacq's swordsmanship?"

"I be agreein' with ye, Alex. She be good, but I be not knowin' how good she be bein' when comparin' to a pack o' pirates." He paused a moment, continuing to catch his breath, then continued, chuckling, "I be rememberin' the first time, Jacq an' me be practicin' our sword fightin' on the roof o' the, at that time, vacated barn beside the inn. What a time that were! It were a once a week occurrence I be supposin'."

"You two practiced your swordsmanship," Alex gasped, "on rooftops? In the middle of the night?!" Her eyes grew, an astonished expression conquering her face as she gawked, glancing between Miata and Crevan.

Nervously glancing at Murtaugh, Miata laughed halfheartedly. "Maybe that be one o' the things Jacq be tellin' me to ne'er tell ye?" He gave her his best smile, blatantly feeling utterly horrible about spilling this news to her apparently unaware ears. At first he was certain she was furious. However, as she stood staring, saying nothing, Miata began to wonder what it was she was actually thinking. "Be ye…angry," he stopped briefly, trying to be delicate, "Alex?"

"Angry?" Alex repeated in a low, somewhat husky tone. "Why would I be angry? If you found out five years after the fact that your sister and her friend were up playing cutlasses on rooftops without you, would *you* be angry?"

Blinking, Miata shrugged, glancing to Murtaugh for help.

"So," Crevan broke in, smiling dazzlingly in Alex's direction, "Miss Alex, what does this Captain Ming want your sister for anyway? He's most notably called a scourge of the seven seas by those who don't know much about him, and far worse by those who do. They say, if he continues as he is, he will be one of the most well-known and greatly feared pirates to sail in our time."

"I do not know," Alex said with a sigh, allowing the conversation between her and Miata to drop quietly off into nothing. "It does not make any sense to me at all. As it is, the only way he could possibly know of her is by hearsay, which, to me, would not be enough to go chasing a poor girl all over the countryside."

"Perhaps it was whatever the hearsayer said…?" Crevan responded, taking another bite of his apple and munching it contentedly.

"I do not know." Alex sighed. "It is all rubbish to me." At this, she slid down the wall, sinking to a seated position on the floor.

"I be sure we be findin' out these answers soon enough," Miata said, sticking the tip of his sword into the floorboards. "Soon enough…"

Chapter 9

An awkward hush rose up like mist from the sandy terrain between Audric Schellden and Jacqueline Taylor Luray as they stood apart. His face contorted repeatedly from a combination of embarrassment and disappointment. "I-I'm sorry, Jacq..." He moved away from having her trapped between his body and the inn's wall. "I...I couldn't bear the thought of never seeing you again after you leave this island. I know your crew, which I can't believe you're with, plans to leave on the morrow. I just wanted a kiss...for old times' sake..."

"Well," Jacq retorted, popping off the wall with her elbows and shoulders, "you've had your kiss. May you rest in peace."

"Jacq, it's not like that...I'm not like that..." he returned, straightening to his full height and crossing his arms. "Be honest with yourself, Jacq. What do you think of me?"

A smirk twisted her lips. "You? You're a pirate, Audric. You always have been. But, before you joined a crew and got yourself a nickname and such flimflam, you stole hearts instead of gold and jewels." Strands of hair shook loose from under her bandana and fell into her face, which she cast aside with a twitch of her head. "It *is* like you, and you *are* like that.

I *did* love you once, and you knew it. The reason I fell for you to begin with was probably because you smell of adventure, but now I know it was folly from the beginning. Michael was right about you." At this, she leaned menacingly into his face. "You broke my heart, something that should have been more precious to you than any rocks or coins you could ever find. Yet, here you are in all these fancy clothes and pretty hardware." She gestured to his attire. "Nay, Audric. You are the reason you're not getting a second chance with me. You fooled me once, but you shan't fool me twice." Backing away from him, she crossed her arms and stuck her chin out in determination. "In this relationship, you are the only one that will bear the shame, because I will not let *you* make a fool of *me*."

"Who is it that has earned your affections, then, huh?" he asked, scoffing. His inflection and glare suggested he'd taken offense at her argument against him.

"No one officially," she returned, twisting away from facing him.

"Officially? What in the name of stars and seas does that mean?" he asked in a demanding tone.

"It means it's none of your business, is it? You're not my father...You're certainly not my brother...You're not even a good mate. Besides, why do you even care?" Grinding her teeth together, she hated that a part of her felt a touch of flattery at his indignation.

"I care because there is a bloody someone that is preventing you from taking a chance with me!" he replied, spreading his arms in a wide welcome to her.

At that moment, a barmaid poked her head out the door and called alluringly, "Oh, Audric! I thought I heard your voice! Why not come in and visit with me! I haven't seen you in here all day!"

"Jocelyn! Oi!…I'm a might busy right now…I…Uh…" He glanced back at Jacq, panic in his eyes.

"You know…You're right, Audric." Jacq smiled, backing away from him as he stood perplexing between the barmaid and the faux pirate. "There is someone preventing us from being able to get back together…" Licking her chapped lips, she looked down at her boots, a sad smile creeping onto her face, then glanced up at the darkening sky, remembering her assurance to Bahari that she'd return before dark.

"Wha-? Who?" he asked in a fervent plea, waving Jocelyn back inside.

Pausing a moment, she shook her head, a dull ache settling in the scar on her shoulder. "You."

"But…Jacq!" Running his hand down his face, he moved to take a step forward.

However, a large body bumped into him, pushing him off his balance so that he had to catch himself on the corner of the building to keep from falling. Looking up, he saw the tall, broad figure of a man, arms folded sternly across his chest. "Shakina is done with you."

Turning her back to Audric and waiting for her new friend to join her, Jacq smirked to herself. *Bahari…*As she stood, she lifted her watch to the heavens and saw the first star of the evening wink at her. She smiled; it winked again. With Audric's statement about her having to have a special someone to not choose him echoing in her mind, she let out a ragged sigh. "I may not have a man to call my own," she said in a low mutter to herself, "but my reasons are my own, and they are adequate!"

Her jaw tightening, Jacq's mind began to whir with

internal arguing. *How can I even have a man to call my own when I don't even know if any of the ones I fancy actually share an interest in me?*

Don't be a simpleton! Who cares about that right now? I need to get off this forsaken island and away from that bloody poor excuse for a man!

Alex is likely worried sick…Now is not the time to lose focus on what my mission is, especially over Iron Audric Schellden. The last thing I need to do on this rock is go mad.

She glanced back in the direction of Audric. "Well, maybe not the *last* thing, but close enough…"

"Shakina?" Bahari's voice interrupted her. "Are you well?"

"I'll be better once we get away from this poor excuse for an inn," she replied, casting her gaze once more behind her.

Audric, standing uneasily watching after her, made a hopeful motion towards her.

"Good-bye, Audric…" she called so distantly she wasn't even sure he could hear her, a strange pit forming in her stomach. "May you find happiness somewhere…" Then, turning away from him, she and Bahari struck out for Esperanza's ramshackle cabin.

Audric kicked at the sand. "Bloody Crevan…He was right. She *was* more than I ever could have imagined." Heaving a sigh and rubbing the back of his neck, he too glanced up at the star, which was now being joined by others. "Well, Jacq, may you, every once in a while, remember we are under the same sky and think of me." A smirk tilting his mouth, he slowly made his way back to the inn doors. Then, glancing once more at her retreating figure, he shoved open the doors, calling loudly, "Jocelyn! Where's my rum! I haven't had a drop o' liquor all day!"

After they were far enough away that the noises of the inn were becoming no more than a muted racket, Jacq chuckled. "Thank you, Bahari." Scuffing her feet at the sandy path, she glanced up at the treetops. "I'm afraid he had been being quite persistent all afternoon. I almost couldn't break his heart, but I'm sure it will mend fast enough."

"You know him?" Bahari questioned, a hint of disgust ringing clearly in his deep voice.

"I thought I did once..." she said in doleful admittance.

"You love him?" he asked, his face wrinkling and scrunching up at the thought.

"I did once," she answered in a faraway voice as they traipsed across the island. "We had some mates in common. My mate, Miata, and another chap named Murtaugh. That was a very long time ago."

Watching her face as she spoke, he knowingly nodded and concluded, "And sometimes the past is the only place it belongs?" In his shrewd, wise eyes it was easily visible that he believed some things had no use or need to resurface once they had been buried with the silt and sand of time. And, somehow, he had correctly perceived such was the case with the subject at hand.

"Aye," Jacq agreed, a deep gratefulness at his kind understanding washing over her. Breathing in the evening air, she suddenly felt a strange sense of relief, as if she'd been wearing a corset and someone had cut it open, allowing her to breathe again. Alex would hate to hear her mocking corsets... *Alex...* Her short-lived amusement with herself came to an abrupt end as the two walked in silence together, Jacq engrossed in the options she had at hand. As the soft glow from Esperanza's home drew near, she took a deep breath and looked over at the silent titan beside her. "Bahari, would you ever desert Ming and the *Wind Hawke*'s crew?"

"So," Alex spoke in the quiet stillness of the evening, "where precisely are we going?" Watching with intrigue as Crevan took in the oceanic scenery, she leaned on the railing of the ship beside him. She found she was quite happy to be wearing a dress again, although, to her surprise she had secretly found the trousers and blouse to be quite comfortable.

"We are bound for the pirate haven in the Isles of Scilly," he replied, not moving a muscle. "It's not what anyone would call a town for a lady. Definitely not a place you'd want to raise a family, that much I can assure you." Glancing over his shoulder to look at Alex, he smiled when he saw her blinking, perplexed at his detailed response. Turning his head back to look out to sea, he added, "On the bright side, everyone will tell you just about anything about anyone else, and if they seem a little hard to persuade, a little color or a little rum will convince them to divulge the information that they know. Loyalty's not usually their strong suit."

"I see..." Sighing, she followed his gaze out to the horizon. "Well, it is not as if we are making plans for settling there. I just want my sister back."

"Are you paying Cap'n Adams to carry you on your journey to fetch Jacq?" he inquired, suddenly taking greater interest in their conversation, and rotating to face her. "Are you financing this voyage?"

"Actually," Alex replied, smiling rather smugly, "Mr. Dunne is helping me to finance it. He has been very kind, very hospitable, and very generous towards me. Despite what you

and Miata may think, he is quite a gentleman in my direction."

"Of course he is," Crevan agreed with a chuckle, his handsome features accentuated by the glowing lanterns in the night. "You're young. You're attractive. Presumably you have no suitors…Or have recently lost your suitor…You're not poor. What reason is there," pushing off the railing, he sidled up very close to Alex, close enough to feel her body heat, "for him to not be interested in you?"

"I-I was seeing someone," Alex confessed, feeling her heart rate increase rapidly with his nearness and her entire body blushing though he was not even touching her. "But, when my sister was kidnapped and the search began, I learned Mr. Dunne had known him. He was the absolutely, undeniably, most perfect gentleman I have ever met in all my life."

"What happened to him?" Crevan questioned, his curiosity and interest climbing.

"Mr. Dunne told me that he had…" Alex paused, still not having fully accepted or processed the information, "…died." Her eyes glossed over with a wet, gray hue. "I could not believe it when he first told me, but he has been such a perfect gentleman about so many other things that I-"

"He actually told you this chap died?" Crevan verified skeptically. "He actually spoke the words himself?"

Stopping for a moment, Alex thought back. The conversation flashed semi distortedly before her minds eye, but her voice rang clearly in her head…

"And how is he?"

Followed by Nicholas saying, *"Oh…Well, he's…"*

Her heart almost stopping its rhythmic time keeping, she heard her voice replay in her mind, *"Is he…dead?"*

Then, his voice comforting her, *"There, there, m'lady. I was*

not expecting you to come to that conclusion. Most ladies in your position never believe their men die."

How could this have happened? Was it really possibly she had made all the assumptions and he'd just chosen not to correct her? Or maybe he didn't know either way? "Oh, Mr. Murtaugh..." she gulped, catching herself on his arm and the rail. "What have I done?"

Looking a little uncertain as to what she was referring to, he returned, "I'm not really sure...Why don't *you* tell *me*?"

"I...I was the one that said James Monroe was dead! I...I thought Mr. Dunne was implying it, but he never said it." Her jaw moved up and down, but no words or sounds were emitted. "I have been behaving like a strumpet!"

"James Monroe? Miss Alex!" Crevan retorted, snapping her out of the beginning of a panic vortex. "Calm down! We must finish this conversation. Miata was going to tell you of my suspicions regarding your Mr. Dunne, but he couldn't bring himself to do it, so I will."

Helping her sit against the side of the ship, he took a seat beside her and continued. "Miss Alex," his voice lowered even more, "as I heard it, Nicholas Dunne worked aboard a ship with James Monroe. Mr. Dunne served under Mr. Monroe and was being evaluated for some questionable behavior. In fact, Mr. Monroe was positive that Mr. Dunne was associating with pirates on the side, selling information to them.

"After Mr. Monroe discovered this, he reported it to a Cap'n Turner. Cap'n Turner asked his boatswain, a bloke who used to be a pirate, to find any evidence to back up Mr. Monroe's accusations. Six months later, Mr. Rackham, the boatswain, approached Cap'n Turner in private, and Mr. Dunne was dismissed from the ship with a warning shortly thereafter."

"Upon my word!" Alex gasped. "How long ago was this? How do you *know* these things?" Her mouth was dry, and her heart began to pump even faster. Her head started to feel as if it was expanding, pressing so terribly hard on the sides of her skull, banging hard on the walls, screaming to be let out… In the darkness of the night, she stared at him, begging for answers with her silence.

"I think I heard of his falling out only about four or five weeks ago," he responded, looking up at the stars as if they kept track of such things for him. "And, I know these things because I, believe it or not, have a lot of mates in a lot of places. Plus, at the time, I was helping out a blacksmith mate of mine who did some work for some of the lads aboard Cap'n Turner's ship, the *Sea Dragon*."

"How do I know *you* are telling me the truth?" she asked, suddenly feeling skittish and distrustful.

"You could always ask Mr. Dunne yourself if you don't believe what I've said, although he will undoubtedly avoid the question by telling you that I'm a coward and not worth listening to." He smiled, turning to look out at the sky between the rails. "The truth is, Monroe came to me to find out if I knew anything about any secretive work Dunne was up to, and, to be brief, I had information for him. Dunne, with his sources, found out. He was furious." Crevan laughed, looking back at Alex. "I am certain he loathes me."

"If that is the case," Alex said, anger blossoming in her eyes and a whole new part of her personality unfolding dramatically before Crevan's eyes, "he *shall* be sorry. But, what I wish to know is, how did he know about James and I? Nothing is official between us. Even our courtship has been odd because he has been away at sea for the majority of it." She stared at him in want of answers.

"Well, he spoke of you to me, though not by name. I imagine he speaks of you to many, which, of course," he said with a smile, watching Alex's cheeks go from being a perky pink to crimson in less than seconds, "is quite a compliment, I might say. Most ways I figure, our Mr. Dunne saw you and was, at first, just naturally smitten with you. However, when he found out you were Mr. Monroe's lass...Well, I imagine he couldn't resist." With that, he took her hand and helped her to her feet.

"If what you say is so, then I should fancy to speak with him of these indiscretions immediately!" Tossing her hair over her shoulder with an entirely new comportment, her eyes sparked as the initial lighting of a match.

"Nay, nay, nay, Miss Alex!" Crevan advised, clambering in front of her to stop her. "That, I'm afraid, is a very bad idea."

The fire in her eyes glowed menacingly, asking wordlessly why this was so.

"Think of this...If he knows for certain you're no longer interested in him, and, quite frankly, a little upset, he may become angry and advise our Cap'n Adams to turn this little dinghy around without the finding of your dearly beloved sister." As he spoke, he leaned closer to her, backing her against the rail.

At his reasoning, the crackling inferno in Alex's eyes diminished, and her anger simply slipped below her usual pleasant disposition. "Very well. I shall wait." Eyeing him from under her brow, she added, "And if you are not telling the truth, *you* will be sorry."

He chuckled a little apprehensively. "What is that supposed to mean, Miss Alex?"

She tilted her chin back, continuing to gaze at him, inches away from his face, a cool, even gaze that did not, in any way, give him cause to doubt her underlying promise.

"Miss Alex," he responded, taking her hand gently in his. "I have been around long enough to know good people when I meet them. I know what good people deserve. Jacq doesn't deserve to be stranded with a group of pirates, separated from people that she loves and that love her back enough to use everything and everyone at their disposal to find her."

Her eyebrow arched at this.

"I will find your sister," he continued, holding up a finger and stepping closer to her, again invading her personal bubble of space, "of that you can be certain." Then, giving her a teasing wink, he turned and walked away.

As she stared after him, a small chuckle rocked her small frame and a smirk curved her mouth. *Why, Mr. Murtaugh... You sound as if you-*

"Miss Luray?" Nicholas Dunne's voice startled her as he began clunking up the stairs that led to where she stood by the stern of the ship. "Miss Luray, are you quite all right? Crevan wasn't troubling you, was he?"

"Troubling me?" she repeated, turning to face him with her usual sweet smile.

His handsome face was creased with concern visible even in the dim light.

Are you perhaps concerned about what he may have told me? she pondered internally. "Whatever could you mean by that?" she asked inquisitively, Crevan's comments whispering in her mind. Smiling placidly, she waited patiently for his response.

"I simply mean that fellows such as he will often try

to entreat a proper lady with tales of grand adventures and derring-do."

Her eyebrow arced.

"I'm not accusing him, of course, but I just want you," he scooped her hand into his, giving it a gentle kiss, "to be careful, m'lady."

"I try to be, Mr. Dunne," she noted, watching him straighten from the small gesture of concern and affection. "Jacq finds my level of cautiousness to be quite tedious and, as she once stated, 'a very efficient way to lead a dull and dreary life.' Tell me, Mr. Dunne, do you think me to be so tiresomely wary?"

Laughing uneasily, he shrugged. "I don't find anything about you tiresome or dull, Miss Luray. In fact, I find you more and more fascinating every day." Walking to the railing, he sighed. "I only wish I had more to offer to a lady such as yourself...I would give you everything about me for a sliver of your heart." About facing, he saw Alex practically choking on his admission. "Oh! I've upset you...I'm so terribly sorry. I will go now. I apologize for offending you, m'lady. I didn't mean t-"

"Mr. Dunne..." Alex said, breathing raggedly as she moved to the spot at the rail of the ship he'd just vacated. Her eyes glazed over with the increasingly tumultuous mountain of emotions that were gnawing at her nervous system. "I cannot afford to ponder my potential love interests until my sister is safe. It would be a great help to me if you did not bring it up again until after she has returned." As she stared up at the stars, Alex thought she saw one of them wink at her. *Jacq...* Blinking a little, she found this amused her. Two more winked, and she felt suddenly relaxed, though she had not realized until then that she had been tense. "I hope you can understand this and are not irreparably offended by my request."

"Of course, Miss Luray!" he agreed, his search for a glimmer of hope coming up positive. "I will keep my thoughts on this matter to myself until you are ready to talk of such things again." Beginning to trudge down the stairs, she heard him abruptly stop and clear his throat. "Good night, m'lady."

"Good night, Mr. Dunne."

The pale morning light stretched out its fingers, rolling up the blanket of stars it slept beneath at night. An unfriendly silence swelled and eddied on board the *Wind Hawke* that morning as she floated out to sea, leaving the pirate haven in her wake. Bland, insipid clouds, similar to the new cook's food, swirled in the sky, shying away from the reddish sun as it peeked over the horizon, sloshing its buckets of rays all across the landscape as it moved.

Seeing the ruddy toned beacon of daylight rise gallantly to the sky, a roguish smirk formed Jacq's lips. "Red sky at morning…" Glancing over towards the Captain's quarters in the aftcastle, she saw Bahari standing beside the door looking austere as he watched the ever mounting celestial ball of fire.

Inside the room, the adamantly superstitious Captain Ming was pacing and staring out at the dawn of the new day. Opening his door, he saw the girl standing off by the rail and yelled, "Oi! Jacq! My quarters! Now!"

Sighing, Jacq turned to make her way to the captain's cabin. However, when she spun about, she saw Jean-Pierre either admiring or mocking Red Handed Jesse – she couldn't tell which. Then, noticing Jean-Pierre was gesturing at his cheek, a mischievously plucky grin turned the corners of her mouth. Sashaying up beside the saucy Frenchman, she nodded towards Jesse's face and inquired, "Mr. Smith, how did you come by that cut on your cheek?"

"Cut, says I?" he asked, glaring at her crossly. "It be a mere scratch, says I!"

"It's practically an incision!" Jean-Pierre retorted in laughter. Then he turned to Jacq. "He doesn't know how he got it – he gets drunk and loses consciousness. He can never remember what happened – at least so he says…" Slapping him heartily on the back, he earned himself a glare from the shorter pirate as his mirth about the whole thing came pouring out in the form of roaring laughter.

"Hm…" Jacq returned, her expression remaining constant. "Pity." Watching him out of the corner of her eye as she sauntered past them, she discreetly reached up and touched her chest an inch or two below her throat, tracing the elevated outline of a circle beneath her jerkin with her fingertips.

Early that morning, before she and Bahari struck out for the ship, the benevolent Esperanza handed her a medallion about a quarter the size of her palm on a leather strap that kept it close to her throat. "This medallion," she had told her, "is the symbol for *los santos* – the saints – in *España*. Carry it with you always to bring good fortune to you and those you care about, and maybe you could remember me too."

Smiling, Jacq pulled in a big breath of air and continued her casual stroll to where Captain Ming was hovering by his door.

However, by the time Jacq had reached Bahari's side, Ming had closed himself into his room. Biting her lower lip

to try and reduce her wide smirk, Jacq inquired of Bahari, "Is there a problem with his captainship?"

Turning a rather bewildered look towards Jacq, Bahari said in an agitated tone, "I did not understand a word he spoke. It was in a foreign tongue."

Gesturing towards the sun, Jacq chuckled. "There's a saying…Red sky at night, sailor's delight. Red sky in morning, sailor's warning."

"Truly?" Bahari laughed, his brows arching as he glanced at the closed door of the captain's cabin. "That is very interesting in a language I understand."

"Isn't it though." Jacq snickered. "Does he still wish to speak with me?"

"I believe so," he said with a sigh, knocking on the door to his cabin.

Ming peeked out.

"Shakina is here," Bahari reported tersely.

"Very good," he said, nodding and walking to his table. "Send her in."

Brushing past Bahari, she stood, feet shoulder width apart, head tilted a little back and to the left, hands clasped behind her, awaiting the pirate captain's conversation.

"Come in and guard the door," he commanded Bahari. Then, turning to Jacq, he smiled. "Yer turnin' out to be a fine addition to the crew." As he paid his compliment, he looked over her new garb while pacing around her. "A finer looking pirate I never found. Soon enough ya will get yer locket back." He paused, eyeing the katanas hanging off of her. "Ya fancy the swords I gave ye?"

An internally mocking smile plastering itself on her face, Jacq nodded. "They are the best swords I have ever held in

my hands. I thank you for giving them to me, though I am still uncertain as to why you did so. I intend to use them," her gaze fell upon her locket, dangling about his neck, "as wisely as possible."

At this, Ming's lip twitched slightly and he paused his pacing. "I were busy listenin' in at The Haven and heard a bunch o' fools talkin' about bounty they were wishin' they could be havin'. So, we're gonna be claimin' those prizes ourselves. We be lookin' to intercept an' relieve a Spanish Galleon by name o' *Santa Jacinthe* and a merchantman by name o' *Madeline's Mark* afore the month is over. Keep up this kind o' behavior, ya might earn yerself a promotion afore long." Then, stepping aside, he gestured for her to leave.

"Aye, aye, Captain," she returned, authentically in shock. Nodding in his general direction, she then strode out onto the deck.

However, as soon as Bahari shut the door behind her, she shook her head and scoffed. *Promotion? What tomfool rubbish is that?* Her mind paused its laughing for a moment as her new earrings swayed and tapped against her jaw, and a very sobering thought began to formulate, trickling upwards from the pit of her stomach. *Am I really that good of a pirate?*

Nay! It cannot be! Shaking her head, she reminded herself of Esperanza's words. *He only has me aboard ship because I am apparently the most able bodied of my father's children...Stop toturing yourself!* Rolling her eyes, she ascended to the stern of the ship, behind the helmsman, and leaned on the rail to continue watching the gorgeous sunrise that promised foul weather on the horizon. Despite how everyone else felt aboard ship, she couldn't help but smile.

As she turned and tromped up the stairs to the poop deck,

Ming twisted around to Bahari and questioned, "What did she think of The Haven?"

"I think she was ready to get back to the sea," Bahari replied truthfully in his syllable enunciated, rumbling voice. He nodded in affirmation about his thoughts.

"Very good!" Ming chortled, bobbing his head up and down in approval. "I did not see much of either of ya while at The Haven. What were ye about?"

"I was keeping an eye on her, Captain. I wanted to be sure she would remember to return to the ship." He crossed his arms assertively, keeping his cold stare even and unemotional.

"Very good," Ming agreed, nodding and beginning to pace the floor again, his black hair shimmering with his movement. "Continue to watch her. Her ways are strange to me. An' if anything starts to go wrong, let me know straight away."

"Aye, aye, Captain," Bahari agreed, opening the door. A discreet, smug smile played onto his face. "Aye, aye." Taking an aloof stance at the base of the stairs opposite of where Jacq was staring out across the waters, he folded his arms over his chest, and proceeded to observe the crewmen scurrying about the decks.

Noticing him take up this position, Jacq smiled to herself. "The predictability of superstition is phenomenal," she said, casually continuing to watch the sky as the glowing orb rose higher and higher, spreading its warmth in rays of light. Reaching up and touching at the bandana that was still tied about her head, Jacq sighed. "Where are you, Alex? What are you about, anyway?" A small, almost sad smile creased her face. "And how, dear sister, are you faring with Miata?" This thought made her chuckle a little, just imagining the two of them trying to work together.

"Jacqo!" Jean-Pierre interrupted her musings. "What are ya doing, lass?"

Pivoting to look at him, she was slightly surprised to see him a little distraught. "Nothing, I suppose. What's troubling you?"

"Our minstrel, we just found out, doesn't speak our language. At all." He sighed. "He speaks French."

"Jean-Pierre," she giggled, shaking her head. "You're French! What do you mean you-"

He eyed her.

"Oh…Aye, I recall your story. Well, what do you want me to do about it? I can't speak French any better."

"Sing with him?" He grinned sheepishly, begging and pleading with his eyes.

"What! No! You cannot make me do *that*!" She gasped, backing away from him and clutching the rail.

"Ming asked…" His expression admitted regret. "I'll even try and sing along with ya if you want," he offered desperately.

She couldn't have looked any less interested if she tried.

"Come on, Jacqo," he asked. "The lads sing along, but they're uneasy with the mornin' sky and all…"

Rolling her eyes, she stared at him.

"Please…?"

Heaving a belabored exhalation of breath, Jacq shook her head and asked, "What kind of music is he playing?"

"Mostly he plays sad tunes on the fiddle," Jean-Pierre answered in a disappointed tone. "Seems that's about all he knows, or he's hoping to drive us all mad." At this, he smiled cheerlessly. "Right now, either one is possible."

Pondering this a moment, she again shook her head and shrugged. "Where is this musician?"

Clasping his hands together in elation, Jean-Pierre gave her the biggest smile she had ever seen. "Jacqo, I'll make this up to you."

A few seconds after he scampered off, he brought her the now very annoyed looking man with the fiddle who was yelling, "*Vous êtes tous idiots ignorants!*" Then, turning to see Jacq, he smiled and greeted, "*Bonjour, mademoiselle!*"

"Well, now he actually says something I understand," Jean-Pierre commented with a frown. "Give us something fresh, Jacqo."

Laughing at the buccaneer, Jacq looked the minstrel over and smiled politely. Motioning to his fiddle, she began to tap her foot, humming a tune for him to play. Listening to it a moment, he was quickly able to slide the bow across the strings in a singsong fashion that matched her rhythm and pitch. Nodding, she applauded, "Very good, *monsieur*. Now," holding up her fingers, she counted, "play this in sets of four."

Pausing his playing to focus on her request, he then bobbed his head up and down saying, "*Oui, oui! Bien sûr je peux faire ceci, mademoiselle!*" Holding his head high, his mop of hair all falling back with this gesture, he began to play the new tune.

Exhaling begrudgingly and glaring slightly at Jean-Pierre, who smiled sheepishly, she cleared her throat, and on the right note, began rhythmically and loudly, "*Pirates and rogues, corsairs and buccaneers!*"

All the shipmates tuned their ears to her.

"*Yo! ho ho Hey! ooh-ooh-ooh*," she continued, a little less loud, and a little more singsongy, continuing in the same rhythm.

This part, Jean-Pierre sang back at her, gesturing for the

others to sing along as well for the line.

She paused for a moment, trying to think of her next line. "*A tale to tell have I! Incline your ears!*"

All those who hadn't yet been paying attention, obeyed her, and even Ming came out of hiding to hear what she had to say.

"*Yo! ho ho Heave! ooh-ooh-ooh.*"

This time, Jean-Pierre and the rest of the crew echoed the line.

A smirk couldn't help but form on her face. Using the deck as a stage, gesticulating with her arms and inflecting with her voice, she improvised and sang the rest of the ditty with the crewmen echoing her on the pull lines in the chorus.

"A ship sets sail across the ocean blue
With a scourge of a captain and his cutthroat crew
Yo! ho ho Hey! ooh-ooh-ooh
But as anchor's weighed and the course is set
A red sun rises, and the crew begins to sweat.
Yo! ho ho Heave! ooh-ooh-ooh

Pirates all! Drink your rum and cross your blade
Yo! ho ho Hey! ooh-ooh-ooh
Every debt has a time it must be paid
Yo! ho ho Heave! ooh-ooh-ooh

Darker become tales as more tales are told
Tales of lusting for treasure and loving gold
Yo! ho ho Hey! ooh-ooh-ooh
But when greed and miscreants sail the sea
There is nothing less to expect than treachery
Yo! ho ho Heave! ooh-ooh-ooh

Seems like the world is short of things unknown
Yo! ho ho Hey! ooh-ooh-ooh
There are secrets that sleep with Davy Jones
Yo! ho ho Heave! ooh-ooh-ooh

These pirates drown their sins in rum and ale
They fear Davy Jones less than death in jail
Yo! ho ho Hey! ooh-ooh-ooh
But when time is up and the devil's done
They'll ne'er escape, no matter how long they chase the sun.
Yo! ho ho Heave! ooh-ooh-ooh
No matter how long they chase the sun."

Bowing gallantly, Jacq smiled at the crew, many of who stood in awe at her ability to rhyme on the spot, for none of them had ever heard the recitation of this sea song before. Smiling at the fiddler, she bowed her head slightly in his direction and concluded, "Thank you."

"*Pas c'était de problème à tout!*" he said, seeming very pleased. He extended his hand formally, and watched in slight confusion as she grinned a little uneasily and gave it a good, firm shake. After she released his hand, he turned to look at Jean-Pierre, who clapped him on the back, grinning largely at the duo's success. "*Obtenir vos mains de moi, vous sale bête!*" he yelled at the pirate, slapping his hand off in annoyance. Then, marching to the rail of the ship, the musician began to play a lighter, upbeat tune for the listening pleasure of the company.

"See, I understood that last part too," Jean-Pierre said, sighing and shaking his head.

Jacq laughed and kicked at the deck boards. "Don't ask me to do that again."

"It was a mighty interesting ballad, Jacqo," he noted as she watched the fiddler saw away on his instrument, to the delight

of the men aboard. "Did you really make it up yourself? On the spot?"

"I did," she answered, continuing to watch the fiddling Frenchman rather than face him, an amused lilt to her voice.

"Even the bloody captain came out to hear and see you perform. I think he was quite impressed." Twirling in front of her as he meandered off, he winked.

Crossing her arms, she sent him a glare before returning to watching the musician. Then, gazing off towards the horizon, she cleared her throat and smirked. "*No matter how long they chase the sun…*" She paused for a moment then, and a cunning smile formed her lips.

Meditatively twirling a quill around and around between her thumb and index finger, Alex lightly tapped her chin with the feathery end and sighed heavily. Setting the writing utensil down, she got up, paced back and forth across her room, and then returned to her seat. Holding her head up with her hand, she drummed her fingers a few moments on the tabletop in front of her, and then pushed the chair back again, standing up and frowning. "I wish this ship would not sway so much! It makes it nigh on impossible to concentrate…" Pacing back and forth again, she traced the grain of the wood that made up the walls of her room, and then returned again to her seat. Plucking the quill off of the table, she leaned forward, biting her lower lip and preparing to write when a short *knock knock* interrupted her thoughts. "Come in!" she called, dropping the utensil back to the table.

Opening the door with mild trepidation, Miata cleared his throat and peeked in. "What be ye up to, Alex? Ye be stayin'

in yer room all mornin'…Be there somethin' wrong?"

"No!" Snatching up the parchment she had been laboring over, she hid it behind her back.

"What be that?" he asked, motioning at her back.

"It is nothing…" she fibbed, smiling lightly.

"Ye be no good at lyin'," he retorted in a playful tone of voice, sliding into her room and shutting the door behind himself. "Be lettin' me see, Alex."

"No!" she said with determination, thrusting her chin out at him, though a very faint smile could be detected in the lines of her face.

"Come on, Alex…" he requested good-naturedly. "Be ye needin' to be keepin' secrets from me?"

Chewing lightly on her lower lip, she huffed out a breath of air. "Promise you will not laugh?"

He nodded.

Taking a deep breath, she pulled the paper from behind her back and handed it to him.

Taking it with care and a smirk, he glanced down at it, but his forehead furrowed immediately. Blinking several times, he tilted his head and said, "Alex, I be not understandin'."

Glaring at him, she grabbed the paper back and turned away with an injured look on her face. "It is a letter of apology to James Monroe."

"That be fine, Alex," he returned, scratching his forehead, "but all ye be havin' on there be the letter D…?"

"Shh!" she said in a whisper. "I cannot decide if I should address it *Darling James*, or *Dearest James*." She stuck out her lip.

Crossing his arms, he shifted all of his weight to his left leg and stared at her, trying desperately to keep himself

composed. "Well, I be no expert on writin' letters o' love, but I be thinkin' that if I were receivin' a letter from a lass I be carin' about, I be not carin' so much about the *Darlin' o' Dearest* part so much as the *Miata* part." He offered up a supportive smile.

"Thank you, but that is not all too helpful in helping me to decide which one to use." At this, she sat back down at the table, laying the letter-to-be out in front of her.

Leaning on the wall beside the table, Miata stared at it a moment and added with a shrug, "Well, if ye be usin' *Darlin'* all spelled out proper an' all, then it be lookin' a might fancier than *Dearest*."

She stared up at him.

His smile changed from supportive to uncomfortable, but that was his only thought on the matter he had to offer – at least that she would want to hear.

Then, after a few seconds, she nodded. "Very well. Thank you, Miata!" Picking up the quill again, she sighed. "Now, please leave me so that I may be able to finish this, and please be sure to let me know straight away if there is any sighting of a ship?"

Nodding, Miata grinned amiably. "O' course, Alex." Then, sauntering to the door of her tiny room, he stepped back into the corridor. *Darlin' or Dearest, eh? Be that what she be spendin' all mornin' worryin' about?* Snickering, he found that instead of finding it ridiculous he actually thought it a little endearing. Shaking his head, he began a slow, clunking gait up the steps. As he was about to reach the top, however, a shadow fell onto his path. "Oi, Murtaugh! Ye sh-" He stopped abruptly as he looked up, finding Captain Adams standing akimbo before him, blocking most of the top of the steps. "A-Ahoy, Cap'n!" He gulped. "What be ye about?"

"Miata, lad! I've been thinkin' ever since I saw ya, that I'd seen ya afore," he said good-naturedly at him in his loud, booming voice. "I be thinkin' it be time we be havin' a wee talk, aye?" His broad grin and large form convinced Miata that he had little more than no choice in the matter.

The younger man strained a weak smile onto his face. "O' course…"

"Ah! I knew ya were a good lad. Now, come with me!"

As the captain's engulfing shadow retreated with his figure, Miata grasped the rail, certain he was about to pass out. *He be knowin'! I be as good as bein' dead! This be terrible… terrible! There be nothin' good that can be comin' from this…* As he hoisted himself onto the main deck, he noticed out of the corner of his eye Nicholas Dunne standing nearby wearing an aloof expression. His heart rate increased. *He be turnin' me in, eh? Well, two can be playin' that game!*

"Miata, lad! Over here!" Captain Adams' booming voice called out, bolstered by the morning quiet of the ship.

"I be c-comin', Cap'n!" he returned in counterfeit cheerfulness, glowering at Nicholas Dunne who was too preoccupied to notice his expressions at all. He approached the large man, looming over the rail opposite of Nicholas Dunne and casually watching the wake being created by the bow of his boat. Miata cleared his throat. "Cap'n?"

"Come closer, lad," he said with a chuckle. "No need fer us to shout…"

Miata crept closer, praying the man would not behead him in one fell swoop, and gingerly rested his forearms on the rail.

Once Miata was leaning beside him, Captain Adams said in a lowered tone, "Now, the reason I called ya here wasn't to talk about the fact yer the lad who stole from me that evenin'

many a year ago…"

Miata paled immediately, and he knew it had been good of him to not lean over the rail, for at that moment, he may have fallen into the deep. *Be he sayin' that not be the reason o' our conversation?* Though he felt nauseous, a small amount of color returned to his skin. Shaking his head to try and clear the raging phobias that welled up inside of him, he focused on what the captain was saying.

"Now, listen here, lad," Captain Adams continued. "Mr. Dunne has been actin' a might peculiar as o' late. I be thinkin' it has somethin' to do with that bonny Miss Luray we have aboard. I be thinkin' he be distracted from his duties an' this an' that, so I be askin' a favor o' ya."

"Aye, Cap'n?" Miata asked edgily, still pondering why he was not wanting to be repaid for what was stolen years ago.

"Be keepin' that lass at a distance. I be likin' her fine, but that lad be needin' to keep his feet on the ground, an' he seems to be unable with her in such close quarters." At this, he turned and looked Miata square in the eye. His small gray eyes gave the younger man no reason to believe he might not be serious. "Yer wonderin' why I be not wantin' to be repaid what ya stole from me?" Straightening and interlacing his thick fingers in the small of his back, he returned to watching his ship cutting through the water.

"Aye," Miata admitted, trying to swallow the brick that had formed in his throat.

"I were a poor lad meself once," he noted, peering momentarily at Miata from behind the large arc of his massive shoulder. "I remember what it were like, needin' food an' other such necessities an' not havin' it. Why," at this, he chuckled loudly, "I don't even remember how much ya took, lad. An' ya be helpin' make an honest man o' me. After yer sleight o' hand, I were havin' to talk to a man who be offerin' me a job." Smirking down at the stunned seafarer before him, Captain Adams nodded. "I just be hopin' ye be treatin' said bonny lass like a proper lady." Then he nonchalantly turned and casually strolled back to stand beside the helmsman, leaving Miata entirely baffled.

Chapter 11

Morning merged eventlessly into afternoon. Gentle golden rays shone down benevolently and the clouds that were in the sky were few, far between, and friendly in appearance. The saltiness of the sea seemed to sit especially strong in the air. A dull, muggy sensation rolled itself back and forth through the atmosphere as if teasing seafarers, knowing they could do nothing to prevent its coming or going. Although many of the men aboard continued to hum and softly sing the little song Jacq had graced them with earlier, a strange silence still sat about the ship, like heavy dust in an old, abandoned house.

"Ahoy, Cap'n! A boid off da port soide!" hollered the man in the crow's nest. As his words rang throughout the ship, the crew exploded into a mass hustle. Shipmates were running this way and that, clambering to the rails to see, shouting back and forth at each other.

"Hand me a scope, Pike!" Ming commanded, holding out his bejeweled hand. Just as the device came into contact with him, he snatched it up and extended it in one slick movement with his wrist. Then, putting the end to his eye, a mocking expression blossomed onto his face. "By the powers…"

"What is it, Captain?" Jean-Pierre inquired, snaking on the railing of the poop deck in front of the short, snippy man in anticipation.

"*Damasu!* It be our next target!" He snorted gleefully, jeering at what he saw. "Change course, Pike. We take her down."

"Aye, aye, Captain!" Jean-Pierre agreed, not sounding overly thrilled, but obliging regardless. "Master Ugary!"

The well fortified helmsman turned his dark eyes to peer at the pirate.

"Bring her about!" He gestured in the direction Ming had been looking.

Sitting under the stairs below where Ming and his head crewman were standing, Jacq rose and slunk over to the portside railing. Peering out with her naked eye, she noticed this up and coming victim vessel was significantly smaller in size than they were. "That's not a merchantman or a Spanish Galleon," she commented to herself in a mutter. "Blackguard! You will not be sinking that ship…Not today…" A wry, clever smirk molded every feature of her face. Returning to her spot beneath the stairs, she began to hum and sing softly to herself,

> "*A is the anchor that holds a bold ship,*
> *B is the bowsprit that often does dip,*
> *C is the capstan on which we do wind, and*
> *D is the davits on which the jolly boat hangs.*"

Stopping suddenly, she peered between the steps that shrouded her from the remainder of the ship. Her expression, dull but smug, enveloped her demeanor. Sliding out from underneath the staircase, she wove her way through the elated assortment of seamen rushing about like rabid strays.

Turning her sight upwards, she took in the clouds swirling in the distance, and then noticed the *Wind Hawke* was fast approaching her prey. At this, she glanced at Bahari, who nodded. Then, ever so coolly, she ambled down to where her new room was in the forecastle, still singing barely above a whisper,

> "*Oh, hi derry, hey derry, ho derry down,*
> *Give sailors their grog and there's nothing goes wrong,*
> *So merry, so merry, so merry are we,*
> *No matter who's laughing at sailors at sea.*"

Wedging herself into a corner of her room, she pulled out from the pocket of her jerkin the scrap of paper that George Brandon's song was scrawled onto. She'd taken a moment while at Esperanza's to write out the last two lines, just as she had promised him. Tracing the letters with her fingers, sang in a whisper,

> "*E is the ensign, the red, white, and blue,*
> *F is the fo'c'sle, holds the ship's crew,*
> *G is the gangway on which the mate takes his stand,*
> *H is the hawser that seldom does strand.*"

As she sang the last line, a tear rolled down her cheek, and she closed her eyes, letting her mind recall all the pain she had pushed aside and run from for so long.

"Alex! Alex! Alex!" *Bam! Bam! Bam!* "Alex! Alex! A-!"

"What?" she asked in a snap, flinging the door open with such force that she almost knocked herself over. "You are liable to bring the entire crew down here making a ruckus like that…!"

Pointing towards the ceiling, Miata said between gasps, "We be…be spottin'…the ship…the ship o'…ship o' Cap'n… Cap'n Ming…"

"Oh!" She straightened in shock. "I am guessing, judging by the hue of your skin and the tone of your voice, theirs is bigger than ours?"

"Bigger?" He laughed, grabbing her wrist and proceeding to tow her up the stairs. Once they were topside, he pushed through sailors rushing madly about from stem to stern. "It be like…like David an' Goliath…a mouse an' a cat…a rabbit an' a bear!" As they reached the rail, he pointed a long, shaky finger towards the fast approaching ship.

"How can we be sure Jacq is on that ship?" Alex asked, taking in the grandiose vessel. As she spoke, the wind began to pick up, tugging at her skirts and pulling her hair loose from its fastenings and on it was the distinct scent of…rain? Looking towards the heavens, she saw the sky darkening as clouds seemed to come rushing in from every direction. The sea began to swell and become unsettled, crankily shoving the boats around in a display of its disgruntled attitude. Glancing out at the oncoming ship, Alex looked up at the clouds, gathering above it, watching them take form in mere moments.

She turned to look at Miata, who simultaneously whirled about to look at her, and they said in unison, "Jacq!"

Nodding, patting Miata on the back, and then looking at the sky once more, Alex turned and shoved her way towards the hatch to go down to her room again.

"Alex! Where be ye goin'?!" he called after her in confusion.

"To put on slightly more appropriate attire! You did leave that sword in my room, did you not?" she called back, smiling. As she whirled away, the clouds ripped, and it began to rain.

"*Curses!*" exclaimed Captain Adams, coming up behind Miata with the rain rolling off his oily hair. "What be the reason for this storm?!"

"Actually, Cap'n," Miata said nervously, "it be a sign."

"A sign o' what? Bad fortune?" he ranted, glancing at the fast approaching East Indiaman.

"Nay, Cap'n!" Miata shook his head, blinking in the increasingly heavy downpour. "It be meanin' Jacq be aboard that ship." He pointed.

"What? Did Circe herself bless the lass?" he asked in disbelief. "An' where did that bonny Miss Luray run off to?" Shaking the water pointlessly from his head, he looked about for Nicholas Dunne.

"She went to be puttin' on some more appropriate attire, Cap'n!" he reported, grinning. *For once...*

As Alex went careening around corners and rushing to her room, she felt a grip unexpectedly on her arm. Screeching to a halt, she turned to find rain soaked Nicholas Dunne, clinging to her arm, water beaded on his skin and running off his drenched hair. "What is going on, Miss Luray?" he called to her over the rising upset of the ocean waters. "What are you doing?"

"My sister is aboard that vessel, Mr. Dunne. I intend to get her back!" she returned, smiling as the rain continued to flood down on them, seeping through her hair and the fabrics of her clothes. "Help me get her back?"

Nodding, Nicholas Dunne released his hold on her, and turned to find himself square with a tall, darkly clad man.

Glancing up, he wasn't entirely surprised to find Crevan smiling at him from under his hat. "Good day, mate!" The Irishman winked.

Below, Alex hurriedly threw on the brown trousers that were just a might too big, the beige colored blouse with lacy cuffs, the long jacket she nimbly buttoned up, tall boots she could barely get to stay up, a belt she cinched tight, and a tricorne to top it all off. Pausing briefly before she exited her room, she inhaled deeply and put her hand to the hilt of…"Oh!" Scrunching up her nose and pursing her lips into a frown, Alex thrust her hands down onto her hips. "Ugh! Where is that sword?"

"Pike!" Ming called out. "Do ya think that bloody old *shōnin* cursed us?" He sneered violently at the continuously accumulating torrential clouds above them and the tempestuous deep below them.

"Who? Father Brandon? I don't know, Captain!" he shouted back, squinting through the rain pelting his face.

Straining to peer around the ship, Ming grimaced angrily at what he saw. All of the sopping buccaneers, though quite eclectic and easy to differentiate between when dry, were nearly impossible to distinguish one from another. "Where is that *shōjo*?" he asked in a furious tone.

"You mean Jacqo?" Jean-Pierre glanced around. "She was just there!"

Snarling, the captain leaned into his face and ordered, "Bring her!"

"Aye, Captain," Pike said, glaring as Ming turned his back. About facing, he nearly ran into Red Handed Jesse. "What do

you want?" he questioned, his lip curling at the closeness of his fellow pirate.

"I be willin' to be helpin' ye locate Pigeon, says I," he offered, his eyes sparking as the nickname rolled off his tongue.

"It's not that big of a ship, mate," Pike retorted, looking down in annoyance at the stocky curmudgeon. However, noticing Ming turn to glance at him out of the corner of his eye, Jean-Pierre shrugged and added, "But if you want to keep an eye out for her on deck while I search below, then feel free."

"I be keepin' a weather eye, Pike, says I," he assured him, nodding smugly.

Looking Smith up and down in disgust, Jean-Pierre brushed by him to carry out the search. *Okay, Jacqo... Where are ya?* Glancing about, his skin prickled as he could feel the incessant stare of Red Handed Jesse on his back. His mouth involuntarily contorting into a scowl, he marched off to Jacq's room in the forecastle. As he approached the slightly inset door, the waves began to pick up and rock the boat more violently, growling angrily.

"Jacq!" he yelled out to her. "Jacqo! Are you in there?" Not hearing a response, he threw his weight against the door a few times, managing to pop it open on the fourth try. As he entered, along with buckets of sloshing water, a shadow rose against the wall. Pushing the door shut behind him, he drew his sword.

Across the waters, *Anne's Triumph* was getting tossed mercilessly by the waves, and her crew was suddenly glad that Captain Adams was such a relentlessly meticulous man when it came to keeping his boat in good condition. "Miata!" Alex called out. "What is going on?"

"I be not knowin', Alex! It be seemin' our Jacq be most

upset!" he returned, snatching her arm and pulling her to the railing. Then, looking over her attire, he nodded in approval. "Ye be lookin' fine and mighty convincin', mate!"

"Yes, well," she called back over the pouring rain, "I do not feel very convincing at all! I feel as if I am the biggest fraud that has ever set foot on a boarded floor!" she said, chagrin coloring her voice.

"It be not matterin' so much, Alex," Miata assured her, pulling her right up next to him so he did not have to shout. "So long as ye be willin' to be facin' things is what be matterin' more than yer ability to be facin' things."

"I hope you are right," she said over the torrent.

"O' course I am! Yer not alone, Alex." He gave her a kind smile, despite the hostile weather.

"Where'd that bonny lass run off to, Miata?" Captain Adams yelled, coming up behind them.

Alex looked up at him from under her dripping hat.

"Wha-! By the powers!" He chuckled, clapping Miata on the back. "Miss Luray, yer a mighty handsome sailor!" Then, looking at the fast coming East Indiaman, almost upon them, he cracked and popped his knuckles. "Miata, yer gonna be helpin' ready the cannons."

"M-Me?" His eyes growing in utter astonishment. "B-but I be not knowin'-"

"Lad, ye'll be fine. Because of these infernal winds, I need another link in the chain, ya might say! We'll knock 'im dead...He'll never know what hit 'im."

"How can ye be so sure?" Miata whimpered, squinting through the rainstorm.

"Lad, I were the best gunner Cap'n Ming ever had! An' I be the one tellin' ya when to fire, now get those cannons loaded!" He nodded, patting Miata's back one last time before lumbering off to go bark out more instructions to other crewmen.

Miata and Alex exchanged glances. "Whatever ye be doin', Alex," Miata requested, glancing at where he knew he needed to stand to yell out orders to the gunners, "keep away from the rails and don't be fallin' off the ship?"

"Wha-! You are not going to fire upon that ship, are you? Jacq is over there!" Alex yelled after him, pointing in angst.

"Were ya not listenin', Alex? Cap'n Adams were the gunner aboard that ship...He be knowin', more likely than not, how to be stoppin' that ship as safe as could be possible for our Jacq! Be not gettin' washed overboard!" He clasped his hands together in a full body plea before tearing himself away to the position he needed to be in.

Looking down at the men, keeping the powder dry as they went sloshing around with the cannons and the cannonballs, Miata cleared his throat and mustered in a voice much louder than he knew he could, "Ahoy, mates!" All the men turned to look at him. "Cap'n Adams be orderin' the loadin' o' those cannons! Away with ye!"

Everyone stared at him until a rough looking man of an undiscernable age squinted up at Miata, and then turned and called to the rest of the gunners in a pinched, rough voice, "Are youse all deef?! Be doin' what the man be sayin'!"

"Aye!" they yelled, turning to work like the gears in a clock, meshing as the cogs – each man doing his job deftly in nigh perfection.

Turning back to Miata, he waved. "Me name be Ahearn Bronston, Master Gunner o'er these powder monkeys! If youse be needin' anythin' o' any kind whilst ye be relayin' the orders,

be sure to be lettin' me know!" Then, returning his attentions to the gunners, he began walking amongst them, inspecting their work.

"And what, exactly, do you think you're doing, Mr. O'Keeffe?" a voice hissed in Miata's ear, nearly making him jump overboard.

"I be followin' orders," he returned unusually tersely, whipping around to find Nicholas Dunne glaring at him, just as he had suspected. "The Cap'n be orderin' me to be a part o' his command relayin' on account o' the storm." Realizing Dunne had used his newly discovered last name, though, he straightened despite the foul weather.

Seeing this confrontation, the gunners slowed their work to observe the encounter.

"I don't think there's really a problem, mate," Crevan's voice broke in between them, grinning. "Isn't that right, *Mr.* Dunne?" he inquired with a wink.

Disappointed, the gunners went back to work.

Miata's eyebrow arching in confusion, he glanced between Crevan and Nicholas, asking, "Be the two o' ye talkin'?"

"If you're lucky, we'll discuss this later," Dunne replied, sneering and turning, his rain soaked cloak hitting Miata in the leg.

His confused glance transforming into a threatening glare, Miata put his hand on his hip and retorted softly, "Ye be the one who be lucky if we be talkin' later!"

"Miata!"

He looked up to find Captain Adams staring down at him from beside the helm.

"Are those guns, ready?"

Miata looked for the scruffy looking master gunner. "Mr. Bronston!"

The gunner gave him his attention.

"Be those guns ready?"

"They be!" He nodded.

"They be!" Miata passed along, nodding in affirmation. He noticed out of the corner of his eye the foreboding figure of the much larger *Wind Hawke*. His spirits sank a little. *By the powers...It be the ship o' the devil hisself, risen from the ashes...* His forehead broke out in a sweat.

"Miata! Fire the portside!" Adams yelled.

"Fire the portside!" Miata repeated.

"Fire the portside!" Bronston echoed.

As the fire belched out from *Anne's Triumph*'s cannons, the ammunition cracked into the sides of the East Indiaman, sending shudders through her timbers. "He fires upon me?! *Damasu!*" Ming growled, turning like a wolf with its hackles lifted in angry aggression to Red Handed Jesse who happened to be standing nearby. "Where be Pike? Have Peg Leg Paul ready those guns!"

"Aye, aye, Cap'n, says I!" he agreed cheerfully, happy to do Pike's job. As he pushed his portly form past other crewmen so he could call down to Jean-Paul amongst the gale forces, a glint caught his eye and he cried out, "Cap'n! Look, says I!"

Ming turned to find himself following Red Handed Jesse's pudgy finger to the sight of Jean-Pierre and Jacq sword fighting atop the forecastle. "What in the bloody-" Stray water from an outraged wave splashed over him, drenching the already saggy plumage of his hat. "What be they doin'?" He started muttering curse words in his native tongue, shaking his saturated locks like a cat.

"I be not knowin', Cap'n, says I!" Smith said. "Should I be findin' out, says I?" he inquired eagerly. As he asked, another

volley of cannonballs hit the ship, two of which hit the side railing, taking out Scotch and half his boarding crew.

"Nay!" Ming retorted furiously. "Ready our guns afore they blow us to the netherworld!"

Across the ship, on the deck that created a roof for the forecastle, Jacq taunted and yelled at Jean-Pierre, "It doesn't have to be this way, you know!" Angry tears accompanied the raindrops streaming down her cheeks.

"Oh, Jacqo!" He laughed, circling her. "Ya know it can't be any other way!"

Seeing a bucket out of the corner of her eye, Jacq slowly began to back over to it. "If I did know it couldn't be any other way," she retorted coolly, "I wouldn't have suggested it."

Noticing she was against the railing of the deck, he lunged at her, but was quite disheartened when she slid out of the pathway and the blade stuck into the board. His eyes grew, and he tugged ferociously on the grip of his sword, but to no avail.

"You know," she added, coming up beside his ear, bucket in hand, "you'll have to teach me how to do that sometime. I can never get it to stick." Smiling, she shrugged and ran to the other end of the forecastle, closest to *Anne's Triumph.*

"Jacq!" he yelled after her, giving a couple more hard heaves on his sword before it finally loosened enough that he was able to coax it free. "Jacqo! Wait! You don't know what you're doing!" Sheathing his sword, he raced to catch her as she was madly tying a rope, which he noticed extended up to the yardarm, between the bucket and a heavy barrel. As she pushed the barrel down the stairs she stood at the top of, she hopped in the bucket and reached down to slash the rope connecting the bucket to the ground. However, as she did,

Jean-Pierre hopped on beside her.

"What are you doing?" she asked in irritation as they shot into the air.

"I could ask the same thing about you!" he retorted, glancing down at the shrinking deck boards.

Glaring at him, she hopped out of the bucket and barely landed on the rope rigging of the *Wind Hawke*. "Isn't it obvious?" she asked between clenched teeth, turning to peer about the vessel. No longer crying, she saw the waves began to subside and the rain was mostly a drizzle. She also quickly noticed Ming staring up at Jean-Pierre, Red Handed Jesse trying to shout out orders to the gunners, and Bahari…Where was he?

"Shakina!" She looked down to find Bahari nearly squarely underneath her. "Captain wants to speak with you."

"Ugh!" she scoffed loudly. Lightning highlighted the clouds and thunder clapped in the sky, but the waves continued to calm.

At that instant, Alex, who was still clinging miserably to the rail, looked up and saw the thin figure clinging to the ropes. "Jacq?" she asked, hardly able to breathe. "Jacq, what are you doing?! Jacq!" she called out, waving her hat and jumping up and down.

"Don't waste your breath, Miss Alex," Crevan said coming up beside her. Glancing about and noticing Nicholas Dunne working his way their direction, he added, "Come with me." Guiding her to the railing where a bunch of other men were crowded around, he handed her a rope and whispered, "Now, don't let go until I tell you."

Tilting her head, Alex glanced around in disorientation. "Wha-?"

"Ready, men!" Adams' voice yelled into the air from a short distance away.

"Aye!" the men around her—including Crevan—responded. He grabbed the rope and wrapped his arms around her.

"Board!" the burly captain shouted.

Suddenly, Alex's eyes grew as Crevan, squeezing her tight, backed up and ran, along with the rest of the men, off the edge of the ship. "Wha-? Wait! No, no...*Aaaaaaaahhh!*" she screamed, clinging more to Crevan than to the rope.

At her scream, Miata glanced up, first at where the captain stood and then unknowingly at Crevan and Alex swinging across the short distance to the East Indiaman amongst the posse of others. *Ha!* He chuckled to himself. *That be a might funny if Alex-* Glancing at where she no longer stood at the rail, he stopped short, his smile dropping as he considered the possibilities. "Alex?"

As Jacq hit the deck beside Bahari, she also heard the squeal. Glancing up, she saw the incoming band of opposing buccaneers landing not too far in front of her, and in their midst, someone who did not quite fit in...The sailor hit the deck, having been sharing a rope with another crewman, and spun about wildly as though utterly lost and immediately began yelling at her fellow crewmember. "Alex?" she asked breathlessly. "Is it possible?"

"Alex?" Bahari repeated, crossing his arms.

"Aye..." She nodded, moving forward and pushing all of the sailors, whether with Ming's crew or otherwise, aside. "Alex is my sister!"

"Sister?" Bahari followed her, shaking his head. "Here?"

A short distance in front of Jacq, Alex was still shouting

at Crevan. "How could you bring me over here? What were you *thinking*?"

Winking, he nodded to his right, in the direction he knew they had previously spotted Jacq. "I told you I'd find her."

As Alex turned, Jacq pushed her way through the last layer of swordsmen and time seemed to slow to a halt. Even though pistol shots were being fired, men were crying out in adrenaline and pain, and swords were clanging all around them, the world seemed to fade to a muddled din. All the bad in life was suddenly outshone by the good, allowing no shadows to darken the two young ladies' paths, and a chasm that seemed to be endless was suddenly merely a footfall deep. "Alex!" Jacq called out, throwing her arms wide.

"Jacq!" Alex returned, running to meet her halfway. As they collided into an embrace, the waves settled back into the sea. The clouds ceased their torrential saturating of the world beneath them, and began to recede and dissipate into a brilliant blue sky. All the sailors, superstitious crewmen of both vessels alike, stopped and glanced around, gulping in a sudden head rush of apprehensive utterances and thoughts. Releasing each other the twins backed up and took one another in.

Then, her forehead contorting, Alex was the first to speak, "Your hair?!"

"Your clothes?!" Jacq counter questioned, returning the expression.

"Earrings?" Alex asked in disapproval, nodding towards the dangling hoops.

"A sword?" Jacq returned skeptically, mock grimacing.

Grinning, they laughed and hugged again. Simultaneously, the two crews realized they weren't fighting anymore and returned to their brawling.

"This way!" Jacq called, pulling Alex, followed by the two men, off to the side a small ways away from the mass free-for-all.

When they paused, Alex gestured to Bahari. "Who is your friend?"

"This is Bahari," Jacq introduced, motioning that he come closer. He bowed, letting his smile alone be his greeting.

Then, noticing the tall, handsome Irishman who'd been looking her up and down, she gasped. "Michael Murtaugh?!"

A devilishly charming grin broke out upon his face. "One and the same."

"We have some catching up to do, mate!" she said in a tone that could have been either playful or threatening – he wasn't sure which.

"Aye, that we do, lass," he agreed, continuing to look her over appreciatively. "It's good to see you're still your usual charming self."

Laughing, Jacq shook her head. "I will humor you with a response when you help get me off this wretched ship!"

"And how do we do that?" Alex inquired.

"That," Jacq said with a grin as she pulled out her katana blades, "is an excellent question."

"Heavens..." Alex sighed, unsheathing her own sword. "What have I gotten myself into?"

Seeing Alex produce the weapon out of the corner of her eye, Jacq inquired in an uneasy tone, "You're actually going to use that?" At her inquiry, a pair of unsavory rogues dropped in front of them. Jacq quickly cleared away the one and, when she turned to deal with the other, was astonished to see Alex grimacing over his unconscious body.

Spotting her sister's surprise, Alex shrugged, a smile

curving her face. "I have been practicing."

"I can see that," Jacq returned with a chuckle. Glancing back at the two men with them, she asked, "Ready to take out some dogs?"

In unison, Bahari picked out a nice, sturdy rail that had been gunned loose from the cannon fire, and Crevan relieved both Jacq and Alex's unconscious conquests of their weapons. His eye resting on Jacq's stance and weaponry, the Irishman nodded. "Aye!"

Meanwhile, Miata, still staring after Alex's sail through the air, shook his head and muttered, "By the powers…"

"What," yelled Nicholas Dunne, grabbing Miata up by the front of his shirt, "is Miss Luray doing swinging to Ming's ship with your mate, Crevan?"

"I be not knowin'," Miata retorted, pushing Nicholas off of himself. "An' I can be assurin' ye it weren't any idea o' mine! So, ye be keepin' yer do-goodie fingers to yerself, *mate!*"

"Mr. Dunne!" Captain Adams bellowed down at him. The two squabblers looked up. "Stay here with the ship, lad! Miata, prepare to board!"

"He's going with you?" Nicholas asked, obviously insulted at this.

"Aye, lad. Remember our accord!" Adams warned, shaking his finger. "Keep me treasure safe!" He lovingly patted the boat. "Now, come along, Miata m'boy! We've not got all day!"

Glancing inquisitively between the two, Miata turned, bumping Nicholas in the shin with his sheath. "Aye, aye, Cap'n!" he called up to Captain Adams, throwing his gaze once more over his shoulder to smile at the now scowling Nicholas Dunne. *An accord, eh, mate?* he pondered in amusement. *An what be the meanin' o' that, Mr. Dunne?*

As the crew from *Anne's Triumph* poured over onto the

Wind Hawke, Ming let out a screeching yelp and turned venomously to Red Handed Jesse, who had failed to pass on Ming's orders to fire into the smaller vessel due to the distraction of Jean-Pierre shooting up to the yardarm in a bucket and the sudden calming of the weather. "I ought to run ye through!" the disgruntled captain yelled at him. "Make yerself useful an' get me that lass!" Rancor and malice steamed from his nostrils with contempt and scorn hot on his breath. "Fail me again an' yer head will be hangin' where that bucket," he motioned to where the bucket swayed alone by the yardarm, "be danglin' from!"

"Aye, Cap'n, says I! Pigeon ye be havin'!" Red Handed Jesse agreed, a hint of terror in his voice as he hurried away so fast that he was tripping over himself.

On the main deck, Bahari was discreetly cudgeling his own crew left and right. To his left, Jacq was finding her focus split between watching Alex's fighting style and combating the pilfering goons that happened across her path. Beside her, sending prayers constantly heavenward, Alex kept swinging, telling herself she needed to keep her eyes open. Then, to Alex's left, Crevan was showing off his understated skills in swordsmanship while keeping an eyes on the girls. The four were leaving behind them a wake for the incoming assailants to follow in and do damage of their own to Ming's crew count. Ahead of them, Jean-Pierre, who had seen Ming's anger from where he'd been sitting, was working his way their direction, laying blows and crossing swords with anyone who wandered in front of him – regardless of what ship they hailed from. The sky rang with metallic clangs and indistinguishable whoops and hollers.

Concurrently, Red Handed Jesse was fighting desperately,

teeth grinding, sweat pouring from his brow, to get to Jacq. The dull smell of burnt wood rose up persistently from the depths of the ship, reminding everyone of the volley that had taken place only moments ago. His head still sore from the incident a few nights prior, he found that being juggled amongst all the bodies in the ruckus was giving him a rather painful headache. Of course, he did not doubt for a moment that Ming whispering constantly in his ear, "*Or yer head will be hangin' where that bucket be danglin' from!*" was helping much either. Looking up, he saw between the colliding bodies and weapons that Jean-Pierre was nearly upon Jacq and her party. Then his heart stopped suddenly. Did that peculiarly fighting sailor to Jacq's left look just like her? "By the powers…Thar be two, says I?"

At that moment, Jean-Pierre and Jacq were suddenly face to face. "How was your ride?" she asked, chuckling and giving him a little wink.

"A wee bit unexpected," he returned, grinning at her between the v-shaped window created above where their swords crossed. "But, I'm tellin' ya, Jacq, you need to come with me. After all, you have an accord to settle."

"What is he talking about?" Alex asked in a feisty tone, coming up beside Jacq. "And who is he anyway?"

"He is Jean-Pierre Legard, the Frenchman who can't speak French," Jacq introduced calmly, obviously mulling over his comment.

He sent her a glare as a sarcastic thank you.

"How do I know you will keep your word?" she asked.

"Be not movin', Pigeon, says I!" Red Handed Jesse's voice interrupted loudly, pulling Jacq's attentions away from Jean-Pierre. Her heart sank at seeing Alex at the point of his

flintlock. "I be guessin' she be meanin' somethin' to ya bein's ya two looks so much alike an' all, says I. Be followin' orders, Pigeon, or she be takin' a nice, long visit with Davy Jones, says I."

Her lip twitching and curling involuntarily, she turned to look at Bahari, her breathing increasing at this outrageous demand.

He nodded.

Licking her slightly dried lips, she swiveled to stare at Jean-Pierre.

He nodded as well.

Heaving a sigh as she watched the continued fighting going on around them, she sheathed her swords irritably and retorted in a growl, "Very well. I will go." She noticed Crevan, who had nonchalantly avoided being seen by Jesse Smith and Jean-Pierre, had slunk backwards in the direction of the incoming crewman. "Lead the way, Mr. Smith," she said, challenging him with her inflection and her gaze.

"Pike be leadin' the way, Pigeon, says I," he retorted. "I be smarter than to be listenin' to you!"

She glanced over at Jean-Pierre, a mysterious smirk on her face. "Jean-Pierre?"

He grinned back at her, nudging her ahead of him. "Jacqo..."

Ming's crew parted as the Red Sea as the small entourage trudged with heavy feet to the poop deck where Ming stood, arms crossed and gloating. The noise of the fighting seemed to fade as the group lined up in front of the *Wind Hawke*'s captain, right to left: Jacq, Jean-Pierre, Alex, Red Handed Jesse, and Bahari. Looking the company over, he grunted. "Well done, Pike."

Down the line, Red Handed Jesse nearly boiled over and exploded with insulted rage that Pike had been recognized and he had not.

"I see ye have proven yer loyalties," he noted to Bahari, who bowed obligingly in his direction. Then he paused and looked at Alex. Lifting her chin with his finger, he looked her in the eye a moment.

"I'm down here, Captain!" Jacq taunted, peeking around Jean-Pierre.

Storming over to face her, he retorted, "What be the idea of attackin' yer own crew, Jacq? Have ya no sense of loyalty about ya?" He turned away from her and began pacing.

"Actually, Captain," she replied, "I have a strong sense of loyalty!" In one swift motion, she lunged forward, grabbed one of his own knives, and pushed him forward onto the floor of the deck. "They just don't happen to lie with you."

Bahari leaped forward, cudgel in hand.

Red Handed Jesse joined him, yelping, "Cap'n!"

"Stay back!" Ming ordered, feeling where Jacq's hand held the knife, just a short distance from his throat. "What are ye thinkin', lass?" he cooed at her. "Ya can't be killin' me an' still be claimin' to not be a pirate. If ya do kill me, then yer only provin' that I was right about ye all along. Ya are the bad twin…Are ya the bad twin," he paused pointedly, "Jacq?"

Glowering at him, she looked aside a moment, and then turned back to him, sliding the knife she held carefully along his throat until she heard it scrap against something metallic. Hooking the chain on the tip of her weapon, she pulled the locket out from being tucked inside his shirt. Plucking the locket from where it spilled out onto the deck, she yanked it off and shoved it into her pocket. "This belongs to me, savvy?

And, to answer your question, Captain…I would kill you." She raised the blade slightly above him, and then emphatically, with all of her might, stabbed the knife into the floor she had him trapped on. "But serving on your ship was enough. I refuse to spend eternity in the netherworld by your side as well!"

Raising slightly and drawing her sword, she pointed it at his throat. "You will let us go now, or you will regret it."

"Be those my only options?" he inquired stiffly.

"Aye." Her eyebrow arched at this inquiry, hoping he knew she was nothing but serious.

Waving his hand towards the other vessel, he inquired, "An' why be ye wantin' to serve with those pirates instead o' these?!"

"Because," Jacq returned, laughing and glancing at Alex. "They're not pirates at all." She pushed the sword tip against his throat. "Do we have an accord?"

"I don't see how me agreein' to let ye waltz out o' here is much o' an accord," he retorted.

"You get to keep your life. That should count for something," she replied.

His tanned, chiseled face twitched with an uncharted level of unhappiness. "I be not understandin' ye, Jacq. I can see in yer eyes that ye fancy havin' the power to do devilry."

"I do fancy having the power to do devilry," Jacq admitted, a smirk widening her mouth, "and then electing not to."

"I gave ye that power!" he retorted, glaring at her as best as he could in his position.

"Nay, Captain," she disagreed, shaking her head. "It is a part of me. It always has been. You just tried to manipulate me into liking it."

He growled at this. "Pity those are my only options, but it

seems as if I have no choice in the matter. Go, afore I change my mind."

Glancing at Bahari, who was still standing with the cudgel in his hand, Jacq nodded. "Good day, Mr. Ono." Whirling about, sword still drawn, she walked toward Alex, who's eyes she watched grow in great fear.

"Jacq!" she screamed, starting forward just slightly.

Jacq turned to find Ming, kris dagger drawn and held high above his head, mouth open in an angry war cry, leaping up from the deck and running for her.

Her breath left her as the sight alone frightened her speechless. As she stood there, strangely unable to move, a body collided with her, sending her sprawling onto the floor face down, her katana blade clattering onto the deck, out of her hand. As she hit the deck, another dull thud resounded and Ming landed beside her, his unique, wavy dagger still clutched in his fist, his eyes closed, with a large, bleeding abrasion on his forehead. Shrinking away from the fallen captain, who she was slightly disappointed to notice was still breathing, Jacq looked up to see Bahari, that broken piece of railing in has hand, smiling like the cat who just ate the canary. "Bahari?" she asked.

"He had it coming for a long time," he commented. "I have killed and injured many evil men in my day. Injuring one more will not mar my destiny." He grinned.

"What be goin' on here, says I?" Red Handed Jesse asked, looking between them. He looked down, aghast, at Ming lying on the ground, breathing so shallowly.

Whirling about, Bahari clobbered Red Handed Jesse in the head, knocking him out cold. As he crumpled to the floor between Bahari and Alex, Jacq turned and stared at him.

"Bahari!" He looked at her innocently. "Again? You knocked him out *again?*"

Smiling sheepishly, he shrugged.

Laughing, Jacq leapt to her feet, throwing her arms around him.

Blinking several times in surprise, he glanced at Alex, who was smiling, and slowly began to return the embrace. However, the moment only lasted a few seconds as suddenly Jacq recalled they were not finished.

Spinning away from Bahari and pulling her second sword, she came face to face with Jean-Pierre, who had drawn his own sword by the time she had finished turning to face him. Immediately pointing the blades at each other, she greeted him cordially, "'Ello, mate! What say you to that plan now?"

The corner of his mouth dropped with displeasure at her request. "How do I know you will keep your word?"

Recognizing the exact verbatim of his question, she smiled and answered, "You're just going to have to trust me."

At that moment, Crevan, Miata, and Captain Adams spilled onto the deck. "Drop it, lad!" Crevan called out. "Or it may be the last breath you take."

Jacq nodded, and Jean-Pierre relinquished his sword to her. Bending for her other sword, she nodded at Crevan.

As Crevan came forward and bound Jean-Pierre's hands with some rope he grabbed off the deck floor, Captain Adams turned to the rest of the ship and bellowed, "Ahoy, lads!" Firing two pistols, one to punctuate his sentence, and the other seconds after, he watched as both sets of crewmen stopped their scuffling to give him their attention. "Cap'n Ming is down! I be the new Cap'n o' this ship! An' all the crewmen o' Cap'n Ming be havin' two choices. They be either goin' to the brig all nice an' quiet like, or they be dyin' at the ends o' me crew's swords! The choice be yours!"

As usual with pirates, Ming's crew had no desire to die—even in an act of bravery or loyalty. So, it was no surprise, least of all to Captain Adams, when there was a sudden clamor of clangings and clinkings as Ming's crew's swords and firearms dropped to the floor around them while they stood in stupefaction about the uncanny infiltration of their ship.

Chapter 12

As the now imprisoned pirates were taken to the brig, Jean-Pierre looked sullenly after Jacq, saying things with his eyes that he could not say with his mouth. His brother was no different as he marched down to the brig of the *Wind Hawke*. An overwhelming sense of guilt came over the young woman, and she found she could not bear to watch them descend into the black. Ming, still unconscious, was carried down below by some of his own able bodied crewmen.

"Evil blackguard," she said to herself in a menacing tone. Taking a deep breath, she looked away as he disappeared below. As she did, she noticed Captain Adams talking to Murtaugh and Miata. She smiled over at the two boys nodding and chuckling with the burly ship captain. Then, realizing her sister was not nearby, she glanced around, seeing her small, quaint figure – now hardly distinguishable in her new get up – slanting against the railing, looking at the wake.

Crossing the distance to her, Jacq touched her shoulder. "What's wrong?"

Turning to smile at Jacq, Alex reached into her sister's pocket, producing the locket. "Nothing," she said in her perpetual primness, reaching over and fastening the chain around Jacq's neck. "Everything is fine now. We are together." She forced a smile.

Jacq narrowed her eyes at her reply. "There is something troubling you. I can see it in your eyes. When you are ready to share it with me, I will be waiting," Jacq told her, sweeping her into an embrace. "How did you and Miata fare together as you searched for me?" Letting Alex go, she glanced fondly over at her friend.

"Yes," Alex admitted with an ease that rather stunned Jacq. "He proved to be quite helpful, and, to my surprise, one of the only people I could trust." A small chuckle rocked her body, but glazed over her eyes. "I think I may be starting to see why you – and Amy – fancy him as much as you do, though I do not know if I ever shall admit it to him." A real smile, to Jacq's relief, finally broke onto her face at this comment. "Have you spoken with him yet? He has something important to tell you."

"Does he, now?" Crossing her arms, she eyed him. "What sort of something?"

Grinning, Alex shrugged. "I shall not spoil it. Go speak with him, and when you are through…" She paused, glancing at the ground. "You spoke the truth. There is a matter in which I wish to ask your help."

Bobbing her head once in concurrence to this plan, Jacq touched her sister's shoulder one last time before sauntering over to the group of men. As soon as she was gone, the handsome Mr. Dunne appeared on deck and made his way over to Alex.

Simultaneously, Miata looked up and saw Jacq, his face breaking into a smile. Rushing forward, he scooped her up

into his arms, spinning about with her feet dangling up off the ground. "Jacq!" he whispered into her ear, squeezing her to himself. "Alex an' I were worried we wouldn't be seein' ye again." At this confession, he placed her on the floor so that he could look down into her eyes, holding her face in his hands. "I be glad ye be back, Jacq. Alex an' I be havin' a time together, but, we be missin' ye somethin' fierce."

Giggling at his expressiveness, Jacq nodded. "As am I, mate. Now, what's this I hear about you having something to tell me?"

"Ah!" Letting go of her, he straightened. "It be true, Jacq." Taking a small step backwards, he cleared his throat and said, "Miss Luray, ye be lookin' at Miata O'Keeffe, son o' the late Keegan O'Keeffe an' his lovely wife, Lolita." Bowing, he rose with a glow about him that would rival the sun.

"O'Keeffe? Y-Your last name?" Jacq laughed, covering her mouth in shock. "Oh, Miata! Well, I…!" She paused, trying to absorb the news. "Mr. Miata O'Keeffe…Doesn't sound bad at all now, does it? Haha!" Reaching up, she touched his cheek. "I have never been happier for you, mate. However did you come by this discovery?"

"A kindly woman from the orphanage I were raised in found us. She be fillin' me." His glow lessened slightly, but his elatedness remained strong, giving him a more confident demeanor than she'd ever seen from him.

"Congratulations, lad!" Captain Adams said jovially, his voice as booming as ever. "Now, introduce us to this lass we journeyed across the waters for!"

"O' course," Miata agreed, grinning sheepishly. "Jacq, this be Cap'n Adams o' *Anne's Triumph*. Cap'n, this be Jacqueline Taylor Luray, o', as us mates be callin' her, Jacq."

"Miss Luray," Captain Adams greeted, extending his hand.

"Captain," she returned respectfully, gripping his hand. "I owe you many thanks."

As the captain let go of her hand, she glanced over at Murtaugh who had been quietly standing off to the side, observing her in silent satisfaction. Upon seeing her gaze land on him, a smile pushed up the left corner of his mouth, and he sauntered over as if her eyes beckoned him.

"Michael Murtaugh..." she said as he approached.

"Jacqueline Luray..." he returned in kind.

Biting her lower lip, she fought the smirk tugging at her lips. "However did you end up here?"

Chuckling, he shrugged. "I couldn't stand to know you weren't safe. It also happened that I was in a small fight with a pirate by name of Red Handed Jesse, so I had information too. Leverage to come along, you know." He winked at her.

"Too bad you didn't end him. You'd have done me a great favor," she said with a sigh, unable to lose the smile she had while looking at him. "We have much to catch up on..."

"Aye," he agreed. "I think I-"

"Oi, lads!" Captain Adams' voice interrupted loudly. "Now, I need ye to be helpin' get these two ships ready to sail!" He looked at Jacq. "Back to Penzance or Port Gilgallad?"

"Actually, Captain, Swansea is where we'd request you take us," answered Jacq. She turned to verify this with Alex and saw a handsome blonde man excuse himself from her side. Watching her sister fidget after his departure, Jacq added, "Lads, my sister and I shall leave you to your duties. We have some matters to discuss. Oh! And, their French minstrel is a nice chap, you might see if he'll join you." Then, marching up to Alex and holding out her hand, she invited, "Shall we?"

Nodding, Alex agreed, "Yes." Looping her arm through Jacq's the two sauntered, across the ship to Jacq's room in the forecastle of the *Wind Hawke*.

No sooner was the door shut then Alex sank onto her sister's hammock, head in her hands. "I have done something terrible, Jacq, and I do not know to what extent the damage goes."

"Alex," Jacq said with a sigh, "you're going to have to start from the beginning, because I have no idea what you're talking about."

Sniffling, Alex produced the parchment she'd be laboring over in her room aboard *Anne's Triumph*. "See for yourself." Curling into the fetal position in Jacq's hammock, she watched as Jacq unfolded the paper, displaying the contents to herself.

"Darling James," she read aloud.

"Do not read it aloud!" Alex said in a pathetic whimper.

"Alex, that's all it says..." Jacq commented.

"While I am so glad to have you back safe and sound, Jacq, you and Miata have some markedly similar reactions to things," Alex noted, sounding a little injured.

Sending her sister a glare, she held up the paper. "What is this for?"

"Oh, it really is nothing," Alex insisted, reaching for the piece of paper.

"Alex," Jacq retorted, holding it out of her reach, "if it were truly nothing, I wouldn't be holding it in my hand right now, would I? Now, tell me what this is about? You're acting awfully strange. What is troubling you?"

Tears returning to her hazel eyes, Alex's lip trembled like the lip of a child. She looked away from Jacq.

A sympathetic smile forming her expression, Jacq sat down beside her twin in the hammock, resting her hand on her shoulder. “You know, I’ve been a pirate for the last week and discovered the man I was serving under, Captain Ming, wanted me to be a pirate to get revenge on our father – for putting him in jail.”

Alex turned a wide set of eyes to Jacq. “Truly?”

Shrugging, Jacq nodded. “Can’t beat that, mate.”

Taking in a long, slow breath, Alex composed herself and began, “That letter, though neither you nor Miata think much of its meager beginnings, is going to be an apology letter to James Monroe. I no longer deserve his company, let alone his good intentions.” She stared down at the floor, ashamed.

“*What?*” Jacq scoffed. “What are you *talking about? Deserve?* What kind of rubbish is that?”

“I betrayed him, Jacq! I thought that Mr. Dunne was telling the truth when he indirectly told me James Monroe had passed on, but it was not true. He is still alive, and I fraternized with Mr. Dunne as a little strumpet one could pick up off the streets of London,” she explained, disdain for herself coating every syllable.

“W-What?” Jacq asked in furious tone, bounding to her feet and drawing her swords. “Where is this Mr. Dunne? Is he that man that was speaking to you up by the stern? I shall make him pay for his deceit! Preying on a distraught lass… That’s no gentleman!”

“No, no, Jacq!” Alex pleaded, grabbing for her arm so desperately she spun out of the hammock, landing on the floor on her knees. “It is my fault, do not you see? If I had taken the time to listen to Miata and discover who he was instead of just accepting his gentlemanly charade, then none of this would

have ever happened. James is deserving of someone with more class than I have as it is. I cannot believe I trusted him, Jacq! What does it say about me if I cannot tell the difference between a charlatan and a gentleman?"

Putting her blades away, Jacq knelt beside her sister. "I saw Audric Schellden in the Isles of Scilly."

"You did? That fiend?" She gasped. "How awful, but…W-why do you bring him into this conversation?"

"Because, Alex," Jacq explained with a disappointed sigh, "after all the pain and the heartache he caused me, there is a part of me that still loves him. Quite a small part, I wish to point out, but he doesn't deserve it. Your misunderstanding and despair is very small compared to the relational atrocities of said Audric Schellden." Alex started to look away, but Jacq caught her chin with her finger, adding, "If I can somehow, unexplainably, still have even a sliver of love for *him*…James will *surely* be able to forgive you, if, of course, he's any man worthy of your love."

A small smile began to form on Alex's face. "How I have missed you, sister."

Returning the expression, Jacq said, "Relax. I can sense a turning of the tides is at hand. What was that Captain Turner would say? Sometimes angels fall."

The smile finally breaking loose, Alex exhaled. "I pray this never happens again. You being off running about with pirates, leaving me with Miata…It really was quite dreadful of you."

Laughing, Jacq shrugged. "Miata's not so bad! And you got Mr. Murtaugh along as well? Truly, it is I who is jealous of you!"

The chaotic afternoon faded into a lulled evening, blanketed by a thick layer of clouds that had blown in for the night. They were holding in the warm air that usually fled the sea, only allowing a tiny star to sparkle ambiguously here and there before vanishing again behind the shroud of overcast curtains. Everyone was on board the *Wind Hawke* as it was towing *Anne's Triumph*. Jacq walked about the ship, hands interlaced contemplatively, breathing freedom once again. Alex had fallen asleep almost immediately when they turned in, but after some tossing and turning, Jacq had risen to prowl the decks. Ever so casually, she moseyed down to the brig where a man by name of Hornbeck was guarding the prisoners.

"Ahoy, lass!" he greeted cheerfully.

"Good day, good man!" she responded. "I need a Mr. Legard," she informed him formally. Out of the corner of her eye she saw Ming lying still on the floor, his head wrapped in a bandage with a ruddy spot in it that covered half of his forehead.

"There be two o' them," he noted, scratching at his impressive, graying beard. Both Jean-Pierre and Jean-Paul ambled forward in their small cell at the mention of their shared name. "An' I were just about to retire for the night."

"Hmm," she said thoughtfully. "I'll take them both, that way I won't have to make the trip more than necessary. And then I shall return them once I'm through." She smiled convincingly.

"Under whose orders, lass?" Mr. Hornbeck asked with a yawn.

"Honestly, Mr. Hornbeck, I was hoping to have a moment

alone with the lads. We've," she glanced at the brothers, "a few unresolved issues to discuss."

"Well..." He looked at the pirates. "Yer sure you can take care now?" he asked, looking incredulous.

"Aye, sir." She gave him her most persuasive smile.

"Bah...Very well. If they give ye any trouble, though," he leaned closer to her and lowered his voice, "go fer the throat."

"Aye, aye, sir!" she agreed, grinning and nodding obliging. Looking at the two men as he opened the cell door for them, she repeated, "Did you hear that, lads? One wrong move and..." She drew a line across her throat with her finger.

Jean-Pierre's face merged a smirk and a frown. "Aye, aye, Jacqo."

Motioning the two men in front of her, hands still bound, she tapped the hilt of her sword. "Thank you again, Mr. Hornbeck." Then, pushing them forward, she snapped, "All right, move along now, lads! Hurry up, savvy?"

They ascended the steps, and as they touched air, she gestured for them to make their way along the railing to the small ledge going behind the upper cabins. As they rounded the structure, they came to three heavily tied knots on the railing, spaced about three feet apart. They were, in fact, the knots keeping *Anne's Triumph* in tow. The brothers stared at her.

"I didn't think you would do it," Jean-Pierre admitted.

"Why not?" Jacq retorted, shrugging her shoulders. Picking up Jean-Paul's hands, she began to pluck at his bindings. "I said I would if you didn't resist."

He grinned. "Perhaps I was wrong. Seems you have a little pirate in you after all, Jacqo."

As she finished up his brother's knots, she started on his.

"Oh, I wouldn't be so sure, Jean-Pierre. I'm keeping my word, not freeing some random pirate. Besides, I do not wish to be the one responsible for the hanging of a poor widow's sons."

"You believed that story?" Jean-Pierre asked as the ropes that had been around his wrists fell to the ground.

Her eyebrow rose and she counter questioned, "Should I not have?"

"Well, it is the truth," he admitted, grinning bashfully, "but I reckoned nary a lad or lass believed it. I figured most thought it to be an invented tale of woe."

Jacq chuckled, looking him in the eye a moment. "I could see in your eyes that it was more personal than just a story spun to ensnare its listeners. You may have exaggerated some things, but it is obvious you can't speak French and that you have a strong connection to your brother." She gestured to where Jean-Paul was standing and he beamed proudly.

Taking her chin in his hand, the ebony clad swashbuckler whispered, "Come with us, Jacq. Join us. Be free."

"The kind of freedom you offer is not really freedom at all," she said in gentle rejection, looking away from him. "After being on the island and talking to different people, I've come to realize that it's because when you steal something, you spend your entire life fighting to keep it." Pausing, she glanced over at Jean-Paul and then returned her gaze to meet his. "That kind of a life isn't for me."

Suddenly feeling mesmerized by her soft smile and honest stare, he smiled and leaned a little closer, his mouth just an inch or two from hers. "That's a pity, Jacq."

Clearing his throat, Jean-Paul scuffed his shoes on the deck boards, making the two snap apart. "If we're goin' to get out of here, we better get a move on it."

"Very well, Jean-Paul. Hopefully Captain Adams left a bit

of hardware behind." He looked back to Jacq. "How is this goin' to work out for you, Jacqo?"

Holding up the rope, she sighed. "I suppose you'll have to overpower me."

A wicked smile twisted his mouth. "Well, well, Jacqo..."

"Don't get any funny ideas, Mr. Legard!" she retorted, glaring at him.

"Jean-Paul," he gestured down at his pegleg, "get on with it. I'll tie up our mate here and be along straight away."

Nodding cooperatively, Jean-Paul turned to the girl one last time. "Jacq."

"Jean-Paul," she returned.

Turning, he climbed over the railing and began the crawl across the rope to *Anne's Triumph*. Hanging upside down from it, he scooted with impressive speed across its span to the sloop.

Grabbing up her wrists, Jean-Pierre stole the rope and began winding them around, securing her in a knot.

"Stop smiling," she told him, wearing a good-natured glare.

He chuckled. "I can't." Then, reaching up, he loosed the black neckerchief from around his throat. "We can't have ya screamin', lass. You need to hold it between your teeth," he instructed as he gently tied it around her head. He grinned at his handiwork. "And you even have something to remember me by."

She smirked.

Then, pulling the mock gag out of her mouth, he sighed. "I won't forget ya, Jacqo, or this. If ever you need a less than lawful favor, come find me."

Heaving a sigh, Jacq wagged her head up and down. "Farewell, Jean-Pierre."

"Until we meet again, love." Repositioning the neckerchief in her mouth, he kissed her forehead. Hopping onto the railing, Jean-Pierre turned once more to smile at her. Then, bowing gallantly, he swung down onto the rope and shuttled himself into the darkness.

Watching him disappear into the coal-colored night, Jacq leaned back against the wall, sliding to the floor, listening to the splashing of the ocean on the side of the vessel and breathing in the cool warmth of the summery air. The clouds were thinning, letting the partial moon make an appearance now and again. Reaching to her neck with her bound hands, she felt both the locket and Esperanza's medallion safely beneath her shirt. Smiling faintly at the memory of the kind woman, she sighed and closed her eyes.

"Miss Luray…? What are you about, might I ask?" a masculine voice interrupted her moment of serenity.

Opening her eyes and seeing a lantern approaching her, she held up her hand to shield her eyes from the light, inadvertently showing off her secured wrists. "Is that you, Murtaugh?" Her question was muffled due to the neckerchief in her mouth.

"Jacqueline!" He hurried over to her. "Are you gagged? W-Why are your hands bound?" Kneeling, he took the cloth from her mouth. "Are you unharmed?"

"Aye…" As he took her hands in his and began freeing her wrists, she tried fiercely to think of something to say. She hadn't counted on Murtaugh, of all people, finding her. "I…I tried talking to some of the pirate crew, but I underestimated their desire to escape…"

At this his eyebrows rose. "Oh? Is that so?"

She watched him drop the loose rope onto the floor and

gave him a timid smile. "Aye?"

"I don't know, Jacqueline…It seems unlikely they would have had such a scuffle with you without alerting half the ship – unless you let them get away…?"

"Wha- Michael! Why would I-"

"I'm not even going to ask," he said with a laugh as he sat next to her against the wall.

She glanced at him in the soft light of the lantern, refreshing herself on the ruggedly handsome angles of his face. "It's been a long time," she commented.

"I know." His voice was dejected sounding, and he stared out at the wake of the ship.

Noticing two of the tow ropes suddenly slacken immensely, her eyes grew and she turned to face the Irishman. "Thank you for taking care of and helping Alex and Miata. I can't express my gratitude."

He chuckled lightly at her remark. "Oh, Jacqueline, you know I did it for you." He turned his bright, cerulean stare at her, the way he always did that made her breath catch in her throat. "And maybe a little for Miata. I know how much you mean to him, and he's a good soul with a sad history."

"Aye…" They sat in silence a few seconds. "I saw Audric on the island," she said, abruptly, not even sure she wanted to admit it to him.

"Aye? How is the ol' dodger?" His mood shifted to being a little uneasy.

"He's as much a fool as he ever was, just as you would say," she returned, grabbing up the rope that had been about her wrists so she could toy with it in an attempt to calm her nerves. Another silence ensued as Jacq gathered the courage to finish what was on her mind. "I wished it would've been you."

"Me?" His disposition lifted again.

"On the island with me." She looked up from the rope to find him gazing intently at her. "But this is better." The flame from the lantern danced inviting and dangerously in her eyes.

"Aye?"

She nodded. "Aye."

He looked up in time to see the third rope slack off. "Good."

"Do you mind if I ask you a question?"

"Of course not!" he returned with a chuckle. "What's on your mind?"

"Who is Mr. Dunne and what is he doing on this ship with Captain Adams, helping my sister?"

Sighing, Murtaugh replied, "Mr. Dunne has an accord with our Cap'n Adams. The arrangement is that he works as the good cap'n's unannounced quartermaster for three years without pay. In exchange, after his three years have been served, Cap'n Adams will allow Mr. Dunne to give his name as a positive reference in regards to his reputation. I'm afraid after the occurrence with Mr. Monroe, he was unable to find a decent position aboard any reputable vessel in the immediate area." A gentle smile eased itself into his expression. "Truly, I hope he can build a more respectable life for himself after this."

"And that is why I will always consider you a gentleman," Jacq responded, beaming fondly at him. Then, staring back out towards the ocean, she went on, "I wish you wouldn't have left like you did…Without even a word saying you were off."

"Looking back I wish that too, Jacqueline. But, the truth is I couldn't bear how disappointed you were in me, so I left to right myself." He returned his eyes to look her over.

She was staring down at the twisted rope in her hands. "You're a good man, Michael Murtaugh."

Lifting her chin with his finger, he examined her. He had almost forgotten how she could seem so strong and simultaneously so delicate. Her hair glowed in the flickering lantern light and her eyes shone like stars. Winking at her, he noted, "We should get some sleep."

"Aye," she agreed, smirking back at him, "that we should."

Chapter 13

A shrill whistle startled Jacq and Alex awake, followed by the commotion of feet racing across the decks sounding like a stampede of cows.

"What is that about?" Alex asked, turning to Jacq for answers.

"Oh, no…" Jacq glanced about the room, thinking. "It's the boatswain's call."

Turning a skeptical glance at her sister, Alex's eyes narrowed. "What did you do?"

Looking wide-eyed at Alex, Jacq shrugged. "W-What do you mean?"

"Oh…" Alex shook her head, crossing her arms. "You did something."

Bang! Bang! Bang!

Wincing, Jacq, still dressed from the night before, rose and walked to the door. "Aye?" she answered with the door still closed.

"Captain Adams wishes audiences with Miss Jacqueline straight away!" Nicholas Dunne reported.

Grinding her teeth, Jacq ran her hand over her bandana covered head, casting a glance back at Alex who was still

staring her down in awestruck silence. Taking a deep breath, Jacq turned back to the door. "I'll be out straight away, sir!"

Getting out of bed, Alex re-crossed her arms. "What did you do?"

Spinning back to Alex, Jacq studied her a moment before saying, "Do me a favor and ask me again when I return." Producing her most convincing smile, Jacq then opened the door and slid out onto the deck.

"Jacq! Jacq get back here!" Alex called out, stomping her foot. Huffing in irritation, she shook her head. "She knows I require assistance with my cursed corset!" Glancing at the pile of clothes that consisted of the pants and blouse she'd been wearing the day before and was looking forward to not wearing again, she smirked. "Well, two can play this game."

Out on deck, Jacq had joined the assembly of Miata, Crevan, Bahari, Mr. Dunne, Mr. Hornbeck, and Captain Adams. "It seems," Captain Adams was saying, "that we had a tussle aboard our ship last night, lads, an' a few o' those ne'er-do-well pirates managed to scuttle aboard me ol' ship an' make off with her." He turned angry gray eyes to Jacq. "Mr. Hornbeck claims he turned the buckos over to ye last night. What have ye to say for yerself?"

Shrinking a little at his withering stare, a meek, nervous laugh escaped her. "W-Well," she glanced at Murtaugh who was doing his best to disguise concern with indifference, "h-he did."

Adams' eyes widened. "Explain."

"I-I wanted to speak with them privately, but they tied me up and jumped overboard."

"Overboard onto me ship!" he retorted crossly. "Why didn't ye alert the crew straight away?"

She looked down at this, partially in sincere embarrassment and partially struggling to find a way to get out of this without having to conjur up some elaborate fabrication. "Well, I…I…"

"I found her bound," Crevan spoke up. All eyes swept to him, including Jacq's.

"Go on," Adams said, still looking unimpressed but no longer on the verge of erupting like a volcano.

"It was late. When I found her, her wrists were bound and she had a cloth in her mouth. I talked with her a might, but she didn't give me very much information, so I got her back to her quarters." He glanced over at Jacq who was listening to him, hardly breathing with her heart pounding in her chest. Alex was walking up to stand beside her. "I intended to report finding her in that condition this morning for investigative purposes as to proper crew behavior, but as to the ship, the night was so dark I didn't see she was missing."

Adams eyed Crevan a few minutes before letting out a long, heavy sigh. "Bloody Irishman…" Shaking his head, he ran his hands through his hair. "Very well. It seems there is naught to be done with it for now. But, when we drop our cargo," he glanced at the twins and Miata, "off in Swansea, I intend to be gettin' the ol' lass back." Giving them all one final glare, he waved his hand at them like he was shooing away a fly. "Away with all o' ye. If anythin' else happens aboard my ship, ye be tellin' me straight away, ye hear?!"

"Aye, aye, Captain!" all of them answered in unison, dispersing before he changed his mind and wanted to flog one of them.

"Jacq? Did you have *anything* to do with the escape of those two pirates?" Alex asked as she followed close behind her.

Stopping, Jacq looked over at Murtaugh who had stopped to talk to Miata. As if feeling her gaze, he cast a glance over

his shoulder and, seeing her, winked. Smirking, Jacq stopped and faced Alex. "I don't know that you'd believe any answer I gave you."

Huffing out a breath of air, Alex jammed her fists down on her hips. "There is certainly one answer I might believe."

Grinning, Jacq nodded with her head. "Come on."

As they ascended the stairs to the forecastle, Nicholas Dunne skirted up behind them and called to Alex, "Miss Luray! Please lend me a fragment of your time?"

Both of the young women spun about, Jacq looking unabashedly hostile upon seeing him. Chuckling nervously, he gestured towards the other sister and asked, "Just Miss Alex, if you please?"

Jacq's eyes shifted warily between the two.

Managing a smile, Alex nodded, patting Jacq on the shoulder. "Of course, Mr. Dunne. Jacq, why not go ahead and wait for me. I shall be along shortly."

"Very well, Alex, but, if you need anything," she glowered at him, "be sure to let me know immediately." Smiling at Nicholas Dunne, she added, "Behave yourself, savvy?"

"Heh...Of course." Dunne laughed awkwardly as Jacq pivoted to her left and strode over to the railing to wait for Alex.

"You should pardon my sister's manners. After all, she just spent a week aboard a pirate ship...But you would not know anything about that, would you?" she asked, moving away from where she stood at the top of the staircase.

"No, I...I never served aboard a pirate ship before," he retorted, a hint of annoyance in his voice. "I wanted to apologize for my seemingly inconsiderateness the last twenty-four hours. My duties during the fight between the *Wind Hawke* and *Anne's Triumph* prevented me from attending to personal cares, such as checking on you."

"I see," she returned. Then, breathing a weighted sigh, she slid closer to him and whispered, "Mr. Dunne, I know about you and James Monroe."

He looked away.

"I know that you are not exactly who you have presented yourself as being, and I would appreciate it if you would stop pretending. Who are you?"

Looking back at her, he clenched his jaw, grinding his teeth. Then, squinting up into the bright sunny sky, he responded, "I'm Nicholas Dunne, Miss Luray. I'm a man who, just as every man, has secrets that need not be shared with the world. But," he moved his gaze back to her, "I'm also a man who tries to be a gentleman, and a man who has fallen in love with you." Reaching out, he touched her hand.

Exhaling sharply, Alex pulled away and replied, "I am sorry, Mr. Dunne. Though I am, as I am sure you are aware, rather fond of you, I have to admit that discovering your deceit has given me cause to doubt everything between us. Not only this, but now that I know Mr. Monroe is alive…" She looked away. "Mr. Dunne, you must know that you have no future here." Her eyes began to tear up slightly. "Please excuse me." Whirling away before he could stop her, she fled across the deck to go stand by Jacq who turned and glared threateningly in Nicholas' direction.

Frowning, he growled. *Is there nothing a fellow can do right once he's done one thing wrong?* Unnecessarily adjusting his collar, Nicholas dragged his feet across the ship to return to his station at the captain's side.

It was high afternoon, after four days of uneventful sailing, when the *Wind Hawke* pulled into port at Swansea, north of Port Gilgallad. Jacq and Alex, eagerly clutching each other's hands, waited impatiently for the ramp to be lowered so they might spill onto the harbor. "How glorious! I cannot believe we are really here!" Alex said just above a whisper as the wind gently tossed her hair. "We shall soon meet our father, Jacq! I cannot believe I doubted you that he was still alive!"

Returning the expression with almost equal elation, Jacq nodded, shifting her weight anxiously and breathing deeply of the salty air. "I just hope Amy got on well. I'm sure Bill will be furious." At this, her mouth dropped slightly at the corner.

"Who's Bill?" Murtaugh inquired, coming up beside her as the boat began docking.

"Her bird – a blue-throated macaw, to be precise. He can be a might temperamental," Miata informed, appearing behind him and patting him on the back. Glancing gladly at the harbor, he took in a lung-swelling breath of air. "Oh, Murtaugh, what were the name o' that inn ye were tellin' us about?"

"Bottleneck Inn," Murtaugh and Jacq answered in unison, glancing shyly at each other when they did.

Miata smirked knowingly as he watched them. "Aye, that be the one."

"Aye," Jacq agreed, glancing at Alex. "We'll stop by and see if anyone there has information that would be of value to us."

Miata and Crevan exchanged pleased expressions.

The minutes seemed to drag on as the helmsman guided the ship in and the crew performed all the necessary fastenings

to keep the *Wind Hawke* from floating out to sea unattended. As the ship slowed to a stop in the available port opening, Jacq and Alex all but held their breath, waiting in anticipation.

Wandering up to join them, Bahari nodded towards Jacq. "Shakina."

She grinned back at him. "Bahari."

Then, at Captain Adams' order, they watched the ramp lower – seemingly at the speed of an old overweight cow – until it touched the dock. The moment they were given approval, the group scurried down it, preparing to head towards the local inn.

However, as they began to strike out, Jacq stopped so abruptly Alex ran into her shoulder. "What is it?"

"Is that not the *Sea Dragon*? Captain Turner's ship?" she inquired, pointing to a craft in port on the other side of a sloop docked just above them.

"Is it?" Alex gulped, taking a step forward so that she was beside Jacq.

"I really think it is," Jacq said with a laugh, taking another step forward. "Aye, Alex! I-I really think it is!" she repeated, giggling at the mere idea.

"This way to the inn," Crevan directed as Miata and Bahari got the two girls to turn and follow him. "We can inquire about the *Sea Dragon* in here. Undoubtedly the innkeeper will know many of the answers to the questions you have. If, for some reason, he doesn't have much information, he'll know who does."

As the group entered the crowded Bottleneck Inn, Miata noted, "I be thinkin' Bottleneck be a right proper name for this inn."

Laughing and patting him on the back, Jacq nodded. "Aye..."

As Crevan guided them through the dimly lit, crowded

inn, Jacq couldn't help but peer at their surroundings. The large room was filled with men and women predominately ranging between middle and lower class, including a smattering of slightly higher class men and a heavy sprinkling of rabble. The air was warm but smelled of sweat and smoke with a hint of fish.

"There's the keep," Murtaugh said, jumping forward through the last two rows of seamen between them and the counter. "Ahoy! Pardon me, sir!" he called out.

The innkeeper swiveled around and made eye contact, motioning with a twitch of his head to meet him at the end of the bar.

Nodding, Crevan gestured for the group to follow him, winding through the attendants to reach the innkeeper.

Once they had reached the crowded counter, the innkeeper approached them coolly and in a deep, raspy voice inquired, "What can I do fer ya?"

"We're looking for a man by name of Captain Turner," Crevan said, glancing back at the rest of his company.

"Turner is it?" he repeated in a mumble, squinting out at the patrons. "Turner is a right common name around here it seems. Do ya know his ship?"

"The *Sea Dragon*!" Jacq spoke up. "We saw it docked here right afore we came in!"

"Ah – the *Sea Dragon...*" he repeated, pondering this new information. "Mmm...Not sure I know a Cap'n Turner from the *Sea Dragon...*"

"Are you sure? Captain David Turner," Crevan repeated

"Uh huh." The ragged innkeeper paused to consider the name once more. "Well, he must be a good man if I don't know much about 'im. If his ship is still put to port, then I

imagine 'im to still be around."

"Do you know, perchance, where we might be able to find him outside of this fine establishment?" Jacq asked, offering up her sweetest smile as a plea for any information he could possibly have.

"We really must find him," Alex said. "The sooner the better!"

Looking at the hopeful faces of the twins, he scratched at his jaw. "Erm," the innkeeper said in a mutter, trying to think of something he could tell them. "Give me just a minute." Then, sauntering to the other end of the bar and grabbing at a man at the counter, he asked in a growl, "Do ya know a man by name o' Cap'n Turner? Cap'n David Turner…? Or maybe someone who sails with 'im?"

"Captain of the *Sea Dragon*?" the darkly cloaked man returned.

"Aye, I believe so…" the innkeeper said, gesturing to Crevan to come to him.

"I know of him…" the man admitted as Crevan pushed through the thick crowd to get to his side.

"You know Captain Turner of the *Sea Dragon*?" Crevan asked, jostling his way to the counter beside the man.

"Who are you?" the man asked, spinning about but leaving his hood pulled low over his face so just his mouth and lightly bearded jaw were exposed.

"He's the inquirer," the man behind the counter informed before turning to walk away.

"What do you want with Captain Turner?" the man questioned, turning his attention back to Crevan.

"I have some mates who request an audience with him," the Irishman returned, easing onto his elbow beside the darkly

clad stranger.

"What kind of an audience?" the man replied coolly.

"Personal," Crevan answered guardedly.

"You're awfully closemouthed about the matter," he noted.

"It's not really my personal business, and I don't make a practice of exposing my mates," the Irishman retorted in a cross tone.

"Very well, very well. Pardon the coldness, mate. We are keeping a wary eye these days," he admitted.

"And why is that?" Crevan inquired, his curiosity peaking.

"Personal," the man smiled beneath his hood. "Bring your mates and meet me outside," he instructed. Then, turning back to the bar, he waved coins in the air, "Innkeep!" Rising from the chair, he began weaving his way towards the door.

Across the room, Jacq saw this and began to panic. "Oh... No, no! Alex, wait here."

"Wha- Jacq! Wait!" Alex called, grabbing at her sister's wrist. However, Jacq had already begun to push and shove her way through the noisy men and women.

Rolling her eyes, Alex huffed a sigh and turned to Bahari and Miata, gesturing at the disappearing back of her sister. "Great...There she goes."

Within a few seconds, Crevan made it back to their small cluster. "Very good. The gent at the counter agreed to have a chat with us." Pleased, he glanced around in hopes of approval from everyone, and then noticed they were short a party member. "Where's Jacq?"

Meanwhile, keeping her eye on the tall, hooded man, Jacq slinked through the inn and reached the door before him, slipping out and waiting for him to exit. Snuggling up next to the wall, she waited, and about thirty seconds later the hooded

man entered the street in front of her, turning and quickly walking away from her. "Oi! Begging your pardon, sir!" she called after him, starting forward. "Could you please tell me where the good Captain Turner is?"

He paused his quick stride at the sound of her voice. "Jacq?" He whirled about to face her just as the rest of her company spilled out of the inn.

"Aye…" she said apprehensively, shifting her weight between her feet.

Laughing, the cloaked mysteryman ripped the hood off his head, revealing the black, charmingly disheveled hair of Dante Rackham.

"Dante? Dante Rackham?!" she asked, somewhere between a gasp and a laugh. "Wha-what are you doing here?"

Turning to look at who else was with her, Dante shook his head. "Crevan! Is that you?" he asked of Murtaugh.

"Rackham," Crevan returned with a laugh, shaking his hand.

"Alex. Miata," Dante greeted, giving each of them a respectful nod.

"So, what were you doing in there, mate?" Crevan asked with a confused laugh.

"Well, we've been busy trying to gather information and get the ship properly stocked." Dante shrugged. "The Bottleneck is never low on gossip."

"Properly stocked," Jacq repeated trembling in anticipation as to what that could mean.

"Aye. We are actually preparing to leave on the morrow," he acknowledged with a sigh.

Alex's heart cracked. "L-Leaving?" she asked, touching a worried hand to a flushing cheek. "But I…We…We all have so much to talk about."

"Well," Dante returned frankly with a hint of a smirk, "since you showed up, plans will have undoubtedly changed."

"Is that so?" Jacq asked, tilting her head in want of an explanation.

"Come along," he answered with another laugh, shaking his head. Then, doing his best to seem casual, he put his arm around Jacq's shoulders and gave her a small squeeze.

She could feel her heart skip, but she maintained a cool exterior and smiled up at him. "Dante Rackham…" She giggled, still astonished to stumble upon him.

"It's good to see your face," he stated simply, a twinkle in his eye she was never able to understand gleaming elusively at her. Then, as he released her and began leading the way, he turned to Alex and said, "Alex, I trust you're well?"

"As well as can be expected, I suppose," she answered delicately, clinging to Jacq's side.

Smiling, he looked at Miata. "And you, Miata?"

"Be doin' dandy, Skippy," he acknowledged. Then, gesturing to Bahari, he added, "This be the man what saved our Jacq, Bahari. He were Ming's bodyguard afore he were introduced to Jacq."

"Ming?" Dante reiterated, stopping and staring at the tall dark man. "You mean Captain Ming? Of the *Wind Hawke*?"

"I be Cap'n o' the *Wind Hawke* now!" Captain Adams' voice boomed, startling the collection of young folks as he lumbered up behind them from the docks. "An' we be wantin' to rid ourselves of said scurvy pirate as soon as we can! Who be the man o' town we be needin' to be talkin' to fer that?"

"Captain, come with us!" Dante returned, waving him over. "We were just on our way to see such a man now!"

Swansea was a bustling city bigger than both Penzance

and *Port de Couler de Bateaux.* It had a style similar to Penzance, but somehow felt more regal and dignified. Winsome little boutiques for the opulent buyers lined the streets, suggesting that many wealthy persons decorated the city passageways on a regular basis. Sweet scents and friendly banter cluttered the air, giving the town a very affable, relaxed atmosphere. After they wove their way through a couple buggy dotted roads, the group of seafarers came upon a cozy building with a large, handsomely carved sign out front engraved with the words *Lady Mary's.*

Gesturing towards the door as Dante stopped the caravan, he announced, "Well, here we are!"

"And where, exactly, is here?" Jacq inquired, standing on tiptoe to try and see in the building as Dante opened the door for them and they filed in.

"You'll see," Dante said, smiling at her and walking away from the group. "Stay right here. I'll bring the man out." Stepping lightly towards a door at the far end of the large room, he slipped through it, leaving the party to entertain themselves. As he closed the door securely behind him, he turned to find Captain Turner watching him. "Good day, sirs," he greeted, standing tall and glancing between Turner, James Monroe, and a tall, grayish brown haired man with broad shoulders and a thick neck and jaw line. "You'll never guess who just arrived."

Meanwhile, in the large welcoming room, the bunch stared about at the array of carvings and ship paraphernalia that served as decorations. Jacq was unexplainably drawn to the handiwork of the miniature versions of vessels that lined one of the shelves on the wall across from them. Bahari, being a carver himself, found them to be most intriguing as well. Along with the small boat carvings, there were a large number of books that had to do with sailing, carpentry, and cartography that covered the space the shelves provided. Various ship wheels hung on the walls, reminding those who knew him ever so slightly of Geoffrey Pierce.

Against the wall to the left of the one they had entered through sat a large cabinet, rich and brilliant in color, with a large painting of a beautiful auburn haired woman. Below it, atop the cabinet, a single oil lamp was burning low, casting a warm glow on the painting above. "Who is she?" Alex inquired, touching Jacq's arm. "She is beautiful." As the twins moved to admire the art, Bahari, Crevan, Miata, and even Captain Adams moved to see.

"She is your mother," a strong voice behind them replied.

Everyone whirled away from the painting to look at the voice behind them. There, standing before them, was a naval officer of strong stature, hands clasped behind his back. His skin was tanned and well weathered by salty winds and waves. His eyes were kind and hazel in color, much like Jacq's and Alex's, but they had a hidden softeness to them as he looked at the two girls. Stepping cautiously forward, Jacq smiled politely and inquired, gesturing between Alex and herself, "You knew our mother?"

"He certainly did," Captain Turner spoke up, stepping out from the door Dante had previously used. He was followed by James and Dante.

"James," Alex gasped, her lower lip trembling at the sight of him.

"I am," Captain Turner spoke again, "honored to introduce you to the very highly respected Vice-Admiral Bartholomew Luray of the Royal Navy. This..."

The girls exchanged glances as the captain paused.

"…is your father." He beamed proudly, seeming to feel privileged by simply standing beside him.

The statuesque expression of the middle-aged man's face cracked. "My daughters?" As he asked, he held out his arms to them.

Gasping, though she had believed it to be true, Jacq trembled and she found it hard to move. This was it. This was him. *All those years of wondering, and here he is…Alive and respectable and grand!*

Beside her, gripping her sister's hand so hard her knuckles were white, Alex stifled tears welling in her eyes. Jacq had been right. She had been right! She had taken a chance and was not disappointed. *Our father is a gentleman and a hero! He is more than I could have hoped for…*

Side by side, they walked forward to meet him, each putting a free hand in one of his outstretched ones. Taking in each girl, he shook his head as a smile stretched across his face. "You are both so beautiful," he said in a reverent tone. "I cannot believe it has taken this long for me to finally meet you. Your sister told me so much about you."

"Oh! Where is Amy?" Alex asked, smiling.

"Oh, Amy…" He chuckled, giving each of their hands a kiss. "She is at home on the estate. Your pets," he grinned at this, a smile that looked nearly identical to their own, "are safe with her. Captain Turner and I were actually just going over plans to scour the waters for you. I am so releaved you are both well."

"Is that why you were stocking the ship?" Alex asked just above a whisper, glancing at James.

"Yes, it is, Miss Luray," James returned, sending her a smile.

"Then, will you still be leaving in the morning?" Jacq asked, her gaze turning to look between Dante and Crevan.

"I reckon not," Dante said with a grin, glancing back at Captain Turner.

"Well, that be fine an' all," a forgotten, loud voice interrupted, "but I be havin' prisoners I be wantin' to be rid o'. Now, who be I needin' to be talkin' with about that?"

"That would be me, sir" Mr. Luray spoke up, extending his hand.

"Captain Edward Adams, once o' *Anne's Triumph*, an' now o' the *Wind Hawke*, sir," he introduced himself, taking Bartholomew's extended hand in a hearty shake.

"The *Wind Hawke*? You mean Ming's ship?" Mr. Luray's brows rose in interest.

"Aye! I be wantin' to be keepin' the boat as it be havin' sentimental value, but I be wantin' to be givin' ye the kind souls what provided me with said ship."

"Are you saying you have Captain Ming?" he asked, rubbing at his chin.

"Aye," Captain Adams answered, nodding with a sense of pride.

"How...?" he started.

"Captain Ming kidnapped me," Jacq spoke up. "It took me a while to find out why, but it was because he had sworn vengeance on you by..."

"...turning one of my own children into a pirate," he completed the sentence, cupping his daughter's cheek in his hand and looking at her upturned face. "Aye, Jacqueline, I distinctly remember his cursing. He will stand trial for his crimes against the crown and the citizens of this country." Then, turning to Captain Adams, he requested as he stepped

forward, "Help me escort these captured miscreants of yours to the lockup, and then I shall make sure you get any reward that is coming to you."

"Reward? W-Well, thank ye, Admiral!" Adams nodded, grinning broadly.

"F-Father?" Jacq stopped him, glancing out at the darkening late afternoon sky, "I-I have a matter I must attend to." She touched the pocket of her jerkin, embarrassed that the word had stuck so badly to the roof of her mouth. "Where is the nearest church?"

"Of course, dear." Signaling them all to follow him, he walked outside. "It is quite easy to see," he said as Jacq stopped beside him. He pointed to a steeple that protruded up gallantly far above any other roof in Swansea. As he was showing her the direction, the bells began to ring softly, in a way only church bells can. "Do you intend to stay a while?" he asked, looking between the two.

"Oh, yes!" the girls returned eagerly in unison.

"If we're welcome, of course," Jacq added, suddenly feeling self-conscious.

"Yes, right, of course," Alex agreed, nodding.

"Certainly you are both welcome to stay as long as you wish! Once you have finished whatever it is you need to do, please come back to my shop and wait for me. We can return to the estate together. Your sister, Amy, will be delighted."

"And what of our mates, Miata, Bahari, and Murtaugh?" Jacq spoke up. "Are they welcome as well?"

"Of course! Anyone who would help ensure my daughter's safety is welcome in my home," he said, nodding at the men.

They all respectfully returned the expression, touched the girls would invite them to stay.

"Now," he turned back to Captain Adams, clapping him on the back, "before you feel entirely forgotten, let us rid you of your depraved baggage, hmmm?"

As they went, Alex sighed and touched Jacq's shoulder. "What is this business you must attend to?"

"Much more pleasant than the unattended business coming your way," Jacq replied, grimacing.

Turning to look over her shoulder, Alex's eyes widened in dread at the sight of Nicholas Dunne hurrying towards her. "Oh, Jacq, what shall I do?"

"You shall attend to your unattended business," Jacq suggested in a soft tone, "while I attend to mine. If you finish before I do, feel welcome to meet me at the church." First glaring at him as he came trotting up to them, Jacq turned and sauntered away, her swords swaying with her hips.

"Is all well with you?" Dunne asked as he came to a stop beside Alex, trying to catch his breath.

"Everything is well enough," Alex responded lightly. "But, I have a couple things to tell you."

He paled.

"First of all, I want to thank you for being the perfect gentleman since you met me in Port Gilgallad. You have been very kind and very generous to me, and I shall never be able to thank you enough for the part you played in helping reunite me with my sister."

He nodded, a small smirk playing onto his face.

"And, as Murtaugh pointed out, I am the one who actually said the words that implicated Mr. Monroe had died, but you did not dispute it. So, although I cannot be entirely angry with you, I am quite upset about that."

He opened his mouth, but she held up her hand.

"Please let me finish, Mr. Dunne. If I stop now, I may not be able to."

Heaving a bewildered sigh, he closed his mouth and stared at the cobblestone street.

"I also wanted to wish you well on your journey to repair your reputation as an honest seafaring gentleman, that is, of course, as long as you stay honest. And, lastly, I am a little sad to say good-bye."

At this, he looked back at her.

"As I told you on board, you should know that you have no future here. My heart belongs to Mr. Monroe. He asked me to marry him before he left on this last voyage, before Jacq was taken after we found the treasure left to us by the late Mr. and Mrs. Bumbleridge."

"You found buried treasure?" he asked, grinning.

"Well, I…Uh…It was a mutual effort…" she admitted, smiling sheepishly.

"Miss Luray, I am impressed. You have a way of fascinating me that I have never seen in any other lady before."

Her cheeks reddened slightly at this.

"I hope that one day I will be worthy of winning such a heart as yours, though I very much doubt another shall ever be found." Bowing, he took her hand and kissed it one last time. "And I hope your sister can find the same happiness that you have. Treasure it forever." Then, without question, explanation, or any further conversation, Nicholas Dunne spun slowly about on the ball of his boot and struck out in long, heavy strides back to the dock leaving Alex feeling almost as wretched as she had felt before.

Meanwhile, Jacq was coming up on the church. Pushing the large, heavy door open, she slipped inside. There, just on the inside of the tall doors as she entered, sat a humble wooden box with the word *Offerings* carved into it. Tracing the letters, she pulled out a small piece of paper from her pocket, creased into quarters. Unfolding it, she exposed to herself the words to George Brandon's song clearly and carefully written out in her handwriting with the title, *Just A Closer Walk With Thee* and a subtitle that read, *the words of a man who found his way home.*

"I couldn't part with the leaf he wrote on," she confessed to the box, reading the words again to herself before refolding the paper and slipping it into the slot in the box top. "I will keep it forever." Glancing about the quiet sanctuary that stretched before her, she smiled and whispered, "Good-bye, old mate." Running her fingertips along the edge of the lid, she silently glided out of the church.

As she exited the building, she saw Alex coming up the way towards her looking heavy hearted. Taking a deep breath of the early evening air, she descended the steps of the worship house and made her way towards her sister. Stopping in front of each other, Jacq let out a slow breath of air as Alex glanced up at the church behind her. "So..."

"So..." Alex volleyed, returning her gaze to her sister.

"Did you finish attending to your unattended business?" As she asked, she moved forward, suggesting with her movement that they walk back to their father's workshop.

"I did," Alex nodded, falling in step with her sister, "though it was most unpleasant work. And you?"

"I did what I needed to do," Jacq said, feeling that she'd done the proper thing, though she was not overcome with happiness.

Looping her arm through Jacq's, Alex inhaled a long, deep breath. "We have our father now, and though we will

never know our mother, our father is a start, right?" she asked, indirectly digging for what was bothering Jacq.

"Aye, and a good start indeed," she agreed with a small smile for emphasis. Silence snuck up between them for a moment as they walked, but Jacq's curiosity about how Alex was feeling compelled her to comment, "I'm glad you got Mr. Monroe back. He's a nice chap."

"I am glad I have you back," Alex countered, smirking to herself.

Jacq grinned at her.

Tossing her hair, Alex continued, "I am afraid things might not work out well between us. What if he does not forgive me?"

"If he doesn't forgive you," Jacq returned, "it's because he can't. And if he can't, then he's a fool…"

"Jacq!" Alex scoffed, nudging her with her elbow. "And what of you, sister? Hmm? I see the way you look at Mr. Murtaugh…However shall you choose between the dashing Mr. Rackham and the charming Mr. Murtaugh?"

"What?" Jacq burst into laughter, her cheeks flushing. "Murtaugh? I don't know what you me-" She stopped as she looked over and saw Alex's face. "What is that look for?" She looked away, straight ahead as they rounded the bend, entering the street of their destination.

"I have seen the way you look at each other. There is nothing you can tell me that will convince me you do not fancy him."

Pursing her lips, Jacq glared over at her sister. "Well, isn't that unfortunate?"

Giggling, Alex tucked her arm in, pulling Jacq closer. Down the street, they saw their father, Captain Turner, and

the rest of the men sauntering towards them. Smiling at seeing James amongst them, Alex nudged at her sister. "Come along, Jacq. Let us go home."

As they reunited with the group and headed back to Mr. Luray's estate house, Captain Adams returned to his newly acquired ship to make sure that the carpenter knew to repair the holes bright and early the following morning. As he set foot in the captain's quarters he'd so proudly claimed as his own, he noticed a small bag and a piece of paper sitting on the table that served as his desk. Lumbering over to it, he picked up both items, the bag clinking monetarily as he did so. "Money?" he asked, unfolding the paper.

Then, chuckling, he read aloud:

> *Captain Adams,*
>
> *It is a shame when a boy steals to survive, but when a man steals, it is shameful. I know you do not know the amount I stole from you years ago, but I do. So, here it is, fair and square.*
>
> *—Miata O'Keeffe.*

Looking rather fondly at the little coin pouch, he exhaled a long breath with a smile on his face. "May the good Lord

bless ya, lad...An' yer bonny lasses."

Much further inland, a large house most would consider a mansion sat nestled in a small indention in the earth, as if God had pressed his thumb there to level the land. Inside the grandiose abode was a striking combination of white marble, brick, and a fine red-toned wood. Large, beautiful rugs accented the vast floors, and long banners hung from the walls like tapestries in a castle. A large staircase was not too far from the entrance, leading to a lush and lavishly furnished upstairs with seven opulently adorned bed chambers. The downstairs was well equipped with a modern kitchen, a handsome dining area, Mr. Luray's study – which had an impressive library attached to it, and a ballroom that he used whenever necessary for large social gatherings. Outside, the lavish abode a handsome forest shrouded part of the back and the right side of the building. An attractive garden framed the front and the left side of the manor, equipped with a fountain, well landscaped shrubberies and trees, and an array of beautiful flowers.

Entering the home made Alex's memories of the kind Mr. and Mrs. Thorpe resurface, creating an odd, warm spot in her stomach and a wateriness in her eyes that she easily batted away without anyone taking notice. Jacq, who had never before been in such a refined establishment, found she could hardly breathe. "You live here?" she asked, turning to her father.

"It is like a castle," Alex said in a dreamy tone.

"It *is* a castle!" Jacq retorted.

Laughing, Mr. Luray shook his head. "Without a family, it is naught but an empty house."

"You mean an empty castle," Jacq said, still gawking at the interior.

As the group laughed, a voice from farther within the

house called, "Father? Is that you? Have you and Captain Turner-" Amy, with her bouncing golden curls, rounded the corner from back towards the kitchen with a monkey wrapped about her waist and a bird perched on her shoulder. "Alex! Jacq! Miata!" Rushing over, she threw her arms around each one of them and her father in bursting excitement.

Bill flew to Jacq, clucking in happiness at seeing her and squawking to scold her for leaving him while Frank hopped into Alex's arms, winding his tail around her so tightly she didn't know if she'd be able to pry him off.

"Oh! I have been so worried!" Amy exclaimed in delighted relief, giving out another round of hugs.

"I am so glad you remained safe!" Alex spoke up as she hugged her and then moved to Miata. "I could not bear the thought of putting your life in danger."

"It was brilliant for me to come back anyway!" Amy returned, looping her arm through Miata's and sending him an enamored smile. "I was able to tell Father about you, though I think he thought I had lost my mind at sea."

"It was a lot to consider, my dear," Mr. Luray spoke up in quiet defense of himself. "I had lost hope so long ago, and to think of Miss Margaret's betrayal was..." He paused, as if still trying to process that part of the scenario. "It was a lot to consider."

"Aye! But, here we are!" She grinned giddily and looked at the company once again, suddenly noticing they were all in need of some soap and water. "Oh! Father...Everyone should get washed up and presentable for our first dinner together!"

"Oh. Amy, you are correct." He made a motion with his hand and a friendly looking man and woman seemed to materialize from the wall. "Miss Lydia, these are my daughters,

Miss Alexandria and Miss Jacqueline. Would you be so kind as to tend to their preparations for the evening?"

"Yes, sir," she agreed in a small voice.

"And, Mr. Edwards, see what you can do for," he gestured towards Bahari, Crevan, and Miata, grimacing slightly, "our friends."

At this, the men exchanged self-conscious glances.

Not an hour later, both Bill and Frank were fast asleep and Alex was smiling at her reflection in the room she and Jacq were to share. Lydia had found her a dress of a rich, handsome red color with white sleeves that widened from the elbows down. There was a V shaped white area on the corset bordered with fine detailing, enhancing the naturally sinuous curves of her body. Her hair was fashionably up with a few tresses hanging down along her face. The final adornment was the gold locket gleaming around her neck. As she reached up to touch it, however, she was distracted by Jacq's voice.

"Let go of it!" she exclaimed from behind the tri-fold dressing screen near the back corner of the room.

"Miss Jacqueline!" Scuffling and grunting could be heard as Lydia struggled. "Hold still!"

Rolling her eyes with a smirk, Alex moved from the mirror towards the screen. "How is it coming along?" she inquired, the question directed to Lydia more than to Jacq.

"She is trying to kill me!" Jacq answered between clenched teeth.

"Miss Lydia?" Alex asked again, forcing herself not to laugh.

"She is very uncooperative," the maid commented, "but I think I've got it now."

"How can you possibly find this comfortable? Why can't

I just wear what I usually wear?" Jacq asked in a whiny voice as she came out from behind the screen, touching at her shrunken midsection.

Gasping, Alex put her hand over her chest. "Jacq! You have a waist!"

The corner of her sister's mouth drew back in a grimace. "I also used to be able to breathe."

"Well, you look like the perfect lady." Taking hold of Jacq's hand, she pulled her over to the looking glass, radiating with pride.

Inhaling in surprise, Jacq touched at her hair, which Lydia began styling in a manner accommodating to her shortened locks. The dress Alex had selected, she hated to admit, looked gorgeous on her. It was a deep hued mixture of blue and green with small silvery white sleeves that hung off her shoulders around her upper arms and a matching band of white just above her hips that extended down in a stripe in the front and back that widened until it hit the floor. As Alex had suggested, half the layers of petticoats had been left out since she figured Jacq would have refused to leave the room, and so the skirt hung gently about her. "I-I don't know what to say."

"You can admit I was right," Alex said with a smile, going to collect Jacq's other clothes from behind the screen. However, as she picked them up, a piece of parchment fluttered to the floor. Plucking it off the ground, she turned it over in her hand. "What is this?"

"What is what?" Jacq asked, craning her neck to try and see.

Alex held up the leaflet as she set down the clothes.

"Oh...That was given to me by an old man aboard the *Wind Hawke*. He was a glimmer of hope to me in a world of darkness."

Alex stopped beside her. "Was?"

Jacq looked down towards her feet. "He was killed during the assault of the ship Ming attacked on the way to the Isles of Scilly."

Holding it out towards her, Alex guessed, "Your unfinished business?"

Nodding, Jacq took it back, running her thumb over the textured paper. "Aye."

Offering her a sad smile, Alex leaned forward to give her a hug, suddenly realizing she was missing something. Pulling away, she asked, "Where is your locket?"

Turning away from her reflection, Jacq touched at the medallion around her neck and shrugged. "I-I don't feel I need to wear it here...Is that strange?"

An intrigued expression transforming Alex's face, she shook her head. "No...This is a new beginning." Reaching up, she unclasped the chain for hers, removing it as well. "We should start with a clean slate."

Just then, the door swung open and Amy skipped into the room, a smile of pure delight on her face. "Sisters! Oh, you both look so elegant! Miss Lydia, you are truly the best!"

Blushing slightly, the maid waved the youngest girl off and noted, "As soon as I'm done with Miss Jacqueline's hair you're all to be off. The night isn't gettin' any younger."

Downstairs, the menfolk were standing about in the dining hall, testing out some of Mr. Luray's wine collection. Everyone who was not already somewhat presentable upon arrival had managed to find something to wear. Miata, standing near

Crevan, was donning a dark pair of brownish trousers and a shimmery gold coat, unbuttoned to expose his white blouse. The Irishman, however, had gotten himself a pair of black trousers with black boots that reached to his knees. A black overcoat with silver fastenings, a white shirt lightly laced from the middle of his chest up, and a small coin bound on a short leather strand finished off his look.

Noticing the two, Dante sauntered over, clearing his throat as he stopped beside them. "So, Mr. Murtaugh…" He extended his hand in a polite gesture.

"Aye, Mr. Rackham?" Crevan grasped his hand in a confident shake.

"So, you're mates with Miata, are ya?" he asked, sounding casual as he sipped at his drink.

"Aye, and Miss Luray," Murtaugh added, glancing at Miata, who nodded.

"*And* Miss Luray?" Rackham repeated, his eyebrow arching.

"Aye," Murtaugh continued nonchalantly. "The lass and I were mates a few years ago, but went separate ways for a time. I consider it a great fortune of mine to be included as one of her mates once again."

Shrugging and feigning indifference, Rackham returned slightly under his breath, "Undoubtedly. She is a fine lass."

Glancing at Miata, who was looking skeptically between the two of them, Murtaugh smiled smugly. "She is."

Before their conversation could get any further, though, the butler entered the room, knocking on the doorpost. "Gentlemen! May I present you with the ladies of the evening, the Luray sisters – Miss Amy, Miss Alexandria, and Miss Jacqueline."

The girls filed in as their names were called, receiving

applause from the men who were doubtlessly as happy to see them as they were to know they'd finally be sitting down to eat. Nevertheless, Mr. Luray walked forward to greet them all, escorting each girl to her seat one at a time. As soon as he arrived at the head of the table, the other men in the room filled the remaining available seats. Then, once everyone had laid claim to a chair, Mr. Luray addressed them saying, "Never has my home been so full of grace nor my heart so full of cheer. Your mothers, God rest their souls, would be the proudest women in the world if they were here to see you now. Let us sit and eat in joy and peace."

As they were served food, hastily but perfectly prepared by Mr. Luray's kitchen staff, the long table buzzed with chatter. Amy begged Miata to tell her all the details of the adventure she missed out on and was delighted to find out he now knew his last name. Mr. Luray was astounded at learning more about Margaret McLoflin and her less than comely deeds, coupled with the adventures of his two daughters. Bahari was quite satisfied to listen to everyone's conversations, absorbing the history that surrounded him. Dante spent nearly as much time sizing up Crevan as he did talking to Vice-Admiral Luray and Captain Turner. Crevan oscillated predominately between James and Jacq, while Alex found herself content to sit beside James. However, despite the revelry, Alex couldn't help but notice that while Mr. Monroe was pleasant as usual, his mood was somehow distant, and it worried her. All the while, Jacq floated in and out of conversations, attempting to keep to the ones that were the least invasive and provided lots of smiles and laughter.

As the evening darkened to nearly midnight, Jacq rose and requested, "Please excuse me. I need a little fresh air."

"Of course, dear!" Mr. Luray said, gesturing towards a nearby door. "Feel free to wander the garden."

Nodding in appreciation, she gave the whole company a polite curtsey and followed her father's advice. Once outside in the darkened, moonlit garden, she noticed a bench not far off. Sighing, she trudged over to it, kicking her little shoes off and setting them beside her. Looking up at the stars, she sang in a mumble,

"*So merry, so merry, so merry are we,*

No matter who's laughing at sailors at sea."

"Still singing sea songs, Jacq?" asked the husky yet melodious voice of Dante Rackham, disrupting her.

Inhaling sharply, Jacq looked up and smiled a little bashfully. "And you don't?"

"Maybe once in a while…" Grinning, he sat down on the bench beside her. "How've you been?"

"Well enough. Who wouldn't fancy being kidnapped by a mad, vengeful pirate captain and hauled off to sea without anyone she knows?" She wiggled her toes, hidden by her skirt, in the grass.

"Somehow I imagine you were a might more than he bargained for," he replied, chuckling and admiring her profile in the moonlight.

Laughing, Jacq shrugged. "Perhaps. What of you?"

"Well, I actually went home to see my father. It was long overdue." Pausing, he smiled at her. "You inspired me."

"So, it went well for you?" she returned, kicking at the grass and doing her best to sound indifferent to his stories.

"Aye. My father is well and was pleased to hear of my position aboard such an honest vessel," he returned, looking up at the sky, filled with twinkling dots that shone and sparkled.

Looking back at her, painfully aware she still hadn't turned to look at him, he asked, "So, what are you doing out here by yourself?"

"I was just pondering," she confessed, finally turning to face him. His eyes glistened in the dim lighting, glittering like stars themselves. His face, having not been shaved for a day or two was rugged and handsome while his untamed ebony hair disappeared into the night sky. There was no denying it…She had missed his face.

Enjoying staring at her in the dark of night, he relaxed a little into his seat and asked, "About what?"

"A lot of things. I had a lot of time to think about things while I was trapped at sea, but now that I'm free…" Stopping, she shrugged. "I was so afraid I would never see Alex, or any of my mates again, or meet my father. I saw a good man die at the hands of hapless thieves, and I met amazing people in the darkest of places. I just have a lot on my mind." Smiling over at him, she sighed. "And I've missed you, Dante." At this, she brought her eyes up to meet his again.

Meeting her warm, softened eyes which seemed to glow as candlelight, his breath seeped out of his lungs. Her smile, slightly tilted to the left, spread across her face and glistened. Scooting closer to her and capturing her chin in his hand, he returned, "I've missed you too, Jacq."

Staring up at him in earnest, she leaned forward searchingly and asked, "Truly?"

A twinge resounding from his heart pinched him in the throat at the sound of her question as she stared at him so intently. Gazing back at her, a soft, tilted smiled creased his mouth. "Aye. The ship's not the same without you and your sister aboard, causing trouble and giving us a laugh."

"Oh…Of course," she said, looking away and disguising her disappointment with indifference.

"Jacq?" Alex's voice chirped as the fashionably conscious girl entered the garden.

Jacq and Dante straightened flawlessly.

"Oh! There you are!" She fidgeted awkwardly as the two stared at her. "I…I was hoping to ask you a question, but it really is quite trivial. I-I can speak with you later."

"Nay, Alex! I insist!" Dante exclaimed, rising from the bench. "I was just about to excuse myself. Please stay. I'll be along again in a while." Without hesitation, he darted around Alex and scurried back into the mansion.

"I am so sorry!" Alex said through clenched teeth, rushing over and sitting down next to her twin.

"Fret not, Alex. He confuses me terribly sometimes." Trying to understand how missing her greatly only constituted missing her antics aboard ship, she shook her head. "So, please, what was your question? I'm glad for the distraction."

Obviously feeling terrible, Alex sighed. "It truly was petty. I just wanted to know if you had noticed what a distinguished gentleman our father is, because he is – in every way! It is truly remarkable. I hardly know him and yet I admire him more than any other man I have ever known."

"While I do agree, I do not think that is what brought you out here." Jacq cast a knowing gaze at her sister.

"I told you it was trivial!" Alex reiterated, frowning at the implication.

"With your words, perhaps. However, your eyes suggested otherwise. So, what's troubling you?"

"Nothing!" An awkward silence formed between them as Alex wished Jacq would stop staring at her in disbelief. "Ugh! Very well…It is James. Something is different, but I have yet

to discover what it is. There is something, though…"

Her usual sideways smile shaping her lips, Jacq put her arm around Alex's shoulders and returned, "Miss Luray, I am certain it will reconcile itself. Just remember that however it happens is how it was meant to happen. You just have to believe it and do your best until it gets sorted."

Forcing a grave smile on her face, Alex shrugged. "You truly believe so?"

"Aye. If I didn't, perhaps we wouldn't be here at all," Jacq said, laughing at herself and feeling slightly pathetic all of a sudden. "I have to believe that."

"You are a perfect sister, and I love you," Alex said, smiling over at her and hugging her a moment. "I am so glad we found you!"

Returning the hug in kind, Jacq laughed. "I love you too." Glancing up at the stars again, she smirked. "Would now be a good time to tell you about the escaped pirates?"

Letting go of the embrace, Alex sat back onto the bench. Then, after a short, incredulous silence, retorted, "No." A few moments of amiable silence, light and relaxed, followed her reply. Then, taking a turn to look up at the heavenly bodies, Alex suddenly inquired, "Say, Jacq…?"

"Aye?"

"When you look at the stars, what do you see?" She glanced between the twinkling specks and Jacq.

Smiling, Jacq followed Alex's gaze and thoughtfully replied, "Diamonds in the sky…You?"

Thinking a very brief moment, Alex nodded. "The same."

Just as she answered, Crevan's voice interrupted them. "Pardon me, ladies. I have a dashing young man looking for a Miss Alexandria. Would either of you know where we could find such a lass?"

James, a soft, pleasant expression on his face, eased around the corner. "I would forever be in your debt."

Giggling, Alex rose, touching Jacq's shoulder, whispering, "Wish me well." Then she walked away arm in arm with James Monroe, who somehow had managed to select a dress coat that matched her gown flawlessly.

Watching them saunter away a moment, Crevan then turned back to Jacq, and inquired as he gestured towards the spot Alex had just vacated, "May I?"

At his request, her mouth involuntarily broke into an attractive shape, admitting she was pleased to see him. "Of course."

Striding over, he sat himself down beside her shoes, smiling at the sight of them. "Would it be terribly dull for me to tell you that you cut quite a figure in that dress?" he asked, keeping a straight face though his voice revealed his hidden amusement with his own comment.

"On the contrary, I might feel compelled to be altogether flattered," she answered playfully, burying her smirk of enjoyment at his conversation.

"Truly?" he asked, acting surprised.

"Aye. But, I must warn you that such a compliment would not go unrepaid." She did her very best to sound somber.

"Is that so?" He turned to face her as though he was keenly interested in this facet.

"Aye. I might have to confess that you look rather dashing in that getup of yours." Her expression of faux seriousness began to slip, revealing a small smile.

"Ugh…How dreadful," he commented, still maintaining a straight face.

Giggling, she nodded. "Aye."

"At least it's not one of those puffy monkey suits with all

the ruffles," he said with a sigh, staring out at the garden.

She giggled again, straightening her skirt needlessly, knowing it was her turn to keep up the conversation. The quiet that rose between them was gentle and warm, not as awkward as silences usually go in rather unfamiliar company. As the moment drew on, however, her curiosity began prying and poking at her as she peeked over at his handsome face while he stared ahead of him.After a few seconds of silence, she spoke, "Michael…?"

"Aye?" he returned, glancing back at her.

Turning to better stare at him, she asked the question that had been clawing at the back of her mind. "Where have you been?"

"Oi…" Laughing, he rubbed his barely stubbled jawline and huffed out a weighted breath of air. "Where haven't I been?…I came back to Swansea to finish my apprenticeship with Mr. Smith, but he left a couple years ago to tend to some family business. While he was away, I started traveling to do custom smithing, so I've been all about half of England, lending a hand where I could and picking up a few extra trade skills here and there. I wanted to be a better man, Jacqueline…" He turned to look at her again, his smile completely vainished from his face. "I wanted to be someone a lass would be proud to have in her company."

Clenching her jaw as she thought a moment, she shook her head. "You've always been a bit of a fox, Michael, but you are a *good* man. I sincerely mean it when I say so." She looked away at the shadows being cast by the trees, stretching long across the stately grass. "I wanted to thank you again for helping my sister. I don't know if you understand how much it means to me."

Shrugging, he shook his head. "It was nothing, really. As I told you, I couldn't, in good conscience, let anything happen to you."

"You must've met so many people in your travels," she said, thinking aloud.

"A few I suppose…" Leaning down, he plucked a blade of grass and began spinning it between his fingers.

"Do you have a lass stowed away somewhere?" she asked, finding that she was extremely interested in hearing his answer.

"Nay," he replied, looking over at her. "I've no secret lady hidden away."

She looked down at her fingers, which she had intertwined in her lap and had been wringing anxiously. "I thought, perhaps, you had forgotten me."

"No," he said in a tone of voice that demanded she look up, "Jacqueline…Rather, I thought of you markedly often at times." Returning his gaze to the piece of grass, he was silent a moment. Then, before Jacq could ask him another digging question, he inquired, "Did you…Uh…" He got up from the bench, crossing over to a tree a short distance ahead of them. "Did you notice the view of the city from here?"

"No…" She watched him curiously.

"Oh, well, you can see the whole city from here." He gestured out in the direction of the town from where he was standing.

"The whole city?" she asked, getting up and padding over to where he was to strain her eyes in the darkness.

"Aye." He looked down and noticed her sliding right up next to him.

Feeling his body heat, she realized she had unintentionally invaded his space. Glancing up and meeting his eyes in the dim lighting, she felt her breath catching in her chest. Michael

Murtaugh was undeniably handsome during the day, but the moonlight made him even more alluring.

As he felt his heart beat increasing, he forced his breathing to remain regulated. However, that became progressively difficult as his gaze fixated first on her eyes, then slid to her lips, to her hair, and to her neck…Crevan forced himself to gulp down a lump that had formed in his throat.

She reached a tentative hand up, touching timid fingertips to his jaw. Was her heart racing? "M-Michael…"

Lifting his hand in want of touching her exposed shoulders, he took a deep breath and returned them to his sides, worried the touch of her skin might push his mind beyond control. "Jacq-"

"Oi! Jacq!" another voice interrupted.

Murtaugh and Jacq hopped apart like a person jumps back after singeing his or her fingers on a hot iron. Their gazes lingered, asking silent questions of each other, but not getting any answers.

"I…" Dante stopped abruptly, noticeably bothered at seeing Crevan outside with Jacq. "I'm not interrupting anything, am I?"

"Nay," Crevan spoke up. "I was just telling her how she missed the sight of the city before the sunset." He looked over at Jacq, hoping she would pick up on his cue.

What just happened? Jacq kept asking breathlessly in her mind. However, she quickly realized he was trying to cover for them, and added, "Aye. It sounds like it's just lovely. I'm sad to have missed it." Then, looking back at Murtaugh, her mind screamed. He had always been handsome and confident, but something about him was on the brink of driving her mad.

"Aye…" Dante returned, his inflection obviously

brimming with doubt and skepticism about their claim. "Well, I would have returned sooner, but I got caught up in a bit of conversation." He eyed Crevan who caught the scrutiny out of the corner of his eye. "You know, Jacq, I don't know if I told you yet, but I've never seen you in a dress before. You look absolutely striking. Don't you agree, Mr. Murtaugh?"

Narrowing his eyes, Crevan lifted his chin and replied, "I would wager that to be an understatement, Mr. Rackham."

Dante discreetly threw him another scowl.

What is going on? Jacq asked herself, glancing between the two young men. However, they were both proficient enough at covertly giving each other dirty looks that she didn't catch them.

"Shakina! There you are," Bahari called out as he ambled outside with the three of them.

"Bahari!" She had never been so happy to hear his voice. "How long will you grace us with your companionship?"

Shrugging, the large man hung his head. "Now that I am free, and after helping reunite your family, there is only one place I wish to go."

Jacq stared at him, nodding and knowing exactly what he meant.

"I have missed my family for too long already," he said in a weary voice.

"If there is a way for me to help you, Bahari, just name it. Your friendship and protection have been of great value to me. Esperanza would want you to find them again. So, I owe it to you both."

Smiling in appreciation of her good intentions, he sighed. "Unless you can find me passage home, I do not know, Shakina. But, your sincerity is a treasure to me."

Clearing his throat, Dante commented, "Pardon me, but, we have two very distinguished seafaring gentlemen just inside. If they cannot assist you, I do not know who could."

Nodding, Jacq smiled and grabbed her shoes up off the bench, beginning to put them on one at a time. "And you do owe me a trip, don't you, Mr. Rackham?"

Crevan's expression darkened at this. "I would also be happy to accompany you."

At his statement, Dante flung a disgruntled glare at Murtaugh.

"You are both perfect gentlemen given the right opportunity," she praised them, heading towards the door to go inside the manor.

First smiling smugly at Dante, Crevan then asked, "Where are you going?"

Turning back to give them another grin, this time lit with mischief, she replied, "Why, to see a man about a boat." Then, spinning on her heel, she entered the house.

Murtaugh and Rackham exchanged perplexed glances that quickly degenerated into challenging glares. Clearing his throat, Crevan commented, "She is a fine lass."

His jaw twitching, Dante nodded. "She is."

Bahari turned to face them, his blue eyes pale in the silver light, but no less intimidating. "I did not secure her freedom so she could be fought over like a goat at market. If either of you intend to claim her heart, you had best treat her like a lady and act like a man."

"Aye, sir," they both agreed, glancing at where Jacq had disappeared into the house.

Unaware of the conversation outside, Jacq sauntered into the dining hall, and, seeing that everyone else was still lounging

at the table, she cleared her throat. "Pardon me! Gentlemen!" All eyes swiveled to her. "Is there anyone here who would help us take our mate, Bahari, home?"

Alex and Miata, sitting across the table from each other, turned wide-eyed stares to one another, wordlessly asking each other if they had just heard Jacq correctly.

Sitting back in his chair and folding his arms across his chest, Mr. Luray asked, "And where is that, my dear?"

In unison, both Miata and Alex heaved a sigh and answered, "…Africa."

www.ingramcontent.com/pod-product-compliance
Lightning Source LLC
Chambersburg PA
CBHW020959120726
47905CB00009B/2765